THE HANDYMAN

THE HANDYMAN

A Novel

MAURA K. DEERING

SHE WRITES PRESS

Published 2023
Printed in the United States of America
Print ISBN: 978-1-64742-507-4
E-ISBN: 978-1-64742-508-1
Library of Congress Control Number: 2023906713

For information, address:
She Writes Press
1569 Solano Ave #546
Berkeley, CA 94707

Interior Design by Kiran Spees

She Writes Press is a division of SparkPoint Studio, LLC.

For the Bee

PROLOGUE
1991

On the day of the memorial service, Dennis Griffin stood on the lakeshore, under a cold gray sky, facing the water. The whine of a chainsaw echoed somewhere along the shore. The air smelled like pine, wood smoke, and the coming winter.

When the chill got to him, he went inside.

He avoided the post-funeral supper and went instead to the flagstone entry hall where the guests had hung their coats. He searched through the pockets, stuffing any cash or items of interest he found in his own jacket pockets.

They had arrived yesterday. Dennis had watched from inside the garage as Brenna emerged from the car and embraced her mother, Meg. He'd watched intently as Brenna's little girl, Sadie, stepped out of the back seat but stayed close to the car, looking uncertain, until Meg went to her, scooped her up, and took her inside.

Now, in the front hall, he discovered a black leather purse on a hook behind a dark green coat. The subdued tones of the assembled guests' voices drifted in, but no one came to disturb him. Dennis listened and tried to make out words; he couldn't. He stuck his hand in the purse, rummaging around. He pulled out a red eel-skin wallet, unsnapped it, and found Brenna's driver's license picture staring back at him. She didn't have any cash in her wallet, just photos and credit cards. There was a Mastercard; a Chevron gas card; and a professional-looking wallet-size portrait of Brenna, her husband, Peter, and Sadie seated in a grove of trees, smiling. When Dennis could stand to look no longer, he dropped the wallet back into Brenna's purse.

He sifted through the rest of her things. There was a hairbrush, key ring, packet of Kleenex, pack of Virginia Slims, and a lighter. He spun the wheel on the lighter and it lit up; he put it in his pocket. He removed a snarled ball of hair from her brush and put that in his pocket too. At the bottom of her bag was a small silver flask. Dennis unscrewed the cap and sniffed. He smelled nothing. He took a swig just as he heard his wife calling his name. He tasted vodka.

"Dennis? . . . Dennis?"

The sound of her footsteps got louder. He dropped the flask back into the purse and slipped out the front door into the oncoming evening. He ran silently across the driveway and up the stairs to their apartment above the garage. In the bedroom, he retrieved a leather briefcase (with his initials, *DEG*, embossed on it) from under the bed, and opened it with a small key he got from his sock drawer. He took the hairball out of his pocket and dropped it into the briefcase. He locked it and placed it back under the bed.

That done, he put the key back in the drawer and went back outside, down the stairs, and along the path to the lakeshore. He sat on a log and lit up a cigarette with Brenna's lighter. The air was cold with the promise of snow.

PART ONE
1965–1985

CHAPTER ONE

B renna Riley loved her father's study. It smelled like books and cigars, and the walls were filled with photos of her father as a younger man. He had been a rower at the Naval Academy and had won a gold medal in the 1952 Helsinki Olympic Games. The medal was in a frame and hung next to a picture of nine men standing in a row on a dock, each holding an oar, except the shortest of them who held a megaphone. Their names were written along the bottom of the photograph, including her father's, Jack Riley.

Brenna also loved the picture of her parents when they got married at a wedding chapel in Reno, Nevada. Her mother had run away with Jack from her home in Maryland because her family had not approved of the marriage. Brenna found this fascinating and exciting. She looked at the photo so often she'd memorized it. Her handsome, powerfully built father, with his dazzling smile, in his navy uniform, towered over her dark-haired and petite mother, who was wearing a light-colored suit and a shy but radiant smile. Behind them, off to the left, was the exterior door of the little faux church with a sign that read Silver Bells Wedding Chapel.

⌒

When Brenna was six, she announced to her father, "I'm going to row, like you did."

Her father laughed and said, "Girls don't row."

Brenna resolved, right then, to be the first girl rower.

She and her dad had a special bond. Brenna loved her mother too, of course, but didn't spend a lot of time with her. She knew her mother loved her, but not in the same way her father did, or even the same way her nanny, Mrs. Dalrymple, did. Mrs. Dalrymple, from the time of Brenna's earliest memories, asked her every day, "How much do I love Brenna?" "This much!" Brenna would answer by holding her arms open as wide as she could. Her father worked a lot but always made time for her.

Her mother mostly made time for her father.

Brenna was eight when she first heard them fighting. It was late at night and Brenna was walking, half asleep, to the bathroom when she heard them. Suddenly wide awake, she crept down the hall and stood outside their bedroom.

"It just looked like you and Linda were arguing, that's all," her mother said. Her voice sounded shaky, as if she was on the verge of tears.

"Arguing? I barely know the woman! How much did you have to drink tonight?"

At first, she hadn't recognized her father's voice. He had never spoken to Brenna that way, with such anger and frustration.

"We've known Linda and Stan for at least ten years," she heard her mother say quietly.

"Where are you going with this, Meg?" her father hissed in that weird furious tone.

"It was just an observation. I'm sorry to upset you." Now it sounded like her mother was crying.

"Whatever you thought you saw"—her father's voice was getting louder, and closer! Brenna hurried back down the hall and slipped into the bathroom just as her parents' bedroom door opened—"it was nothing. Nothing for you to be concerned about."

She heard the door slam and her father's feet stomping down the hall and down the stairs.

⌒

By the time she was ten, Brenna had begun to notice things. Like the three of them would be having dinner, and she and her father would be talking a mile a minute—about Brenna's day at school, what he'd done all day at his newspaper job, what books Brenna was reading, what it had been like when Jack was on his navy ship, what it had been like to march in the opening ceremony at the Olympics—and her mother would sit quietly, smiling pleasantly and nodding at the things they were saying, but detached, not altogether present. Her father would pour her wine, but if her mother reached for the bottle herself, her father would stop her and shake his head, saying, "You've had enough."

Or when they were up at the vacation house in Tahoe. Her mother had a small art studio in their San Francisco house and liked to paint the view of the bay from the terrace from time to time, but, at Tahoe, she painted outside every day, capturing the lake and the surrounding mountains in all seasons and all times of the day.

When she was eleven, Brenna overheard them arguing while they were in Tahoe.

"No, absolutely not!" she heard her father shout. Brenna was on the patio eating a bowl of cereal, and his voice boomed from the open window of his study. The sun was just rising above the tops of the pine trees, and Brenna was planning to take the old wooden rowboat out on the lake. She was trying to convince her dad that she could be a rower by practicing every day. Maybe then, he'd buy her a proper rowing shell.

"I don't understand why not, Jack. Gene and Charlotte are here. I wouldn't be alone."

Gene and Charlotte lived in the apartment above the garage. Gene was the handyman and caretaker of the property, and Charlotte cooked and cleaned the house.

"I've been asked to join the painting group in town," her mother said. "I could even show my work in the gallery. I only want to spend a month in the summer here."

"What about Brenna? You're going to leave her alone for a month?"

"It would be in August when she's away at camp."

"I will take August off and come with you," her father said.

"I would think you'd want to be rid of me."

"Oh, no. Not this again, Meg!"

Her mother said something, but too quietly for Brenna to hear the words. She heard a loud thump, like a fist on a table.

"For Christ sakes, Meg! My 'other interests'—as you call them—are nothing for you to be concerned about, not to mention only in your imagination. You will wait to come up here when I can accompany you. And that is my final word!"

Brenna retreated to the boathouse, leaving her cereal bowl on the patio table. Charlotte would find it later. Brenna wondered what other interests her mother was referring to. She loved her father but didn't understand why he treated her mother the way he did. She promised herself she'd never let a man treat her like that, never let anyone control her, dominate her, or yell at her.

When Brenna was thirteen, she succeeded in talking her father into buying her a single rowing shell and teaching her to row. Her boat was impossibly skinny, made of wood, polished until it gleamed. Brenna loved her boat. She kept it at the Lake Merritt Rowing Club in Oakland, and she and her dad would spend at least one weekend day on the water. He was patient with her as he rowed alongside in his own single shell and instructed her on her stroke.

"You're a natural!" he often said, beaming.

"You have excellent boat feel," he said one day.

"What does that mean?"

"It means that you work with the boat and the way it moves through the water, rather than against it. Not everyone has that. In fact, most don't."

She also noticed that a lot of girls rowed, in singles as well as in bigger boats with other girls. Her dad had told her girls don't row. Either he'd lied or girls had only recently started rowing.

When Brenna started high school, her father relented and allowed her mother to spend time in Tahoe a few weeks out of the year to focus on her painting. Brenna had heard him brag to others about her mother's artistic talents, much as he bragged about Brenna's rowing and writing abilities. Brenna wondered again about her parent's marriage. About how her father spoke to her mother so differently than he spoke to Brenna.

But, as she grew older, she didn't give it too much thought. Brenna felt sorry for her mother but knew such a relationship was never going to happen to her. Plus, she was busy and becoming more independent, allowed to take the BART to Lake Merritt with rowing friends and walk to school with the neighbors. Her parents had argued about that—her mother insisting it was safe, while Jack railed about the many dangers Brenna would encounter on the train and walking through Oakland. Brenna was more distant from her mother than ever. If she had homework problems or questions about politics or current affairs, she went to her father. If her mother entered the room and tried to join the conversation, she and her father would wave her off or change the subject to a lighter topic, like what was for dinner or the weather or how nice Meg's flowers looked out on the terrace.

Brenna's, Jack's, or the world's problems were nothing for Meg to be concerned about.

CHAPTER TWO

When Dennis Griffin was five, he had a slight lisp. It drove his father crazy. Dennis and his mother would be talking about something at breakfast, and his father would lower his paper and interject insightful comments like, "Christ, Marian! You need to get the boy to a speech *therapisTHst* or an *orthodontiTHst!*"

⌇

When Dennis was six, he'd gone to a birthday party to which everyone in the class had been invited. The backyard party had devolved into the girls playing *Pin the Tail on the Donkey*, while the sugar-hyped boys ran around and wrestled on the grass. Dennis, usually ignored by his schoolmates, stood between the two groups, participating in neither activity. That is, until Freddy Johnson came up behind him and gave him a wedgie. Of course, everyone saw it and laughed and laughed. He didn't know what to do and stood frozen on the spot, the waistband of his underwear up around his armpits. His mother chose that moment to appear at the back door and rush over to collect him. When they arrived home, his clothes had still not been readjusted. His father took one look at him and burst out laughing. "Well, that about sums it up, doesn't it, Marian!"

⌇

When he was seven, Dennis was finishing his dessert on Christmas

Eve. It was a cake in the shape of a log with leaves made from green frosting and mushroom-shaped meringue on top.

His mother had said, "Dennis, you'll need to get ready for bed soon. You don't want Santa to bypass us because you are not in your bed."

"Santa?" his father said from his end of the table. "For God's sake, Marian. The boy is too old to believe in Santa."

"Zachary!" his mother gasped.

Dennis had heard this rumor at school, that Santa Claus did not exist. It sort of made sense, but he hadn't wanted to believe it. Still, how could one guy—and a pretty old guy—travel all around the world and climb down all those chimneys in one night?

Later that evening, Dennis was wide awake. He wanted to see for himself about the Santa thing. He made his way down the hall toward the stairs. His destination was the Christmas tree in the front hall.

He heard voices and stopped short. He was outside his parent's room. Their voices were low and he couldn't make out what they were saying. Until his father shouted, "Marian, for the love of God, I don't care. You're the one who wanted children, not me. But I will not tolerate a son who is a momma's boy and believes in Santa Claus, the Easter Bunny, or the boogeyman!"

Dennis abandoned the Santa plan and retreated to his room. But he really wasn't all that surprised at what his father had said.

When he started high school, Dennis spent a couple of days a week after school making copies and shredding documents at his father's law firm. Once his father's secretary had asked him to copy some pages from a pile of books that she said were on a table in the law library and bookmarked with colored paper. Dennis found a pile of books on a table in the library and took them to the copy room. He

started copying the bookmarked pages. An hour or so later, the secretary entered the room carrying a pile of books.

"Dennis, I found these in the library. The books I wanted you to
copy?" she said.

He looked at her in confusion.

"Oh dear, it looks like you picked up the wrong pile."

Naturally, his father appeared at the door at that precise moment
looking for his copies.

"Of course, he picked up the wrong pile," his father snarled. "He's
an idiot! This is not the Barnum and Bailey law firm, Dennis! Make
the copies I need and do it now!"

The secretary added her two cents by saying, "I did say *colored*
paper, Dennis." She nodded to the books in her arms, which were
bookmarked with yellow strips of paper. The books Dennis had been
copying had white strips of paper.

Sometimes, if Dennis didn't have school, his father insisted he
come to court to watch him litigate. His father worked for an insurance
defense firm, and the cases were pretty dry, involving defective con-
struction of buildings and endless testimony from expert witnesses.
But his father thought Dennis would learn something by observing.

When Dennis was seventeen, he was watching television one night
when his parents were out. He was rarely allowed to watch TV, and as
soon as he saw the car pull away, he crept into his father's study. He
had a good sightline on the driveway out the window. He positioned
his father's desk chair such that if he saw headlights, he could quickly
shut off the TV and escape undetected.

He turned the dial and settled on an image of a fighter jet flying
over a deep blue stretch of ocean. Next were images of men running
through an obstacle course in the mud. Then there were men in military dress uniforms shouldering rifles in sync.

"The few. The proud. The marines," said a voice-over.

The commercial stuck with him. He'd been a scrawny kid all his life, but that summer he'd started lifting weights in the gym at his father's country club after his shifts as a caddy. He'd grown a few inches taller and had gained more than a few inches on his frame. His clothes no longer fit, and his mother had to take him shopping for new ones and order larger school uniforms.

His mind kept returning to the TV ad. The idea of training hard and seeing other places appealed to him. He had recently found out that he had an aptitude for fixing engines. Earlier in the summer, a golf cart had broken down, and Dennis had looked under its hood and was able to identify a loose cable. The golfers had gone on and on about how he'd saved the day. They must have told Dennis's boss because he was trained to be a golf cart mechanic shortly thereafter. Maybe he could be a mechanic in the marines.

But even though he was now bigger than his father, he had to work up the courage to broach this career idea.

On the first day of his senior year of high school, Dennis dressed in his new uniform and went downstairs. His father was already seated in the dining room, hidden behind the newspaper. His mother appeared from the kitchen with Dennis's breakfast and placed a sheet of paper next to his plate. It was titled "Acceptable schools to apply to." On the typed list were Yale, Stanford, Cornell, and Princeton. His father had gone to Stanford, then to UC Berkeley's Boalt Hall for law school.

He sat down, and his father lowered the paper an inch and said, "Son."

"Good morning, sir. Thanks, Mom," he said, indicating his plate. His mother smiled and sat down at her place at the table. Dennis didn't start eating; he had no appetite. It was now or never.

Dennis cleared his throat and said, "Sir, if you have a minute."

His father set the paper down and narrowed his eyes at Dennis. After a few seconds had passed, he said, "Well?"

Dennis cleared his throat again. "I've been thinking I might want to postpone college and join the military."

"The military," his dad said flatly.

"Yeah, maybe the marines or—"

"Marian!" his father said nastily, his eyes boring into Dennis. "Did you hear that? Dennis has just informed us that he would like to become a marine instead of going to college. Isn't that nice?"

"Now, Dennis. We've already decided that you're going to college," his mother said, pointing to the list. "Then law school. Then you'll join your father's firm," she said in her *and that's that* voice. She turned to her husband. "Isn't that right, Zachary? Isn't that what we decided?"

"It's what *you* decided," Dennis muttered. "No one asked me what I wanted."

His father leaned toward him and said, "What did you just say?"

"Nothing."

"Goddammit!" His father pounded his fist. Cups rattled and coffee spilled onto the table. "You will repeat what you just said."

"Just that you decided I would go to college. No one asked me what I wanted." Dennis really wished he hadn't brought this up.

"No one cares what you want. That's why no one asked," his father sneered. Coffee ran off the table onto the floor. "This conversation, engaging as it has been, is over," his father said, and disappeared behind his paper.

Dennis opened his mouth, but his mother shook her head and hissed, "Don't upset your father."

She quickly got busy cleaning up the spilled coffee.

Dennis sat silently in his seat. It occurred to him that he would make a terrible lawyer if he couldn't even argue a case with his parents.

↬

On the drive to school, his mother never took her eyes off the road. There was no chitchat. No radio. Dennis wanted to ask her to drop him a couple of blocks from the school, but he knew that wouldn't go over well. Most of his classmates—hell, even the juniors—drove their own cars to school. He was the only senior driven to school by his mother, he was sure of it.

She swung into the circular drive at the front of the school, and he bolted out of the car. As he passed by the tight knots of students, he braced himself for their whispering: "*dork*" or "*freak*." But it was different today. They were looking at him as if they hadn't seen him before. He heard someone say, "Look, a new kid." Someone else said, "Is that *Dennis*?"

During first period, he noticed some of the girls glancing at him. This was new. He was usually invisible to them.

As he walked through the halls to his first class, he passed a couple of the guys who smoked out back during lunch and usually had something obnoxious to say when he walked by. One of them was now gaping at him. Dennis, suddenly emboldened by the realization that he towered over the guy, walked up to him and said, "What?"

The guy—Greg, or Gary, or whatever—took a step back and showed Dennis his palms. "Nothin', man. It's cool." Dennis gave him a hard stare, along with each of the three boys with him in turn. He felt something shift deep down in him.

"Oh yeah? Is it *cool*?" he growled.

They all nodded and smiled. Dennis turned and continued down the hall. What had gotten into him? Where did that come from? He didn't know, but for the first time, he felt his power.

↬

During lunch break, he sat outside on a bench reading for his history class. It was warm and sunny, so he shed his blazer, loosened his tie and collar, and rolled up his sleeves. A shadow fell over him. He looked up and saw one of the guys from the hallway earlier.

"Hey, man," the guy said.

Dennis leveled him with what he hoped was an intimidating stare.

"Yeah, so, it's me, Greg. You know me, right?"

"What do you want?"

"So just thinking maybe you want a smoke?" Greg said, tipping his head toward the back of the gym.

Dennis closed his book and stood up. Greg took a step back, which Dennis liked.

"Sure, I'll smoke," he finally said.

They walked around the side of the school where five or so guys were passing a joint around. Dennis had never smoked pot before. He wasn't sure how. He tried to watch the other guys without looking like he was, and he half closed his eyes as he studied them. When the joint came to him, he inhaled and started to cough.

"Good shit, right?" one of the other guys said, nodding and smiling.

"Yup," Dennis wheezed, trying to get himself under control.

Dennis managed to get high every day at school without letting it affect his grades. He sort of had friends now, for the first time ever. He still didn't talk much, not having much to say. But as his last year of high school progressed, he started lying to his parents. He said he was studying at the library when he was at a party in someone's backyard or working out at the gym. Girls continued to notice him, but he didn't know how to react to that. One of them asked him to a school dance, but he said he couldn't make it. The fact that he didn't talk much, along with his ice-blue eyes, imposing build, and unavailability, resulted in a sort of mystique. *Who was Dennis Griffin?* All the girls were talking about him and how to get his attention. It was as if all those years of being an outcast had never happened.

By the time he graduated, spent a summer caddying and fixing golf carts, and packed up for the dorms at Stanford, he had grown fully into his new persona. During his first week on campus, a tall guy approached him and asked him if he had ever rowed. A week later he walked onto the Stanford men's crew team.

CHAPTER THREE

B renna was running very late. Her schedule was tight; she had only an hour between the end of crew practice and her first class. Most days, she didn't have time to shower or change before class and barely had time to throw down some food and coffee.

She was on the rowing team at Stanford as the coxswain for the men's varsity crew. At five feet three inches, with an extensive knowledge of rowing and a low, confident voice, she was well suited to the job. All the men in her crew were more than a foot taller than she, but when she commanded them to stop the boat, saying "weigh enough, check it down!" they dug in their oar blades.

The stroke, whom all the other rowers followed, and whom Brenna sat facing in the boat, was an intense guy named Dennis, who had ice-blue eyes and a strange mix of arrogance and insecurity. She had first seen him at the freshmen crew meeting. He'd been across the room from her. The meeting was in a gym, and he was seated on a weight bench. Brenna was the only woman in the room, and most of the guys were chatting and horsing around. Dennis, however, was doing neither of those things. He had on a sweatshirt with the hood up and had his hands in his pockets. His long legs were stretched out in front of him. Even with his hood on, Brenna saw a strong jaw and the intensity of his eyes—eyes that settled on her for a moment and sent what felt like a jolt of electricity through her. She quickly looked away, unsettled. *What was that?* It was like they'd made a connection, just by looking at each other. She had never felt anything like that before.

The coaching staff entered the gym, and everyone settled down. The head coach introduced himself and his assistant coaches and began talking about the sport of rowing. Brenna tried to pay attention, but she kept stealing glances at Dennis. Even seated, he looked big and powerful. He both scared and fascinated her.

"For those who don't know," the coach said, "We'll be rowing in eight-man boats. We'll field three eights. The fastest eight men will make up the top boat and enter races. The other two boats will not race. You will all have a chance, every week, to make the top eight.

"Our race seasons are spring and fall. We race 2,000-meter sprints in spring and 5,000-meter head races in the fall."

Brenna thought Dennis looked bored, but it was almost as if she could read his thoughts. Like she *knew* he was bored. She tried focusing on the coach again.

"Eights are rowed by four port rowers and four starboard rowers. From the stern end of the boat, we have the coxswain, stroke, seven-seat, six-seat, five-seat, and so on, down to the one-seat, which is called the bow-seat.

"The coxswains—we have three here: Brenna, Charlie, and Steve—are the only ones facing forward so they steer the boat, call the commands like when to start and stop rowing, when to power up on starboard or port, and when to hit the brakes. You will all become familiar with the commands. And you will follow them exactly. Okay, any questions so far?"

Dennis raised a hand and said, "I'd like to be the stroke, sir."

"Not really a question, but noted," the coach said.

⤳

"Something's off on the starboard side," Dennis said, shaking his head. His voice was deep, gravelly. "I can feel it."

Brenna honed in on the starboard rowers until she identified the problematic oarsman.

"Your blade's coming out early, Brian. Fix your timing."

After a few strokes, Dennis nodded. "Better."

At those moments, when Dennis was pleased with her, Brenna would feel as though everything was right in the world. The guy had an effect on her like nothing she'd experienced. She started to realize that she was attracted to him. But it was more than that. It was as if he were a magnet, pulling her in, and she was powerless to stop it.

On other days, Dennis seemed to blame himself for problems in the boat. They'd be stopped for a short rest, and he'd lament, "It's me. I'm off today."

He'd smile in a self-effacing way that Brenna rarely saw, and she'd be sucked into his orbit all the more. Sitting in the stern with him, it was as if they were in their own little universe.

Dennis never blamed her for anything, though, even jokingly. Unlike some of the other guys, Dennis treated her respectfully— professionally, even. A few of the rowers cajoled her and teased her, saying if she would steer better, they would row better. They called her Short Stack and asked her how the hell she could see where she was going with all of their fat heads in the way and mussed her hair when they walked by.

The varsity eight was preparing to race in San Diego in a couple of months and had two-a-day water practices, along with extra land workouts. The varsity eight spent a lot of time together. Brenna loved it. Her experience rowing in the single served her well as a coxswain. From her first outing with a freshman crew of mostly brand-new rowers—except for a Canadian named Peter who'd rowed in high school—she handled the unsteady boat with skill and authority, and she knew she'd found her calling. A few of the guys Brenna had coxed in the freshman eight, including Peter and Dennis, were selected for the varsity eight the following year, as was she.

When she wasn't occupied with crew, she studied communications.

Brenna was in the library when she felt eyes on her. She looked up, and Dennis was standing across the room staring at her with such fierceness that she gasped a little. Recovering, she lifted a hand in greeting. After smoothing his shirt with his hands, he approached her table.

"Hey," he said, "May I sit?" He indicated the chair across from her. She nodded and indicated the chair right back at him.

He folded his long frame into the chair. "What are you reading?"

"An article for a paper. 'Legal issues in journalism.'" She realized that she had never had a conversation with him on a topic other than rowing.

He nodded and pointed at himself. "Political science. Supposed to go to law school."

Brenna was seldom at a loss for words and was generally comfortable around everyone, but Dennis unnerved her, to say the least. He had on a white USRowing T-shirt and his muscular shoulders were evident underneath. There was something not . . . safe—that was the only word she could conjure—about him.

"So, where are you from?" she asked.

"L.A. You?"

"San Francisco. City by the Bay . . . ," she trailed off. What was it with this guy? He wasn't even her type. She normally didn't go for the moody bad boys. She had started dating the Canadian named Peter, who rowed in the two-seat and was the best of them technically. But they were trying to keep that on the down-low.

"My dad owns the *San Francisco Tribune*. I'm supposed to take it over someday," she blurted out.

"Wow. Really?" He shook his head. She wasn't sure how to take that.

"What? You look so surprised. Is it because I'm a girl and girls don't take over businesses?" She heard the defensiveness in her voice overlaying the nervousness.

"No, no, it's not that. I'm supposed to join my father's law firm. Eventually. It's just interesting that we are on similar paths that way."

"Oh. Sorry. Guess I assumed a lot just now." She laughed awkwardly.

"Yup," Dennis replied. They sat silently for a couple of seconds, until he said, "So, would you want to go out sometime?"

She had not expected that. "Oh! Well. I'm kinda seeing someone. But, I mean, it's not serious. I mean, I guess I could . . . ," she trailed off in midstammer.

"Well, give me a call." He slid a piece of paper across the table, stood up, and walked out.

∽

At practice that afternoon, the team was on land. Brenna felt a mix of relief and regret that she wasn't sitting in the stern of the boat with Dennis. Thoughts swirled in her head. *Why was she thinking about him this way? Why had he asked her out?* She knew she should just tell him she couldn't date him. But, at the same time, she kind of wanted to.

He didn't pay any attention to her that afternoon. He slogged his way through the workout with everyone else, which they were doing on the indoor rowing machines called ergometers, or "ergs." Brenna and the other coxswains circulated among the rowers, calling attention to technical changes they needed to make or lapses in power. The coaches watched too, with their clipboards, making notes.

Dennis had the fastest times among the crew on the ergs. Peter was a couple of inches shorter than Dennis and did not have as much power, but his technique made him almost as fast. Peter was waiting outside the gym for her after practice. It was dark, and he stood in the shadows so the other guys wouldn't see him. It had become their usual routine.

Peter was one of the guys who teased Brenna the most, saying that he loved it when she yelled at him in the boat, and when he asked her to a movie, she wasn't the least bit surprised. But it wasn't a serious relationship. They had an easy and casual way of being together. Like this evening, they met some of his non-rowing friends from his classes at a pub, drank a couple of pints, then, citing early practice in the morning, they called it a night.

When Brenna got back to her dorm, she pulled the piece of paper with Dennis's phone number from her pocket. She looked at it for a long time, then walked down the hall to the pay phone.

CHAPTER FOUR

When Dennis returned to his dorm room that evening, he found a note taped to his door saying that Brenna had called. He snatched it up and headed for the pay phone.

When he got her on the phone, he wasn't sure what to say. "Hey, Brenna. It's Dennis calling you back."

"Oh, hey, thanks for calling me back," she said, sounding as awkward as he felt. "So, yeah, I was just calling about what you asked about in the library? Going out?"

"Okay."

"Yeah, so I appreciate you asking me, but, as I said, I'm kinda seeing someone, so I probably shouldn't—"

"Peter. Right."

"You know about that?"

"I've seen you leave practice together. Put two and two together."

"Huh," she said. "Do the other guys know?"

"Don't know."

"I mean, did you tell anyone what you saw?"

"Nope."

"We're kinda trying to keep it a secret. I mean, we're not serious or anything, but . . . ," she trailed off.

Not serious, he thought. *But she was turning him down.*

～

Dennis sat slumped in the six-seat watching dolphins at SeaWorld propelling themselves into the air. He replayed his conversation with his coach (again).

You do fine at stroke, Dennis, but I need you more in the engine room. You're my strongest guy. Peter's rhythm is a little steadier than yours and easier for the guys to follow. Coach had blathered on about how every seat in the boat was equally important, that all eight rowers had a role in moving the boat. Dennis wasn't buying it. The stroke was the most important rower, no question about it.

After Coach had broken the news to Dennis, he'd left the coach's office, walked down the hallway, and punched a hole in the wall. He stomped out of the boathouse, fully expecting to get a call from Coach telling him he was off the team.

But the next day, when he returned to the boathouse, he saw that someone had tacked a poster up over the hole.

An official called their race to the line, and Dennis tried to focus. The San Diego Crew Classic was a big deal, the first race of the spring season, the race they'd been preparing for. It was two thousand meters of all-out pain. The start line was just north of SeaWorld. It was hard not to watch the dolphins sail by while waiting for the other crews to align.

Dennis should be stroking this boat. There was no way they were going to do well with Peter setting the pace. Peter wasn't aggressive enough. He was too nice. Dennis wondered (again) if Brenna had talked to Coach and if that was why Peter had replaced Dennis. Maybe he'd made her too uncomfortable when he'd asked her out. He leaned to the port side to look at her. She had her game face on. Her dark hair was pulled back into a long braid, and her slim frame fit comfortably in the coxswain's seat.

A dolphin arced above her head, and the race starter said, "Attention, go!"

They did much better than Dennis predicted, coming in third.

Dennis grudgingly admitted that Peter had done a pretty good job, keeping his stroke long, holding a steady cadence, then hitting the gas when Brenna commanded it. After they landed their boat just off-shore, the crowd on the beach was cheering at one team or another, and Dennis watched as Peter picked Brenna up to carry her to the beach so she wouldn't get her feet wet. The winning boat tossed their shrieking coxswain into the water. Once the Stanford boat was washed off, derigged, and put on the trailer for transport back to campus, Dennis walked back toward the hotel, working himself into a foul mood. By the time he unlocked the door to his room, he'd convinced himself that they'd have won if he'd been stroking.

That evening, the Stanford crew team took cabs to the Old Town section of San Diego for dinner and a celebration. Beers were moderately consumed during the meal, after which Coach gave a speech to his V-8 crew about a job well done, proud of them all, blah blah blah. When Coach left to go back to the hotel, the tequila shots commenced.

Before too long, the gathering had gotten raucous and some of the guys, including Peter, were pretty drunk. Peter and the three-seat wound up standing on the table singing "We Are the Champions" until the bartender put a stop to it and suggested it was time for bed. The seven- and bow-seats got Peter into a cab, and the rest of them trickled out. Dennis ended up in a taxi with Joe, the five-seat, and Brenna. Joe opened the window and kept yelling "Whoooo!"

In the lobby, Joe pulled both Dennis and Brenna into a hug. "Love you guys!" he said. While Joe hugged them and smashed Brenna and him together, a current of energy charged through Dennis, almost leaving him breathless.

As he watched Joe lurch toward the elevator, Dennis said, "Think I'm going to take a walk." He turned to Brenna. "You're welcome to join."

She looked dazed. "Uh, sure. Okay."

They headed out along a path to the beach, in silence. Mission Bay sat flat and calm beneath a sliver of moon.

"Nice job today," Dennis said, finally.

"You too."

"Your boyfriend did a decent job too."

Brenna smiled a little. "Yeah, he did. I know you wanted to stroke the boat, but I see why Coach put you in six. The boat had a lot more power than when Rich was there."

Dennis nodded. "Yeah, I guess."

They came to a beach log and Dennis sat down. Brenna sat too. They looked at the water. The bus would pick them up in the morning to transport them back to Stanford. Then, back to the grind to get ready for the Pac-10 Championships.

"So, you didn't ask Coach to switch Peter into the stroke seat?" Dennis said.

"No, of course not! Why would I do that?"

Dennis shrugged.

"You really think I would do something like that? I know how much you wanted it—and so does the wall in the boathouse."

Dennis looked at her. "So, you heard about that, huh."

"Yeah. Everyone did. But luckily, some incredibly smart and quick-thinking person covered it up before the coaches saw it," Brenna said, looking down at her feet and smiling.

Dennis glanced at her sideways. "Well, thanks to that smart and quick-thinking person."

They sat in silence for a few minutes, and Dennis could feel the energy building between them.

Finally, Brenna sighed and said, "Well, guess I'll head back." She made no move to stand up and turned her head to look at him. Dennis suddenly, surprising them both, leaned toward her and kissed her. She didn't resist. She kissed him back. They clawed at each other and fell together onto the sand. Soon they started to fumble with each other's clothes, not caring if anyone came along to see them.

"You sure?" Dennis breathed into her ear.

"No," Brenna said, and kissed him hard.

As he plunged into her and she arched into him, Brenna felt that they were one person, permanently bonded. It was only when it was over that she thought of Peter, with a mix of horrible guilt while at the same time feeling fully alive.

"Hey," she said, as she reassembled her clothes. "Please don't tell Peter about this."

"No," Dennis said. "He wouldn't want to know about this."

He offered her a hand up, and they walked back to the hotel. They rode the elevator and, when it stopped at her floor, she said good night and walked away. It was as if they were both in shock or had shared the same dream.

CHAPTER FIVE

As the lone woman on the Stanford men's rowing team, Brenna always had a room to herself when the team traveled. That night in San Diego, she sat on her bed and thought, *What just happened? Why had it happened?*

You know why, she answered herself. *You were—are—attracted to him.*

But she was also a little afraid of him, which was why she said she couldn't go out with him. That and the fact that she was still dating Peter. She liked Peter's relaxed friendliness, his kindness, his capacity for fun. Yeah, he'd kind of embarrassed her tonight, getting so drunk, but it was a celebration. He had stroked them onto the podium.

But Dennis had powered them into the bronze-medal spot. The intensity with which he rowed radiated up to her in the coxswain seat. She could feel his strength, and it felt dangerous. She feared him but was drawn to him nonetheless.

For the rest of that season, Peter stroked and Dennis rowed in the six-seat. They did well at the Pac-10s, winning a silver medal. Brenna and Dennis saw each other at practice, and it was, admittedly, awkward between them. They'd nod at each other or say hello and quickly put as much distance between them as possible.

Peter never acted as if he knew anything about what had occurred on the beach in San Diego. Dennis must have kept quiet. Brenna kept waiting for something to happen. For Dennis to ask her out again, for Peter to confront her, but neither came about.

The following fall, Brenna was asked to cox for the women's crew team, which was working to develop into a competitive squad. She missed the guys but was excited that the coaching staff thought enough of her to ask her to help build the team. She missed seeing Dennis. She thought about him all the time. He was an enigma to her. There was clearly something between them, which had manifested on the beach in San Diego, but neither one of them made any move to pursue it further. So, she and Peter slowly moved into an exclusive relationship, almost by default.

Peter talked about Dennis a lot. They had apparently become good friends.

"Man, that guy's a beast," Peter would often say, shaking his head in wonderment.

"You know, he's making a run for the national team," he told Brenna one day. "He's going to a development camp next summer. I'll bet he makes the 1984 Olympic team. That'd be cool. We could watch him row since the Olympics will be in L.A."

Brenna was very interested in hearing all of this, but she tried not to let on.

During the fall season of 1982, the V-8 lineup had Peter at stroke and Dennis in the six-seat. It had been that way since their sophomore year. Other guys had been rotated in and out of the boat and in and out of different seats, but Peter and Dennis were always in the boat and usually in the same seats.

Dennis began to meet up with Peter and Brenna at a bar or restaurant, sometimes alone and other times with a date. He tended to date rowers—sometimes the rowers Brenna coxed. He'd throw his arm around the back of their chairs, appearing to be listening to them with his full attention. She tried to tamp down the jealousy that worked its way through her.

One early fall evening, Peter and Brenna were walking near campus. Peter was telling her about the boarding school where he'd gone to high school.

"It was pretty great," Peter said. "It was one of two rowing schools on Vancouver Island. The school was right on the bay where we rowed—hey, there's Dennis!"

Peter pointed to an outdoor table at a student hangout bar. Dennis was sitting with a woman but not one Brenna recognized.

As Peter and Brenna approached, Dennis stood up, saying, "Hey, you guys wanna join us?"

Peter looked at Brenna, who shrugged. "Sure."

Dennis appeared to be even bigger than he had been last spring. He introduced his date. Brenna immediately forgot what he had said her name was. She was tall with big hair, big blondish-reddish hair. Dennis talked about development camp and how it was unlikely he'd make the national team this year, but he was thinking ahead to the pre-Olympic regatta in the single. He'd rowed singles a fair amount during the summer, and it had appealed to him.

"Don't have to worry about syncing up with anyone. I'm always the stroke"—he threw a sidelong glance at Peter, who laughed—"I can run my own show."

"I rowed a single in high school, did I ever tell you that? I still have it over in Oakland," said Brenna.

"That doesn't surprise me," said Dennis. He turned to his date. "Brenna is the best coxswain I've ever rowed with; she has incredible boat feel." He swung his attention back to Brenna. "We were a good team in the stern. Till Coach broke us up. Guess that's how you ended up with this guy!" Everyone at the table laughed, Peter the loudest.

"Sounds like he's got a crush!" Dennis's date said jokingly to Brenna.

"Only on you," Dennis said to her, and gave her a side hug.

At the same time, Brenna, who was seated on the other side of Dennis, felt Dennis brush his leg up against hers. She stiffened, and he moved it away. *Don't jump to conclusions*, she thought. *He's a big guy and takes up a lot of space. He probably didn't even notice.*

Then it happened again. And he left it there. His leg up against hers. As they all chatted away like two couples on a double date. Brenna stood up and said she'd be right back.

In the ladies' room, she splashed water on her flushed face. Her heart pounded. *What was happening?* She felt both alarmed and excited. *Did he mean to do that? Was he sending her some signal?* She returned to the table and told Peter she wasn't feeling well. He took her home.

In October, the V-8 traveled to Boston for the Head of the Charles Regatta. Brenna decided to accompany Peter, even though her women's crew wasn't going. The Charles was the biggest regatta in the country, drawing college crews, national team rowers, current and former Olympians, and high school and master's rowers from around the world. Brenna wanted to see Peter row and also experience the weekend. The Stanford coaches thought her going along was a good idea since she would learn from watching the races.

The V-8, plus Brenna and the coaches, took a flight together. Dennis was seated a couple of rows ahead, and Brenna could see the top of his head all the way to the East Coast. They landed at Logan and took the subway to their hotel, which overlooked the Charles River. Peter was tired and wanted to take a nap before dinner. Brenna was energized; she had never been to Boston and decided to take a walk.

The atmosphere was charged. Crews practiced on the river, and groups of people—really tall people—walked around in the waning fall afternoon. She passed one iconic bridge after another, which marked crews' progress on the course: the railroad bridge, Anderson Bridge, Weeks Bridge. Tents were set up on both shores with vendors selling swag, ergometers, and food. As Brenna started across the Eliot Bridge, she saw a familiar profile. Dennis was leaning on the stone railing watching the rowing shells pass underneath. She told herself to turn around and go back to the hotel. But, instead, she found herself walking toward him.

"Hey, stranger, fancy meeting you here."

Dennis turned and smiled. "Is this cool or what?"

She nodded.

"Where's Peter?"

"He's taking a nap."

Dennis considered that for a beat, then said, "Come on. Let's go see Cambridge."

He was amped up, excited to be there, that was clear. It was contagious. They walked toward Harvard Square, stopping in random shops—a record store, a cigar store, a bookstore. Dennis was fun, animated, in a way Brenna had never seen him before.

"I don't know about you," he said, "but I'm hungry. There's a burger place near here I've been told not to pass by."

"Uh, I should probably get back. Peter's probably awake."

"Call him. He can meet us there."

They found a pay phone, and Brenna called the hotel. Peter picked up, sounding groggy.

Brenna explained that she'd run into Dennis on her walk and that they were thinking about dinner.

"Yeah, you guys go ahead. Sorry. I don't know why I'm so tired. I'm going to rest a little more, maybe meet up with the guys later for some food."

"You sure?"

"Yeah, have fun. I'll see you later."

Brenna hung up and told Dennis that Peter wasn't coming.

"Good. We don't have to wait."

They went to a place called Mr. Bartley's, which had been around forever and served burgers named for politicians. It was busy and crowded, and they were seated at a tiny table.

"You look good," Dennis said. "Are you happy?"

"I am."

"You look like you are. Things with Peter have gotten serious, I guess."

"Yeah, I guess they have."

"Congratulations. Happy for you."

Brenna looked for anything in his face that indicated otherwise. Dennis did look happy for her. Suddenly though, his knees brushed against hers under the table. And she felt the electricity.

But they just talked about rowing and the upcoming race.

"It'd be great if you could cox us."

"Don't think that's gonna happen."

"Probably not. Unless Dave gets sick or something." Dave was Brenna's replacement.

"He looked pretty healthy on the plane," Brenna said, but a part of her hoped he might get sick.

It was fully dark by the time they got back to the hotel. It felt as if they'd been on a date. She was both exhilarated and guilt-ridden. Dennis sat down on a bench outside the lobby.

"I think I'll just sit out here for a bit. Maybe smoke a cigar." He held up the bag from the cigar store.

"You're going to smoke a cigar before a race?"

"Nah, I'm kidding. I'll wait till the victory dinner."

She stood in front of him awkwardly. He moved over an inch or so on the bench, creating a little more space. The gesture sent alarm bells through her. She felt herself being pulled in, afraid she was powerless to stop whatever might happen. *Run away!* her brain screamed, *Run away, now!*

"Well, I'm pretty tired. I better go up and see how Peter's doing." She didn't run, but she did walk away quickly.

Peter still felt tired the next day. It was more than jet lag, he thought. "Is there even jet lag going west to east?" he asked Brenna. He said he felt lightheaded, too.

They went to breakfast in the hotel and ran into Dave and some of the others. Dennis wasn't with them. They pulled chairs up and made room for Brenna and Peter. Oddly enough, Dave said he wasn't feeling that well. Brenna felt a jolt of nerves. *Was she going to have to cox after all?* A second alarming and irrational thought occurred to her: *Was Dennis somehow making Peter and Dave sick?*

On race day, everyone felt fine, and the Stanford men's collegiate eight finished in the top ten, which, at the Head of the Charles, was a good result.

As far as Brenna knew, Dennis had never said anything to Peter about San Diego. And as far as she could tell, Dennis had moved on, and it was time for her to do the same. So, when Peter asked her to marry him, she accepted, and they started planning the wedding for early June, right after graduation.

CHAPTER SIX

Jack booked a house in Mendocino overlooking the ocean, where he and Meg would host Peter's family and hold Brenna's and Peter's wedding. He tried to summon some enthusiasm for this upcoming event and the impending marriage. Brenna had brought Peter up to Tahoe last Christmas to introduce him to the family. Peter was nice enough, a little bland, a little too chatty. He chattered on excitedly about skiing Squaw Valley. It wasn't that Jack didn't like Peter. What wasn't there to like? He just had a feeling that Brenna was settling for the first man to ask her to marry him. She had just graduated from college—as had Peter. It seemed too early for Brenna to decide that Peter was the one she would go the distance with.

Of course, he reminded himself, Jack and Meg had married young. And he also reminded himself that he always gave in to what Brenna wanted.

Up until Brenna's birth Jack had been indifferent to the idea of children. But Meg wanted them, and he wanted to make her happy. When he first saw Brenna, as Meg held her in the hospital bed, he felt love surge through him with a ferocity he'd never experienced before. As she grew, she looked more and more like Meg—small-framed, dark-haired, blue-eyed. But she was different in every other way. She was feisty. She was not afraid to take Jack on and argue her point of view.

What made this marriage bearable to Jack was that Brenna and

Peter planned to live in the Bay Area, where Brenna would take on the job of local news editor at the paper. Finally, she and Jack would work side by side, and he would teach her what she needed to know about running the *Tribune*.

At the wedding, Jack met many of Brenna and Peter's teammates. One in particular, who had a powerful build and ice-blue eyes, stood apart from the group. After the ceremony, this young man and Jack ended up side by side at the bar watching Brenna clown around with some of the guys she had coxed. He introduced himself as Dennis Griffin.

"You must be in training," Jack said to him.

Dennis smiled and raised his Coca-Cola bottle.

"So, were you in a boat Brenna coxed? Or did you row with Peter?" Jack asked.

"Both, actually."

Jack nodded.

"Brenna told me you won gold at the Olympics," Dennis said. "I'm trying to make the 1984 team in the single."

"Are you?" Jack thought, *Why wasn't Brenna with a guy like this?* Peter was giving up rowing to open a restaurant. Jack had grave doubts about this plan; it was not easy opening a business, much less in such a risky industry.

"Yes, sir. I may have a shot at the trials. But only one U.S. sculler goes to the Olympics."

Jack and Dennis talked about rowing and Dennis's plans for law school, until Peter's sister, Kristina, approached. Jack introduced Dennis to her and handed him a business card. "Let me know how it goes at the trials. And I can always use a good lawyer."

"Will do," Dennis said. Jack turned to leave the two of them to get acquainted, but Kristina put a hand on Jack's arm. She was a few years older than Peter and had been eyeing Jack since she arrived.

"Now that we're family, I hope you'll dance with me," she said.

Jack didn't know how to politely refuse, so he took her arm and led her to the dance floor. He saw Meg sipping a glass of wine and watching him. Jack nodded to her and gave a *What can I do?* shrug, and Meg turned to talk to Peter's mother.

CHAPTER SEVEN

Dennis finished fifth at the pre-Olympic regatta. It was not a bad result for a first try, but he was humiliated and furious with himself. He decided to quit rowing.

His father had grudgingly indulged the idea that Dennis might compete in the Olympics, so long as he packed up and returned to Yale in time for the start of his second year of law school.

When Dennis returned home from the regatta, his father merely said, "Well, now that all that rowing business is over, it's time for you to focus on the real world. I've got work for you at the law firm until you leave for the East Coast."

"Thank you, sir," Dennis said, and quickly left the house.

Dennis took his father's Jaguar and drove aimlessly around feeling thoroughly depressed. Maybe he shouldn't quit rowing. Maybe he should go to the selection camp to try for a spot in a double- or a four-man boat. But honestly, he had to agree with his father on this one: enough was enough.

Dennis found himself at a junction for the 405 freeway. He swung onto the ramp and headed north. He merged onto the 101 and drove six hours straight until he arrived in Redwood City near the Stanford boathouse. He got out of the car and stretched his stiff legs. *What was he doing here?* He had nothing but his wallet and the clothes he was wearing. It was early summer and there weren't any crews on the water.

He knew that Peter and Brenna had bought a house a year earlier not far from here. He'd been invited to their housewarming party; he hadn't gone but had memorized the address. He got back in the car and drove around until he found the house.

She was home.

"Dennis!" Brenna said when she opened the door. "What are you doing here?"

"Guess I'm a little late for the housewarming party."

They both laughed awkwardly and a little too loudly.

"How are you? How's your training going?"

"It isn't."

"Why not?"

"It didn't go well at the pre-Olympic regatta, so . . ."

"I'm sorry," Brenna said. "Uh. Do you want to come in? Want a beer?"

"Yeah. I do want a beer."

In the kitchen, she said, "So now what? Back to school?"

"That's the plan. I leave in a few weeks."

"You still going to row for Yale?"

"Nah. Think I'm done with it."

"But you're so good." She looked genuinely concerned.

"Not good enough," he responded, shrugging it off.

They stood in silence for a minute or two.

"Is Peter home?"

"He's at the restaurant."

"Oh. How's that going?"

"Okay, I guess. He works long hours. I work long hours. But I love my job. I didn't know if I would, given that it was what was expected of me without my having much of a say in it. But it's a good fit. Do you want to sit down? Let's go outside." She led the way to a backyard patio.

They talked some more about her job, and Brenna told him she was rowing her single again when she had the time. She'd moved it to a boathouse near Stanford.

"Maybe I'll race it as a masters rower," she said, laughing. "I can challenge the eights at the Crew Classic."

Suddenly she jumped up. "You know, when I was unpacking here, I found something I'd always meant to give to you. I'll be right back."

Dennis found himself standing and following her into the house. She walked down a short hall and turned right, and he continued following. She turned as he came through the door into what was clearly her and Peter's bedroom. She was standing at a bureau pulling a photograph from the frame of the mirror above it.

She looked up and held out the photo. "It's the V-8 from San Diego, remember?"

They stood staring at each other in silence, her hand extending a picture of eight rowers holding her lengthwise like a log. Dennis was propping her up by her right arm, and Peter held her head.

Dennis could hear birds chirping outside and the faraway drone of traffic on Highway 101 until his ears started to ring, and he felt as if he were leaving his body.

Suddenly he lunged forward. She dropped the photo as he pulled her onto the bed.

"Dennis! No! We can't!" he heard her say from a long way away. But she didn't fight him. He almost stopped. He even tried, but he couldn't control himself. He'd waited so long for this to happen again. She seemed to feel the same, to be all in. But even as they moved together in a desperate rhythm, he felt a nagging doubt, like maybe she'd wanted him to stop. Finally, she cried out her release and so did he, shortly thereafter.

Afterward, Dennis sat up and put his head in his hands. He was afraid to move. He didn't know what she was thinking. Should he apologize? Say he didn't know what had come over him? He was afraid to look at her.

"I guess you never told Peter about us," he said into his hands when he could no longer stand the heavy silence between them.

"Us? What about us?"

"Just, you know, about San Diego."

"No, of course not." He heard rustling and a zipper.

"Well, maybe you should; now that it's happened again. Now that it seems like we're having an affair."

"Affair?" she said.

He heard the panic in her voice and was still afraid to look at her, afraid of what he would see on her face.

"This is not an affair," she said stonily, and he felt her words like a physical blow. "You just forced yourself on me."

The pain he felt then threatened to overwhelm him. He willed himself to rally. Finally, he looked up at her. She was standing at the foot of the bed, fully dressed. He glanced around for his T-shirt and pulled it over his head.

He laughed. "Well, it didn't seem as if you minded. Not one bit."

Brenna gaped at him.

"Luring me into your bedroom so you could give me a photo you knew I already have?"

"You need to leave now," she said, close to tears. "And I *will* tell Peter what happened today. I might even report you to the police."

Dennis slowly stood up, forcing himself to keep it together. He zipped up his pants. He bent to smooth the bedspread with his hand, then looked back at her.

"And why would anyone believe it wasn't consensual? After San Diego."

"That was a long time ago, Dennis. No one knew about us, and it's not like you ever wanted anything to do with me afterward."

"Oh, now I see. That's what this is about. That I didn't yell 'Stop the wedding!' and demand that you marry me instead of Peter. Is that it?" He smiled meanly at her, and he felt like a monster.

"In your dreams," she shot back, but her shaky voice betrayed her.

"Anyway," he said brightly. "It's your word against mine."

"That's right. And they'll believe me."

"They might. If there hadn't been a witness."

Brenna stared at him.

"Oh. I guess you didn't know."

"Know what?"

"Rich saw us that night in San Diego. He said he was out walking around and, well, came across us on the beach. He asked me if we were now a couple since it was clear to everyone on the team that you had this huge crush on me.

"But, of course," Dennis continued, surprising himself by how easy the lies came forth. "I asked him not to tell anyone. So that Peter wouldn't find out. To honor your request."

Brenna shook her head.

"Rich could have a conversation with Peter now, though. About old times and all."

CHAPTER EIGHT

Brenna kept quiet. What good would it do to tell? It would only hurt Peter. When she found out she was pregnant, she truly had no idea if Dennis or Peter was the father. It really could have been either of them. She thought about keeping the pregnancy a secret and quietly getting an abortion. She went as far as to open the phone book and find a Planned Parenthood in another city. She even picked up the phone to dial the number. But she couldn't do it and hung up.

When she started showing and finally told him, Peter had been thrilled. They had planned on a family. Someday.

Peter told her not to worry. The restaurant was doing well; Brenna's job paid well, and the benefits included generous maternity leave. They'd be fine.

But Brenna felt nothing but dread. What was growing in there? Peter's baby or the child of a sociopath? Because she was sure there was something wrong with Dennis. She realized that fully now. He really was dangerous and only out for himself. He obviously felt nothing for others. She relived the day the baby might have been conceived over and over in her head. Had he really forced himself on her? Had she responded? Deep down she knew she probably had.

She fell into a deep depression. She didn't want to tell her parents she was pregnant. Peter didn't understand why and told her he was worried about her. He hovered. He went with her to doctor appointments and gave her pep talks.

↩

Dennis sat at the counter in a San Francisco coffee shop. It was early morning and raining. His job at the auto repair shop down the street didn't start for an hour. The server approached, and Dennis looked up from reading the menu and blurted, "Brenna?"

The server shook her head and pointed to her name tag. "Deirdre," she said. "Are you ready to order?"

Dennis shook his head to clear it. The server was dark haired but taller than Brenna. "Sorry, you look like someone I used to know."

Deirdre smiled thinly, in an *I've heard it all, so don't even bother* way, and said again, "Are you ready to order?"

↩

The diner was filling up, and he recognized some of the guys he worked with. They took a booth and nodded at him but didn't invite him over. Dennis could tell they were a little afraid of him, and that was fine with him.

Deirdre brought his coffee. Rain continued to fall. Deirdre brought his breakfast, which he ate while watching her move around the restaurant. She brought his check. He put a five-dollar bill down and left.

↩

He went back to the diner a couple more times before work, and if Deirdre was working, she waited on him. One Sunday, he decided to go in and see if she was there. It was still early, and the place was empty except for an old couple in a booth sitting in complete silence. He sat at the counter. Deirdre appeared and said, "Coffee?"

"Yes, please."

She nodded. He saw her smile as she turned away. Returning with his coffee. "You eating?"

"Nah, just coffee."

"Day off?" she said.

"Yup."

She nodded and disappeared in the back somewhere. A guy came in and sat at the other end of the counter. Deirdre took his order, then returned to Dennis and refilled his coffee.

"So," she said. "You know my name. What's yours?"

She smelled like cigarettes. She was probably his age but looked older.

"I'm Dennis," he said. "Do you have an extra cigarette?"

She reached into her apron pocket and pulled out a pack. She pulled two cigarettes out and placed them next to his coffee cup, along with her lighter. Dennis lit one as she watched.

"Kinda slow, huh," he said, just as the cook called out "Order up!" and Deirdre went to deliver it to the guy at the end of the counter. Dennis put the lighter in his pocket.

The door opened and a couple of cops came in, heading for a booth. Dennis, as usual, turned his face away. He'd grown a beard in an effort to be less recognizable in case his father had the police looking for him.

Deirdre returned and said, "Are you ever going to ask me out, or what?"

It turned out that she was a lot younger than he was. She was eighteen, and she had a four-year-old son. She lived with her mother and two younger siblings in Daly City. She took the BART into the city for work. She would not talk about the father of her child. Her son's name, weirdly enough, was Dennis. She called him Denny.

They went to the movies the first time. Their second date was a picnic at Golden Gate Park. She started spending time at his place when she could get her mother to watch Denny. Dennis liked her well enough, but he could tell she was into him. That was fine. He was agreeable to hanging out with her. If she wanted to refer to him as her boyfriend, that was fine too. He didn't care.

He continued going to the diner several mornings a week. Deirdre would wait on him. He would read the paper. He was sick of his job and his crappy apartment. He was starting to get sick of Deirdre and all her complaining—about how her mother wasn't taking very good care of her younger siblings, and how her sister said she sometimes watched Denny when her mother went to the bar, but she was only ten and too young to be doing that, and how her twelve-year-old brother was ditching school, and why didn't Dennis ever want to come over and meet her family?

Dennis was ready for a change. One morning, before work, he was in the diner looking at the job listings in the *Tribune*, and there it was.

"Wanted: husband and wife, or comparable duo, for caretaking, cooking, and cleaning at second home in Lake Tahoe. If interested, call Jack Riley . . ."

Jack Riley. Had to be the same Jack Riley. Brenna had mentioned her family's place up in Tahoe. Dennis still had Jack's business card in his wallet. He took it out and compared phone numbers. They were the same.

CHAPTER NINE

J ack and Brenna met for lunch at Peter's restaurant. He'd named it Ptarmigan after one of his favorite runs at Whistler where he had skied growing up in Canada. As he had explained to Jack, the concept was "'Cascadia.' Food from the region that extends from Northern California to British Columbia." Jack was one of the restaurant's main investors.

At first, Jack had looked down on Peter's idea of opening a restaurant and figured he'd never see the money he invested again, but the place seemed to be doing pretty well. Its location in Mountain View put it in a prime spot to attract customers from the burgeoning Silicon Valley technology industry.

He and Brenna ordered salmon, which the menu said was grilled on an alder plank. "Very Pacific Northwest," Peter said. It was delicious, Jack had to admit. Brenna hardly touched hers. Despite being seven months pregnant—and visibly so—she looked gaunt, as if the baby were devouring her from the inside.

"Not hungry, Bren?"

She shook her head. "Hard to keep food down."

"Listen," Jack said, taking her hand, which was surprisingly cold, "I don't want you to worry. I know you hadn't planned to start a family quite yet, but I will always be here. Anything you need."

She nodded. "Thanks, Dad. I know."

⤳

Jack was back in his office, still thinking about Brenna. He was worried; she was not the same. It was as if the baby she was growing were draining the life out of her. But what did he know about being pregnant? It wreaked havoc on a woman's body. There were hormones, what-have-you. He knew that much from watching Meg go through it. That's probably all it was.

His secretary buzzed. "There's a Dennis Griffin on the line. Says he's a friend of Brenna's and Peter's from Stanford. Shall I take a message?"

"No, I'll take it." Jack picked up. "Dennis Griffin! How did the trials go?"

"Hello, sir. I'm surprised you remember me."

"Of course, I do. I didn't see you rowing at the Olympics, but did you come close to making the team?"

"I suppose so . . ."

"Well, you have another four years to do it. And you're at Yale, is that right?"

Dennis hesitated. "I was."

"Was?"

"Well, sir. My parents were so angry that I didn't make the Olympic team that they said they would no longer pay for me to go to Yale. I had to drop out and start working to make the money to go back to school, hopefully next fall."

"Jesus," said Jack. He didn't know what else to say. *What kind of parents were these?*

"I've been working as a mechanic here in San Francisco, but I came across your ad for a caretaker in Tahoe. I'm interested in the job."

"Really," Jack said. Their caretakers, Gene and Charlotte, had moved out of the area. His secretary had been taking the calls and interviewing replacements.

"I just got engaged," Dennis continued, "To a widow with a four-year-old son, and we thought what a great opportunity this would be to raise him in Lake Tahoe, instead of here in the city. We're planning a Christmas wedding."

Jack decided right then and there to offer Dennis the job. Dennis's parents must be abominable people, he thought, and Dennis deserved the chance to pursue his dream of going back to law school. He admired Dennis for taking the initiative in order to get his life back on track.

CHAPTER TEN

Deirdre's alarm buzzed at six, and she got up and headed down the hall. As was often the case, there were strange people in the living room. Deirdre's mother worked nights as a bartender, but her side hustle was dealing drugs. Cocaine mostly. The phone rang and people knocked on the door at all hours.

Deirdre found her mother in the kitchen, reaching for a beer in the fridge.

"Those people can't stay," she told her mother. "They need to complete their transactions and get out. They can't be here, hanging out all night."

"Fine, fine. Whatever you say," her mother said, but made no move toward the living room.

"And put that beer back. You need to sober up. You need to watch Denny while I'm at work."

Her mother just stood there.

Deirdre sighed heavily, then plucked the beer out of her mother's hand. She went into the living room, and shouted, "Out! All of you!"

Deirdre made coffee and gave her mother a large mugful. She woke up her sister Alana and her brother Tommy, gave them breakfast, and packed their lunches. She let Denny sleep. Deirdre picked up a pile of cash her mother had placed on the kitchen counter. She needed to go grocery shopping after work. She'd use the rest to pay the rent and the light and phone bills—if there was enough left.

At seven thirty, Deirdre, Alana, and Tommy left the house and headed for the BART station.

After depositing the kids at school, Deirdre got back on the train. Her thoughts turned to Dennis. When he'd started coming into the diner, she felt an instant attraction to him. His ice-blue eyes and strength caught her attention. But it was something else, a magnetism about him, a hint of danger, that caused her to look for him every time the door opened.

But she worried that he wasn't all in. He was distracted a lot of the time and often appeared not to be listening to her. He'd occasionally snap at her and tell her to stop whining. She wasn't the only one with problems, he said.

Dennis had said very little about his family, except to say that they once had money, but his father lost it all making bad investments. He said that his parents had basically told him he was on his own, so he'd left home for a new life in the Bay Area.

Dennis did not come into the diner at all that day, and Deirdre felt a sense of dread that she'd never see him again. But, when her shift ended, he was waiting for her outside the back door. She almost didn't recognize him because he had shaved off his beard and had gotten a haircut. He asked her if she wanted to go for a walk. They headed toward the Embarcadero. It was a warm, sunny afternoon, even though Thanksgiving was just a few days away. Deirdre had invited him to join her family, such as it was, on the holiday. He hadn't committed either way. Maybe he wanted to talk about that. Or break up with her.

They turned onto the sidewalk along the water just past the Ferry Building.

Suddenly, Dennis stopped and dropped to one knee.

"Deirdre, will you marry me?"

She stared at him. *What was happening? Was this a joke?*

"I love you, Deirdre. I hope you say yes."

A small knot of people had slowed their pace as if to hear her response. She looked into the ice-blue eyes and at his expectant smile.

"Yes," she said, "Of course I will!"

The passersby cheered and continued on their way.

"I'm sorry I don't have a ring yet. I was hoping we'd pick it out together," he said. "Right now."

They headed to Union Square. At the Macy's jewelry counter, they selected a modest engagement ring with a small diamond. Dennis reached into his back pocket. He started looking through all his pockets.

Smiling sheepishly, he said, "I must have been nervous today. It seems I left my wallet at home."

To the salesman, he said, "Can you hold this until I can come back with the money?"

Deirdre did not want to leave the store without the ring. "I have enough money. I can cover it."

"Are you sure? I'll pay you back right away," Dennis said.

She counted out fives and singles from the tip money she'd earned and the money her mother had left on the counter that morning.

As they walked to her BART stop, he said, "I've been offered a new job. And I asked if they could find work for you too."

"Really? What kind of work?"

"A caretaker job at a family's second home in Lake Tahoe. And when they are up there, they need a cleaner and cook."

"And that's what I would be? The cleaner and cook?"

"Yes. There's a free apartment included with the job. We would live there full time. You can get Denny out of that house and away from your mom and all."

She worried a little about what would happen to Alana and Tommy, but she had to put Denny—and now Dennis, her future husband—first.

As she hesitated, Dennis said, "I know cooking and cleaning isn't great—"

"When do we leave?" she asked, cutting him off.

They couldn't afford wedding bands, and Dennis must have forgotten to pay her back for the engagement ring, but it didn't matter since they soon became husband and wife. They got married at city hall before a judge and two random witnesses just after Christmas and settled into their new apartment at Tahoe in early January. Jack Riley, the owner, had driven up from San Francisco to show them around. Dennis would be responsible for clearing the snow, making sure the house didn't get too cold, running the water from time to time so the pipes wouldn't freeze, gardening when spring arrived, working on various maintenance and mechanical projects, and chopping wood. When Jack and Meg—or often just Meg by herself—visited, Deirdre would shop for food, prepare meals, and clean the house. Dennis would make sure to have a fire going every evening—inside in the huge stone fireplace or, in nice weather, out on the patio.

Deirdre couldn't help but notice that Jack and Dennis seemed to be on familiar terms, as if they'd met before.

As Jack pulled away to drive back to the city, snow started falling, and she and Dennis climbed the stairs to their apartment above the garage. It was spacious and well furnished, with its own deck overlooking the water. It was far nicer than anyplace else Deirdre had lived.

"Did you know Mr. Riley before?" she asked Dennis.

"What makes you say that?"

"It seemed like you were talking like you did. About rowing, someone named Brenda." That name was familiar to Deirdre, but she couldn't place the context.

"You don't miss a thing, do you?" Dennis said with a chuckle. But his eyes were hard. "We met years ago. Back in my other life, once upon a time, I rowed, and his daughter Bren-*na* was our coxswain, briefly."

"Cox-what?"

"She steered the boat and called drills and commands."

"I see," Deirdre said, even though she didn't.

"I remember meeting him at a regatta—a rowing race. He introduced himself to all of us guys and wanted to talk about rowing and whatnot. He'd rowed back in the day. When I answered the ad for this job, I didn't know I'd be working for the same guy. Small world, right?"

"Yes, it is," Deirdre said. "Well, I guess I should head over to the house." Jack had given them a quick tour, but Deirdre wanted to take a closer look.

"Can you hold off a bit? I need to take a look at the tools in the workshop. Jack asked me to look for something and let him know if I found it."

Deirdre finished loading the dishwasher in the Rileys' kitchen and was drying her hands on a towel. She could see Meg Riley out the kitchen window in her customary painting spot from which she had an unobstructed view of the lake. Deirdre's head was still spinning from how much her life had changed.

She poured two cups of coffee and exited through the back door. She took a seat near Meg's easel and set the coffee cups on a folding patio table.

"Thank you, Deirdre," Meg said. It was early April and midmorning. When Meg was in residence, she and Deirdre had fallen into a routine of having coffee together when Meg took a break from painting.

"How's it going?" Deirdre asked.

Meg turned the easel toward Deirdre, took a seat, and sipped her coffee. "You have a gift for coffee making," she told Deirdre.

"It's the cinnamon. I add just a pinch."

Deirdre surveyed Meg's work. The early spring scene of Lake Tahoe in the morning light was partially complete. Meg's detailed style captured the still-snow-covered peaks, along with the snowy patches along the lakeshore. The water was depicted as dead still, even though a breeze was starting to ripple it now. Meg had told Deirdre that she liked to get out and paint early before the wind picked up in the afternoon. This was her third series of seasonal Lake Tahoe views at different times of the day. A local summer music festival had commissioned her to paint this series for their promotional posters.

"You're such a great artist," Deirdre said. "I've never had the talent for that sort of thing."

Meg smiled. "You have other talents."

"Yes, my cinnamon coffee is world famous." They clicked their coffee cups together.

Deirdre loved it when Meg came up on her own. Meg tried to make it up once a month, although she'd missed the month of March because her daughter had delivered a baby. Deirdre didn't mind it when Jack was there too, but she and Meg had hit it off from the start. To Deirdre, she was like a friend or even the mother she wished she had. She relished these mornings, when Dennis was working somewhere on the property and Denny was at school, and she could spend time with Meg.

CHAPTER ELEVEN

B renna stared into her four-month-old daughter's face, as she had every day since Sadie was born. The baby was blond, and she had Brenna's blue eyes. Other than that, she couldn't tell whom Sadie looked like. Nothing in her features suggested anything one way or another. It seemed that Brenna would either have to tell Peter he needed to take a paternity test or wait until Sadie got older and see if she looked more like Peter or Dennis. The first option was out of the question.

Brenna tried to bond with Sadie, but it wasn't working. Sadie wouldn't breastfeed and cried most of the time. Peter was the only one who could calm her. Brenna had to pump milk for Sadie and feed her with a bottle. Even after she went back to work, she had to close her office door a couple of times a day and pump away.

Her parents fell hard. They were always available to babysit, dropping everything at a moment's notice to drive to Redwood City. Jack and Brenna had been close from day one, but Jack had certainly not been this involved with her care.

She was afraid that her relationship with Meg was repeating itself with Sadie. Failure to bond. Distance. Daddy's girls. Brenna felt terrible about this realization but didn't know what to do about it.

Peter had to be Sadie's father. There was just no other way around it.

Eventually, Brenna talked herself into believing that Peter was most certainly Sadie's father. She started to feel better. She began to come out of her fog. She and Peter took Sadie over to her parents' San Francisco house on the Fourth of July, where they could watch the fireworks over the bay.

Meg and Jack remarked on how much better Brenna looked. Peter put his arm around her shoulders and squeezed.

"And this beautiful child," Meg said, extending her arms toward Sadie.

Brenna handed Sadie over, and Meg carried her out onto the terrace and gave her a tour of the flowers, saying their names as they went.

Peter barbecued chicken and Jack mixed up a pitcher of sangria. Brenna was feeling more like herself—joking and laughing with her father—as Sadie traveled from lap to lap. They talked about getting back into their singles soon, maybe even car-topping the boats up to Tahoe this summer.

"Oh, I keep forgetting to tell you. There's been so much going on," Jack said. "You'll never guess who our new caretaker is up at the house."

Jack glanced at Brenna and Peter in turn.

"You actually want us to guess?" Brenna asked.

"It's an old friend of yours from Stanford. Dennis Griffin."

Brenna dropped her glass; it shattered, and sangria spread across the stone floor. The noise startled Sadie, who began to cry. Brenna quickly stood, took her wailing daughter from Meg's lap, and hurried upstairs to her old bedroom, shutting them inside.

She dropped to the bed, trying to quiet Sadie. Her diaper bag was on the floor and Brenna reached for a pacifier, which Sadie had recently started accepting, thank God. Sadie quieted, sucking away, as Brenna held her. Through the open window, she could hear Jack saying, "I'll take care of that, Meg. Sit down." And Peter saying, "I better go check on them."

Brenna guessed she had less than ten seconds to pull herself together.

Peter knocked lightly and opened the door.

"Hey. That scared you didn't it, Sadie, my little lady," he said, smiling.

"Sorry, I just lost my grip on the glass," Brenna managed.

"Want me to take her? I can give her a bottle from the fridge."

"Sure, thanks." Brenna said, "Haven't had alcohol in a while. Guess it went to my head. I'm going to lie down before the fireworks."

She handed Sadie to Peter, and he blew her a kiss, closing the door as he went.

Brenna lay back on the bed. Dennis Griffin was the new caretaker. *How on earth had that even happened?* They were planning a trip to Tahoe in a few weeks, the whole family. There was no way she'd be able to go with Dennis there.

She sat up and reached back into the diaper bag. She unzipped an inside pocket, pulled out a silver flask, and took a long drink from it. Lying to Peter had become a habit, just like her drinking.

CHAPTER TWELVE

The Rileys came to Tahoe in early August—all of them. Dennis and Deirdre had met them in the driveway as they exited the car. Deirdre couldn't help but feel like Dennis and Deirdre were "the staff" in a movie greeting the wealthy family as they arrived at the country house. And that's what they were.

That image was shattered a bit when Peter pulled Dennis into a bear hug. Brenna, however, hung back, holding the baby, and simply nodded to Dennis. Introductions were made, and Meg invited them all inside. Dennis begged off, saying that he and Denny had wood to stack.

Deirdre went inside with them, offering drinks. The Rileys settled on the patio, and Deirdre brought a pitcher of iced tea.

Jack excused himself briefly and returned with a glass of something stronger. Brenna soon did the same.

"Sit down, Deirdre. Join us!" Meg said, "Deirdre is my wonderful companion when I'm up here alone."

Smiles all around. Except for Brenna. She looked pale and tense, taking quick sips from her drink. Deirdre was struck by some of the similarities she and Brenna shared: the same hair color, same build (although Deirdre was a little taller), and, to some extent, similar features. Deirdre suddenly recalled the first day Dennis had come into the coffee shop. *Had he called her Brenna?*

". . . and the rowing team. I'll show you. I'll be right back." Meg had been saying something to Deirdre, but Deirdre had not been listening.

Meg went into the living room and returned a couple of minutes later. She stood just outside the circle of chairs looking confused as Peter chattered away about Brenna's coxing days. Brenna looked as if she wanted to disappear.

Peter stopped and said, "What's up, Meg?"

"The photo of the crew with you all holding Brenna and the one of the wedding toast are gone." She turned to Deirdre. "Did you happen to move any of the photos that were on the mantle?"

She didn't say it accusingly, but Deirdre felt herself stiffen. "No, I didn't."

"That's odd. Well, they'll turn up, I'm sure."

Deirdre went to the kitchen to refill the iced tea pitcher. After she took it out to the patio, she offered excuses about needing to start dinner and made her exit.

During the Rileys' visit, Deirdre noticed Dennis and Peter hanging out quite a bit. When he wasn't working, Dennis included Peter in his outings with Denny. The Rileys had brought two slim rowing boats on top of their car. One morning, Jack got Dennis, then Peter, out in one of the skinny boats, with himself trying to keep up in the old rowboat. Soon it became a regular game, with one of them rowing a skinny shell and another trying, futilely, to keep up in the rowboat, sometimes with Denny aboard. Deirdre would hear their shouts and laughter and could watch from the Rileys' kitchen window. From a distance, it was hard to tell Dennis and Peter apart.

Deirdre never observed Brenna joining any of the outings, even though Meg had said the other rowing boat they'd brought was Brenna's. Deirdre concluded that Dennis and Peter had at one point been good friends, although Dennis had never talked about him. Brenna, on the other hand, eyed Dennis warily. There was no question about that. Clearly, something had gone on between them. Maybe they'd had a relationship?

Dennis had just finished reading Denny a bedtime story, and now he and Deirdre sat out on the deck—Dennis with a beer, Deirdre a cup of tea.

"So, you and Peter were friends at school?"

"We rowed together. I told you about that."

"No, I don't think so. You said Brenna was the cox, uh, thing—"

"Coxswain."

"Yeah, but I don't remember you mentioning Peter."

"So, what's your point?"

"Nothing," Deirdre said, "I was just curious."

They sat in silence for a minute.

"Were you and Brenna good friends?" Deirdre asked.

Dennis looked annoyed. He took a deep breath as if to compose himself.

"As you just said," he said, clearly agitated, "She was our cox-thing." He said "cox-thing" mockingly.

"Cox*swain*," Deirdre corrected him, attempting to lighten the mood. It didn't.

Dennis stared at her. "Where are you going with this?"

"Nowhere, Dennis. I don't see why my asking you these questions is such a big deal."

"It's not a big deal," Dennis hissed. "Can we just not talk about this?"

"Fine," Deirdre said, and stood up to go inside. Obviously, it was a big deal. Obviously, he and Brenna had dated.

When Jack and Meg were away and it was just the three of them on the property, Dennis liked to suggest that they move into the house. *Who would know?* He had said it again this morning.

"Come on, Deirdre. Don't you want to experience life as a fancy person?"

"No. I'm fine with our apartment. It wouldn't be right."

"What do you know about what's right? Raised by a crack-whore mother, no idea who your father is, having a baby when you were barely out of junior high." He walked away shaking his head.

He had been saying demeaning things like this ever since the Rileys had left a couple of weeks ago, acting as if he were better than she was. Sometimes he criticized her appearance. How she looked older than she actually was, how she wore frumpy clothes. He clearly was losing his attraction to her and barely touched her anymore.

He was a good father to Denny, though. He liked to read to him before bed and take him fishing, on hikes, and out on the lake in the rowboat. But since the Rileys had left, he'd sometimes been a little short with him. Telling him he was too old to cry, that he had to learn to be a little man, toughen up. Denny would often cry harder, and Dennis would storm out of the apartment and drive away in his truck.

Deirdre finished vacuuming the house and returned to the apartment. She could hear Denny crying even before she finished climbing the stairs. This was only the second week back from summer break, but the after-school meltdown was already becoming a routine.

When she opened the door, the first thing she saw was an overturned chair in the dining area. The second thing was Denny's lunchbox on the floor. A very bad meltdown was clearly in progress. She went into Denny's room and found him in the closet, head in his hands, inconsolable.

She knelt down. "Hey, hey, little man—"

"Don't call me that!" Denny lifted his face. He had lowered his arms and Deirdre could see bruises on each of his upper arms peeking out from the sleeves of his T-shirt. "Did someone grab you?" Deirdre pulled Denny to her and hugged him as he continued sobbing.

She picked him up and walked to Dennis's and her bedroom where she found Dennis sitting on the edge of the bed, his head in his hands as Denny's had been.

"What happened to Denny?" she said. But she was afraid she knew.

Dennis shook his head, then stood and faced her. Denny wriggled free and ran back to his room. His door slammed.

Deirdre shook. "You did this."

"He ran away from me when I tried to pick him up at school. I had to chase him through the playground. He almost ran into the parking lot before I caught him. He could've been run over! Then he screamed all the way home. I had to make it stop! I just shook him a little!"

They stared at each other until Deirdre backed out the door, opened Denny's door, picked him up again, and left the apartment. Dennis didn't follow.

Deirdre walked into town. She had no idea where they were going to go. She had left the house without her wallet or a sweater for Denny. What was she going to do? She stopped just before the bridge that spanned the Truckee River. There was a bench there, and she sat down. Denny, clearly exhausted, lay on the bench with his head in her lap. Soon he was asleep. As the sun disappeared behind the mountains and the temperature dropped, she had no choice but to pick Denny up and walk back home.

Dennis's truck was gone when they got back. Deirdre put Denny in bed, realizing too late that he probably hadn't had anything to eat since lunch. She didn't have the heart to wake him, though. She picked up his empty lunchbox, righted the dining room chair, and went out to the deck. It was growing dark and very chilly, but she didn't care.

Before long, headlights swept the driveway. Dennis appeared at the bottom of the stairs with a bouquet of flowers. She had no choice but to forgive him and believe his promises that it would never happen again. She had nowhere else to go. She had briefly thought of calling Meg and telling her what had happened. But what would that accomplish? The Rileys wouldn't want to become involved in their family drama. They might fire Dennis—and her too.

Maybe Dennis just hadn't realized how hard he had grabbed Denny.

PART TWO
1991–1999

CHAPTER THIRTEEN

Deirdre started volunteering at Denny's elementary school when the Rileys were in the Bay Area and there wasn't much to do in the main house. She often felt isolated and bored in the apartment and needed to be around other people. She and Dennis were plugging along. She hadn't found any physical evidence that he had grabbed or shaken or physically handled Denny again, but he was sometimes impatient with him and said degrading things to him, like calling him "useless" and telling him to use the brain God gave him and not be a "dumbass." Denny would try to shrug it off, but the hurt in his eyes was obvious.

One day, Deirdre was called in to speak with the principal of Denny's school. Deirdre learned that he sometimes bullied the other kids. He was big for his age, so he got away with it. All Deirdre could do was promise to talk to Denny.

That afternoon, when she and Denny were driving home, she asked him, "Everything okay at school?"

Denny shrugged but said nothing.

Deirdre waited. Finally, he said, "I wanna ride my bike to school by myself. It's lame that you drive me."

"Are other kids teasing you?"

Denny laughed. "No way. They're scared of me. Buncha pussies. Dennis said that eleven-year-old boys whose moms take them to school are momma's boys."

"Denny," she said, pulling off to the side of the road and looking at her son. Denny sat slumped in his seat. "Has Dennis been hurting you?"

Denny turned away. "I could ride my bike. Or drive."

"What do you mean, you could drive?"

"I can drive Dennis's truck. He's teaching me. And he's showing me how to fix stuff if it breaks."

She didn't want to believe that Dennis was hurting him, so she chose not to. Even though she was not excited that he was teaching Denny to drive, maybe that meant they were getting along.

As for her own relationship with Dennis, he was often distant and preoccupied. But at other times, he seemed like his old self. She loved him but felt trapped, nonetheless. She still sensed something between Dennis and Brenna when Brenna visited, even though they were rarely within ten feet of one another. That, in and of itself, aroused Deirdre's suspicions. Brenna wanted nothing to do with Deirdre. She was polite, but when Deirdre happened to come upon her in the house, Brenna would quickly make an excuse and head elsewhere.

Deirdre made a deal with Denny that if he stopped bullying his classmates, she might let him ride his bike to school. She continued to volunteer at his school because she enjoyed it and so she could keep an eye on him. She got to know some of the other moms, most of them well-coiffed, tan, and athletic. There were three in particular who often volunteered when Deirdre did. The group's apparent leader, whose name was Sheila, approached Deirdre when she was dropping Denny off in Dennis's truck one morning. The truck was new, provided by Jack for them to use.

Deirdre felt as if the prom queen was deigning to speak to her. She had not had this sort of high school experience, having dropped out at age fourteen with frequent truancy prior to that. But she'd seen *Pretty in Pink.*

"Hey!" Sheila said, leaning into the truck's open window. "Some of us have a little walking and coffee group if you want to join us. Tomorrow maybe?"

Deirdre ended up walking to a bakery with them one or two times a week. Sheila seemed to have money, and her two friends, Sara and Jen, probably did too. The three of them talked about skiing together in the winter. Jen told Deirdre that Sheila lived in a big house overlooking Squaw Valley.

"You'll have to ski with us next winter. We have so much fun! Especially at *après.*"

"Great!" Deirdre didn't know what *après* was and had never skied a day in her life. But she'd worry about that later.

They didn't talk much about kids or husbands except to say that Jen was separated but her husband, a lawyer, was still supporting her; Sara was married to a real estate developer, whom she said cheated on her all the time, but she didn't care in the least; and Sheila's husband was an investment banker who spent a lot of time in San Francisco.

"Works for me!" Sheila quipped.

When asked what Deirdre's husband did, she said he was a property manager.

On the last day of school before summer vacation, Denny's class had a party, and the parents were invited at the end. Deirdre went, of course. Sheila sidled up and said, "We're going boating tomorrow and you're coming with us."

"Uh—"

"No excuses! Just the girls."

"I think Dennis might need the truck tomorrow."

"I'll pick you up."

Deirdre told Sheila generally where she lived and said, "I'll wait for you out by the road."

Deirdre stood dutifully by the road the next morning until Sheila pulled up in her shiny truck. The other two were meeting them at the marina, she said.

"Hey, isn't that the Rileys' place?" Sheila asked.

"Uh, yes. They're our neighbors."

"I love Meg Riley's paintings. Have you met her?"

"Once or twice."

They pulled into the marina parking lot, and Sheila led her to a dock with a locked gate. Sara and Jen were waiting.

"Whoo-hoo!" Jen said, "I love boating!" She held up two six-packs of wine coolers.

Having grown up watching her mother abuse pretty much everything, young Deirdre had shunned alcohol and drugs herself. She drank only very rarely now.

Sheila entered a code into a keypad and opened the gate. They made their way to a midsize powerboat, climbed aboard, and Sheila took the wheel. Jen cracked the wine coolers. Deirdre hesitated, but then said, "What the hell!" and accepted the cold bottle. The other three women cheered. The first gulp went straight to her head, so she slowed way down, sipping periodically while lounging on the boat cushions and taking in the sun. *This is all right,* she thought.

Sheila careened around the lake, leaving a large wake behind them.

Sara suddenly yelled out: "The *Queen!* The *Queen!*"

Off to port was a paddleboat, the *Tahoe Queen*. It took tourists back and forth between the north and south shores of the lake.

"Gotta moon it," Sara said.

"What?" Deirdre watched in horror as Sara and Jen started unzipping their shorts. "No, no, no—"

"You drive then!" said Sheila and pulled Deirdre toward the wheel. Sheila had one hand on the wheel and was unzipping her shorts with the other. "Take it, Dee!"

Deirdre grabbed the wheel. She didn't know how to drive a boat. The throttle was fully forward, and they were speeding along and bouncing over the whitecaps. Deirdre had no choice but to rise to the occasion and approach it as she would driving a car. That seemed to be the ticket.

She steered them toward the *Tahoe Queen* and Sheila yelled, "Pull up alongside!" The three women lined up on the port side of the boat and, as Deirdre slowed their speed a little, they dropped their swimsuit bottoms, screaming with laughter. A few tourists stood on the *Queen*'s deck gaping at them. Deirdre couldn't help but laugh with them as she pushed the throttle all the way forward again and roared away. Hell, this was *fun!*

Deirdre drank another wine cooler as Sheila drove them back toward the marina a while later. Sara had brought some chips and guacamole, so she ate some of those. The four women joked and laughed as they bumped their way across the water. Deirdre felt more alive than she had in years, while at the same time fully relaxed and stress-free. She wished they could stay out here forever.

Deirdre drove to the market after she got home from the marina. She had the beginnings of a headache, but they were out of everything at the apartment and Dennis made it very clear that grocery shopping was her job. She mindlessly filled a cart and got in the checkout line, but when it was time to pay, she couldn't find her wallet. She rummaged around in her purse, but it wasn't there. Irritated, she left the store and drove to school to pick up Denny. She ran into Sheila in front of Denny's classroom.

"Was that fun today or what?" Sheila said.

"Yes, it was the most fun I've had in a long time," Deirdre said. "But I can't find my wallet anywhere. It might've fallen out of my purse when we were on the boat."

"Shoot, that's a bummer. Ryan has an orthodontist appointment, but I can try to swing by the marina later to check."

"Thanks. That would be great. I need to get to the grocery store sometime today."

"Hmmm, we have to drive down to Reno . . . You know what, why don't you stop by there." Sheila reached into her bag and wrote something on a Post-it note. "Here's the gate code and the slip number," she said, handing the Post-it to Deirdre.

Denny grumbled about having to drive to the marina, but once Deirdre had entered the code for the gate and they were walking down the dock he perked up.

"Man, when I grow up, I'm gonna buy me one of these."

"'Buy one of these,' not 'buy *me* one of these,'" Deirdre said absently.

Deirdre found the boat and stepped aboard with Denny in tow. As she searched for her wallet, Denny played with the boat's steering wheel, pretending to drive. "Hey!" he said, "Is this your wallet?"

"Yes!" Deirdre shouted, relieved. "I must have lost it when I was driving."

"*You* know how to drive this?" Denny said, gaping at her.

"It's not hard. It's like driving a car."

A couple of weeks later, Sheila called to invite Deirdre on a hike, along with Jen and Sara. They met at Sara's and left the kids with Sara's nanny. Sheila drove them to the trailhead, and they hiked to a small lake that wasn't well known to tourists. Deirdre hadn't been on a hike since she was a kid. It was gorgeous. The cool of the forest in the morning gave way to the warm afternoon as they emerged into the granite-scape of the lake's basin. They had the place to themselves, and the deep blue water beckoned. Before Deirdre could even put her pack down, the other three had stripped down and jumped in.

They shrieked and yelled about how cold the water was while calling for Deirdre to join them.

"Nah, I'm good," Deirdre called back, laughing. She sat in the shade and drank some water. She pulled a granola bar from her daypack and ate it, watching her friends clown around, their laughter echoing off the rocks. Sheila's pack was nearby, and Deirdre kept one eye on her friends while sliding it over to her with her foot. She unzipped the small outer pocket and took Sheila's keys, placing them in the bottom of her own pack. She zipped up Sheila's pack and returned it to where it had been, then jumped up.

"Okay! I'm coming in!" The other three cheered as Deirdre pulled off her clothes and ran for the icy water.

When they got back to the trailhead, Sheila rummaged in her pack for her keys.

"Damn it! What did I do with them?"

The other three watched as she dumped the entire contents of the pack onto the ground. Of course, there were no keys.

"They musta fallen outta my pack. Luckily, I've got a hide-a-key to get us home," Sheila finally said, and reached under the back bumper.

CHAPTER FOURTEEN

Brenna had worked her way into the job of managing editor at the *Tribune*. Jack was gradually stepping back from his position at the paper and was working with Peter on opening a second restaurant. Brenna enjoyed her job and put in long hours. Sadie spent a lot of time with her babysitter, Mrs. Nash, a grandmotherly woman who drove in from the East Bay each day. Sadie loved her, which helped alleviate Brenna's guilt for working so much and for her inability to embrace parenting the way she thought she would—and should. Peter worked long hours too but was happy to spend his time off with Sadie. Brenna preferred taking a long bath with a bottle of wine.

One evening, Peter brought it up: Brenna's alcohol consumption.

"I love you, Bren," he said. "You know that, right? But I don't recognize you anymore. How much are you drinking each day?"

Brenna tried to think this through. She kept a bottle in her desk drawer at work (*what self-respecting newspaper editor didn't?*) and had a couple of drinks at the end of the day. No earlier than five or sometimes four. Then, at home, she'd open wine for her and Peter to have with dinner.

"Four drinks, I guess," she said. *Maybe five*, she thought. *Six tops.*

"Okay," he said, looking doubtful. "Do you think that's a bit excessive?"

"I don't know. Most people seem to drink that much."

"Do they? I don't. Your mother doesn't. Your dad . . . well, I guess he does. But he's a big guy. Someone your size—"

"You drink wine with me every night," she said. She sounded defensive, which was not how she wanted to sound. She just really wanted to talk about something else. Or go to bed.

"I do," he agreed. "You open a bottle. I have one glass. You drink the rest of it." His tone was kind, and factual, but not accusatory. It made it hard for her to argue, which she guessed was the point.

After digesting their conversation for a few days, she went to a lunchtime meeting of Alcoholics Anonymous in the basement of a church near her office. It was as she had expected: a room full of folding chairs that smelled like old carpet and weak coffee. Many of the attendees were professionals like herself, but most were men. Others looked as though they slept on the streets. The men in suits and ties talked a lot in the meeting. About how their higher powers were guiding them, making their lives infinitely better—not perfect, but better. There were still bad days, but the good days were becoming more frequent. Some looked at Brenna, who had been identified as The Newcomer, as they concluded their shares and said things like: "keep coming back," "it works if you work it," and "let go and let God."

Brenna decided AA wasn't her thing and tried to sneak out right after the meeting ended. But someone touched her arm as she headed for the door. A woman close to her age, dressed in workday clothes, was smiling at her. She extended a piece of paper to Brenna.

"I'm Abigail," she said, "And this is my phone number. Call anytime if you want to talk, meet for coffee, whatever. I work a few blocks from here."

⁓

Brenna didn't go back to the meeting, but something about what the people had said there stuck with her. Each time she drank, she heard them saying, "I know now that I'm powerless over alcohol."

Was Brenna powerless? She didn't think so. She was good at her job. She usually woke up feeling fine; only occasionally did she have a headache or sour stomach. She took care of what she had to take care of—getting Sadie ready for school, dropping her off, catching the train into the city, taking Sadie to birthday parties and arranging playdates on the weekends, attending school functions, getting dinner ready or at least grabbing takeout on her way home from work.

But when four o'clock rolled around each day, she felt compelled to open the bottom drawer of her desk where she kept the bottle of vodka, pour a finger or two into her coffee cup, and relish the feeling of the day's stress slipping away. Was this powerlessness?

Or was it the photo on her desk of Peter and Sadie and the knot in her stomach each time she glanced at it. Was that powerlessness?

She finally called Abigail and they met for lunch. Brenna found herself telling her all of it. About Dennis and Sadie and Peter. The whole story. She started going to the lunchtime meetings every day. Abigail offered to sponsor her and work the steps with her. Brenna got her thirty-day chip at the monthly birthday meeting. Cake was served afterward. She went back to work feeling a sense of great accomplishment. There were no vodka bottles in her desk anymore.

Peter and Jack left for a scouting trip to look at potential restaurant sites in the Sierra foothills and the Reno–Tahoe area. Brenna called in sick and went for a long drive. She was taking action, turning her life around. Her higher power was guiding her and driving away her demons. She was no longer powerless.

That night, when she had just finished putting Sadie to bed, the phone rang.

She picked up. "Brenna?" Jack's voice broke.

"Dad? What's wrong?"

Jack drove down from Tahoe the next day and came straight to Brenna's house in Redwood City. He stayed two nights in the guest room and spent a lot of the time with Sadie.

"But didn't dad know how to swim?" Brenna heard Sadie ask him. Jack and Sadie sat outside on the patio with the kitchen window open to the warmth of the late fall afternoon. Brenna had opened a bottle of wine and was sipping from her glass, trying to summon the energy to call for a pizza to be delivered. Not that anyone was hungry.

"He did. You're right about that," Jack replied. "But the lake water is very cold. And that can cause even strong swimmers to go into shock and drown."

"What's 'go into shock'?"

"It means that the cold water makes you sort of freeze up and you can't move very well, and it makes it harder to get back in your boat."

"So, dad couldn't get back in his boat. And he drowned."

"Yes, sweetheart. That seems to be what happened."

Brenna looked out the window at them, and she could see Sadie's shoulders shaking as Jack held her.

Jack, Brenna, and Sadie crawled along amid the morning rush hour on the Bay Bridge, then merged onto I-80 and headed through the brown, oak-treed hills of the East Bay, and then into the dusty, dry Central Valley. Brenna sat silently in the passenger seat beside Jack and tried not to think about how much she wanted a drink or about Sadie or Peter or about how things had gone so horribly wrong. She was unsuccessful on all counts.

Brenna looked back at Sadie, asleep in the back seat. Something about the tilt of Sadie's head caused the knot in her stomach to reemerge—if it ever really left. It was Dennis's jawline she saw. Brenna turned away. They were passing through the eastern suburbs of Sacramento and beginning the ascent into the Sierra foothills.

Sadie was only six, but she was taking Peter's death hard. Her dad had been her rock, her island of stability when Brenna wasn't. Sadie had reverted to wetting the bed and sucking her thumb. Brenna didn't blame her, but she was worried. Not only about Sadie's mental state, but also her own, which was hanging by the thinnest of threads. Exhausted, Brenna drifted off to sleep herself.

Brenna awoke with a jerk at the sound of the car tires crunching on gravel. Out the window, the midday sun slanted through the trees and lit up Lake Tahoe. There was Meg, waiting near the front door of the house. Brenna looked around for Dennis but didn't see him anywhere.

The memorial service the following day was to be followed by a gathering at the Rileys' house. The day dawned bright and sunny, but storm clouds soon rolled in from the west, turning the sky a gunmetal gray; the temperature plummeted, and it felt like snow was coming. When Brenna was drinking her coffee that morning at the dining table, with just a little something extra in it, she watched Dennis in the adjacent living room arranging logs in the big river rock fireplace.

As she, Peter, and Sadie made the trip to Tahoe several times a year, she'd almost gotten used to seeing Dennis. Almost. He was friendly to her, greeting her with a nod, but kept his distance. He and Peter had gotten along as well as ever during their visits.

Jack and Brenna still kept their rowing shells in the boathouse. Jack was spending more time in Tahoe and liked rowing in the still mornings. Brenna was too busy to row her boat in the Bay Area and was fine keeping it at Tahoe, although she hadn't rowed it in years. In the summer and fall, she'd sometimes see Dennis in Jack's boat out on the water, like this morning; she knew Jack had given him permission to use it anytime. Peter as well.

Dennis stood up when the fire was going and saw Brenna watching him. He approached her at the table.

"Brenna, I'm so sorry. I can't believe this happened," he said.

Brenna nodded but couldn't look at him directly.

"Deirdre sends her condolences. She's volunteering in Denny's classroom this morning but will be back in time for the service."

Brenna didn't know how to respond to that. Deirdre and Brenna were always cordial to each other but had never had a real conversation. Sometimes Brenna noticed Deirdre staring at her. When Deirdre noticed Brenna noticing, she'd quickly avert her gaze. It was not lost on Brenna that the two of them were similar in appearance.

"Well. See you later," Dennis said, and left.

Her body still reacted to him, she noticed with annoyance. Her heart would beat faster, and she'd feel a nervous energy rippling through her—that same connection with him. Even after all this time.

Brenna made it through the service, largely because she was distracted by Sadie's fidgeting. She kept whispering questions loudly to Meg: what was the minister saying, who was that man over there, how long was this going to last? Meg patiently whispered back and tried to calm her.

Dennis sat nearby with Deirdre and Denny. Denny seemed equally fidgety, complaining under his breath in a slouchy preteen way, and Deirdre kept shushing him. Denny had a nasty countenance, in Brenna's opinion. At one point he stuck his tongue out at Sadie, who burst into tears. Dennis cuffed Denny on the ear. Meg took Sadie outside.

CHAPTER FIFTEEN

The morning after her dad's memorial, Sadie sat cross-legged in front of the television in Jack's den, eating cereal and watching cartoons. She stared hard at the Road Runner beeping on the television. If Sadie thought about her dad being dead, she would start crying, so she tried not to think about it.

Something outside caught her eye, so she stood up and went to the window. It was Mr. Griffin pushing a wheelbarrow full of dirt toward Grammeg's garden. She slipped out through the sliding door onto the deck and descended the stairs to the front yard. The grass was wet, and her slippers were soaked through by the time she caught up with Mr. Griffin. He was shoveling dirt out of the wheelbarrow into the planting beds.

"What're you doing?" she said to Mr. Griffin.

He leaned the shovel against the wheelbarrow. "Good morning, Miss Sadie," he said bowing low to her. It made her laugh, even on this sad day. "Your grandmother—what do you call her? Grammeg?"

Sadie nodded. She had four grandparents: Grandmother Karin, Grandfather Gunner, Grandpa Jack, and Grandma Meg, but she'd shortened *Grandma Meg* to *Grammeg* because she said it most often. She liked all her grandparents, but she loved Grammeg the best. Even more than Mrs. Nash, her babysitter in San Francisco. And she really loved Mrs. Nash. She loved Grandpa Jack too, but he was pretty loud and "over the top," as Grammeg said frequently.

"Well, your grandmother wants to plant bulbs for next spring, so I'm getting things ready for her."

"Oh. But she's not 'my grandmother,' she's 'Grammeg.'"

"Fair enough," Mr. Griffin said with a chuckle.

"What are bulbs?" Sadie asked.

"Some flowers grow from them—tulips, daffodils—"

"Sadie!" Her mother was rushing across the lawn toward them. Sadie rolled her eyes in what she thought was a pretty good imitation of Denny. Mr. Griffin burst out laughing.

"Sadie! Come back inside right now," her mother said, grabbing her hand and tugging her toward the house.

"Morning, Brenna. See you later, Miss Sadie," Mr. Griffin said. Her mother ignored him. Sadie turned to wave goodbye, and he winked at her. Like they shared secrets.

Her mother pulled her toward the kitchen door and clucked about her wet slippers and pajamas. "Take those slippers off before you go inside, then go upstairs and put on some clothes," she ordered.

∽

Sadie was in her room, still in her pajamas, brushing her doll Cindy's hair when her mother stuck her head in the doorway.

"Sadie, I need to talk to you."

She pushed through the door and sat on Sadie's bed, patting the place beside her. Sadie sat.

"I know this has been a hard time for our family. It's just you and me now, Sadie, and I need to get back to the city next week. There are a lot of things to do about your dad's business and estate—"

"What does 'estate' mean?"

"It means . . . it's not important. Listen," her mother said impatiently as if Sadie hadn't been, "I've been talking to Grammeg, and how would you like to stay here with her for a while? It would mean starting first grade here, not at home. I'd be up to visit at Thanksgiving, Christmas . . ."

"I wouldn't go to first grade at home? What about my friends?"

"You'll make new friends. Here."

Sadie considered that. She supposed that was true.

"What about Mrs. Nash? Would she still take care of me?"

"No. Grammeg will take care of you."

"I guess that's okay."

"All right, then," Brenna stood up. "Didn't I tell you to get out of those wet pajamas and put on clothes?"

"They're not wet."

"Sadie. Just do it."

Her mother left the room, and Sadie practiced another Denny eye roll. She loved her mother, but she wasn't around that much. Her dad used to say that her mother was "stressed" a lot. Her dad worried about her mother, so Sadie did too. Now her mother was going to leave her here. With Grammeg.

Sadie picked up her doll. "We're going to stay here, Cindy. Isn't that nice?" She hugged Cindy and smiled. "Don't worry. Grammeg will take care of us, and we'll make new friends at school."

CHAPTER SIXTEEN

B renna and Jack had just finished meeting with Peter's business attorney in San Francisco to sign papers authorizing the sale of the restaurant. Brenna was on her way home and stopped at the liquor store for some wine.

She needed this time to think things through. She'd left Sadie with her mother three weeks ago and felt both guilty and relieved. She loved Sadie; she really did. But she couldn't deal with parenting right now. Not that she ever could.

Oh well, she thought as she drove, *it's a familiar pattern: daddy's girls.* There was a difference, though. Brenna had always sensed that Meg had wanted to be close to Brenna, but they just were so opposite in temperament and personality. Brenna, on the other hand, was far more emotionally distant from Sadie than Meg had ever been from Brenna. And on that note, Brenna pulled into her driveway, went into the house, and reached for the corkscrew.

Brenna intended to start going to AA meetings again, but she just hadn't done it. The allure of descending into oblivion with a bottle or three of wine was too strong. Only alcohol could drive all the bad thoughts from her mind. She didn't know if she'd be up to going back to work, even part time.

She called Sadie before it got too late.

"Hi, Mama," Sadie said when she got on the phone. "At school today, Miss Fern farted and the boys all laughed. I got invited to a birthday party and Grammeg's going to take me to buy a present tomorrow morning and the party's in the afternoon. There's going to be horse rides . . . ," Sadie chattered on, sounding perfectly happy. Brenna consoled herself with the thought that maybe she had made the right call, leaving Sadie in Tahoe.

After saying good night to Sadie, Brenna started to dial her AA sponsor, Abigail, as she had almost every night. Halfway through dialing, she hung up, as she had almost every night, and took her glass of wine, along with the bottle, outside to the patio. She knew she should eat something but really couldn't summon the energy.

The next morning, Brenna was hungover and disgusted with herself. She finally went through with calling Abigail, and they made an appointment to meet later that day. After Brenna hung up, the phone rang. It was her father. His voice sounded odd, uncharacteristically tentative.

"Bren," he said, and sighed deeply. "Your mother got a call from Sheriff Tanner up in Tahoe. He said someone had reported seeing a rower out alone on the same morning that Peter had . . . Anyway, the caller said he was off Dollar Point in a ski boat. He saw the rower coming and slowed down. Then another powerboater came along and apparently didn't see the rower and sent a pretty sizable wake toward the single. And it went over."

Brenna was gripping the phone and feeling her knees start to buckle. She made it from the kitchen counter to a chair, while her father continued talking. "The caller in the ski boat said the other boat just kept going, didn't even stop. The caller pulled up alongside the shell, which was still flipped, and the rower was hanging on to it. He asked the rower if he needed help, and the rower told him he was fine, that he'd be able to get back in. That flips happened all the time."

"And you think it was Peter," Brenna said flatly. She thought she might be sick.

"That's what the sheriff's office thinks, yes. The guy said that when he drove away, he could see that Peter had righted the shell, so off he went. Anyway, he said he took his kids on vacation, and when he got home, he saw the notice in the paper about Peter and how he'd . . ."

"Drowned." Brenna finished his sentence for him.

"He said he felt terrible, that he should have stayed and helped." Jack paused and sighed heavily again. "He also said that he'd told the sheriff that the driver of the other boat was all in black, including a ski mask and goggles. He thought that was odd." He paused again. When Brenna didn't say anything, he said, "At least now we have a better idea of what happened."

"Yay," Brenna said in the same flat voice.

"I just wanted you to know, sweetheart. Your mother wasn't sure I should tell you. But you have the right to know—"

"It's okay, Dad. I'm okay. But I need to go now."

It was not yet noon, but Brenna opened the bottle of vodka she kept in the freezer. She blew off her meeting with Abigail.

CHAPTER SEVENTEEN

Meg steeled herself and entered Jack's den, where he was watching football. He was spending a lot more time here in Tahoe. She surmised that Jack's other interests in the city held less appeal for him, but she wasn't sure why. She didn't want to bring it up and, instead, decided to just accept that he was settling into a quieter, less eventful, life. Jack loved her; Meg knew that. He had said that his return to the *Tribune* would be short-lived. Depending on how it went, he was prepared to hire someone to work with Brenna as assistant managing editor, if need be. Brenna might not like that, but it may have to happen, he said.

Jack turned down the volume on the television when Meg came and sat in the chair next to him.

"Jack, I think it's time we let Dennis go. I'm not comfortable with him here anymore. We can give him a generous severance, and maybe he can go back to school."

"What? Why? What about Deirdre? That means she'd be gone too."

"I know. And I'm worried about her. I think Dennis might be abusing her. And Denny as well."

"No," Jack shook his head, a shadow falling over his face. "You're wrong, Meg. I know you've become close with Deirdre, but you can't concern yourself with their family business."

Meg took a deep breath. She was not going to give in this time. She pulled two photographs from her sweater pocket and handed them to him.

He studied the photo. "Is that Dennis rowing?"

"No, it's Peter. See the other one? It's Peter launching off the dock. He was rowing away from the dock, and I thought it might make a nice painting, with the light and the mountains behind him. I don't remember taking the photo where he's farther out, but I guess I must have. There's something else in that one. Do you see it?"

Jack reached for a pair of glasses and examined the picture.

"In the lower right corner."

"I see. It looks like a log . . . or like the bow of the rowboat. It was probably Dennis in the rowboat trying to catch Peter."

"Exactly," Meg said. "Jack, these photos were from the morning Peter drowned. So, if Dennis was on the water with Peter, why hasn't he told anyone? Was he there when Peter flipped? If so, wouldn't he have tried to help him? Maybe he even caused Peter's boat to go over, Jack."

"How would he have done that? Peter was waked by a powerboat."

"I don't know," Meg said. "Maybe he rowed somewhere where he had access to a powerboat. Or maybe he saw it happen and didn't try to help or even tell anyone what he'd seen."

Jack looked at her as if she'd gone mad.

"Meg," Jack said sternly. His temper was not nearly as short as it had been in the past, but his patience was not infinite. "I am 100 percent certain that Dennis did not row to some mysterious location and jump into a powerboat. And I doubt he was even on the lake at all. I remember having seen his truck heading down the driveway that morning. And about the bruises you've seen; people get bruises. Denny's a kid, and Deirdre does a lot of physical work."

"But," he continued, his tone softening. "If you don't want to be here without me, come back to the city. Sadie can stay with us there. Or you can stay with Brenna and Sadie in Redwood City."

Meg had considered this. But moving Sadie to San Francisco didn't seem like a good idea. Too much change. Tahoe was Sadie's second home. She had her own room here. And Meg had to admit, it would be less stressful here than managing school and activities in the city; Meg knew that from experience.

Jack peered at the photos again. "It's probably a log," he said, handing the pictures back to Meg.

"I'm sure you're right." Meg looked at the picture again, trying to see a log, trying to believe what she'd just said. But, to her, it didn't look like a log; it looked like part of the rowboat.

CHAPTER EIGHTEEN

Deirdre sat in the bakery drinking coffee with Sheila, Jen, and Sara, who were talking about Peter Anderson's drowning.

"That's your neighbors' son-in-law, right?" Sara asked. "Did you see the article in the paper?"

Deirdre nodded. The article had said the sheriff's department presumed it to be an accident, but that some witness had seen a powerboat wake a rowing shell on that same day, causing it to flip. *What if they investigated? Would that mean an arrest? Jail? Maybe prison?*

"Such a freaky thing to happen, don't you think?" Jen said.

Deirdre nodded again. She had to get out of there.

Sheila was suggesting that they go hiking the next week before it got cold and snowy.

"I don't know if I can," Deirdre said, "Mrs. Ri—" She stopped herself. *Be careful!* she admonished herself. "I volunteer taking care of a neighbor lady, and she's not feeling well."

"Oh, she'll feel better by next week," Sheila said as if her saying it would make it so. "We had such a blast last time!"

Deirdre remembered. She also remembered taking Sheila's keys from her backpack. The keys were now in her jewelry box, along with the Post-it note Sheila had given her with the gate code and marina slip number. She'd need to move them to Dennis's briefcase. The one with his initials that she'd found under his side of the bed. The one he opened with the little key he kept hidden in his sock drawer. The one in which he kept two framed photos—one of Brenna and Peter toasting each other at what looked to be their wedding, with Dennis in the background. The other of Dennis and seven other guys, standing in a line and holding Brenna sideways.

"We'll meet at the school, and I'll drive," Sheila was saying.

Deirdre looked at her blankly.

"For the hike." Sheila snapped her fingers in front of Deirdre's face. "Earth to Dee."

"I can't. I'm sorry. I have to go," Deirdre said as she stood quickly and exited the bakery.

Dennis might get angry if she took too long getting the truck back. Ever since Peter's memorial service, he'd been alternating between rage and contrition.

"You need to control your kid," he'd hissed at her just a few days ago. He had an iron grip on her arm and was pressing his fingers into her flesh. "You spoil him. And I will not tolerate a son who is a momma's boy."

Tears welled up in Deirdre's eyes and she tried to free herself from Dennis. He suddenly seemed to realize he was hurting her and quickly released her arm.

"Deirdre, I'm sorry," he said, looking confused, as if he'd just woken up. "I don't know what happens to me, why I get like that."

She had noticed Meg glancing at her arm, at the bruises Dennis left. Dennis always said he was sorry after he'd hurt her. But he would soon find out what it really meant to be sorry.

CHAPTER NINETEEN

B renna went back to work, but it was difficult to focus. Sometimes, her hangovers were so bad she would drink a shot or two of vodka at her desk. To take the edge off. Just a little hair of the dog. It was the only way she could get through the day.

She still called Sadie every night before she'd drunk too much. Sadie seemed to have settled in just fine up in Tahoe. She chattered on each evening about what had happened at school, what she was going to be for Halloween, what Denny had done or said, what she and Grammeg had for dinner.

"Love you and miss you, Mama," Sadie would say at the end of each call. Brenna wondered if that was true. She was a complete and utter failure as a parent. Surely Sadie must agree.

After ending the calls with Sadie, she'd hit the wine in earnest, trying to quiet her mind of its endless cycle of thoughts—Peter, Dennis, Sadie. Eventually, she'd pass out. Then get up and start all over again.

This was no way to live, she thought. *She had to do something.*

⤙

Brenna drove through the Central Valley on a clear and chilly day. The Sierra range was visible in the distance, dusted in snow. It was the Sunday before Thanksgiving, and she was on her way to Tahoe. She was anxious about seeing Sadie. And Dennis. And about what she was planning to do. Her hands shook, and she took a swig from her flask of vodka. Just enough to steady herself.

A few weeks prior, Jack had hired a young woman named Clara, who'd moved from Chicago, where she'd worked as a news editor. Jack had said that she was there to assist Brenna during her "difficult time." But it was obvious that aside from being worried about her, Jack was concerned about her performance as managing editor. He'd been pulling back from the paper prior to Peter's death but was back almost full time lately.

Brenna had heard the rumors circulating. Her staff was concerned about her. Finally, Jack came into her office one afternoon. He sat in the chair across the desk from her.

"Bren, I think you need to take some time away. Clara is ready to step in for as long as you need, with help from Jim. I'll be checking in with them regularly."

Brenna looked at the floor.

"It's for the best, sweetheart. And once you've had a chance to truly grieve for Peter, you can come back."

Brenna just nodded. She couldn't look at Jack. She knew he was right. Nothing was working. She had to dig herself out of this hole.

Brenna arrived in Tahoe just before dinnertime. Jack would be joining them in a couple of days. Meg and Sadie emerged from the house to greet her.

Meg embraced her and then stepped back. Sadie stood next to Meg looking hesitant.

"Hi, Mama," Sadie said. She'd grown a little.

Brenna leaned down and opened her arms and Sadie stepped into them. The hug felt a little mechanical. *But what did I expect?* Brenna thought.

"We're having lasagna for dinner," Sadie said. "Deirdre makes it, and it's really good."

Dennis had appeared at some point, Brenna realized, and was carrying her bags from the car into the house. He nodded to her on his way past. "Good to see you, Brenna," he said.

The three of them followed Dennis inside. He started upstairs with the bags, but Brenna stopped him.

"Just leave them. I'll take them up later."

Dennis put them down, nodded to her again, and headed for the door. Sadie had gone into the kitchen. Brenna could hear her chatting with Deirdre.

"Brenna?" Meg was looking at her with concern. "I asked how you are feeling."

"I don't know, Mom. I don't know."

Meg pulled her into another hug.

Once Brenna extracted herself, she said, "I'm going to take my stuff upstairs and rest a bit. Don't wait for me. I'll eat later."

"I'll have Deirdre fix you a plate."

Brenna escaped to her room. And her flask. Soon she was out cold.

Brenna slept until nearly noon the next day. She awoke feeling physically better than she had in a long time. She hadn't slept like that in months. She knew she had to get it together. She knew how to do it; she just had not yet picked up the phone to call the local AA chapter for a meeting schedule. She promised herself she'd do it that day.

The house was quiet. Sadie was at school. Brenna made her way to the kitchen. In the refrigerator, she found a plate of lasagna with plastic wrap over it. She assumed that was her dinner. Her stomach growled, and she ate it without heating it up.

Next, she went in search of her mother, guessing correctly that Meg was in her studio, a glassed-in porch on the south side of the house that she used during cold weather. The sun streamed in through the window reflecting off the lake.

Meg looked up from her easel and smiled. "So glad you slept in."

"Me too. I needed it."

Meg patted the seat of a chair next to hers on the other side of a small table. Brenna sat down.

"Are you hungry?" Meg asked.

"Just ate. Last night's dinner."

"Ah. Deirdre brought it up to you last night, but she said you didn't answer her knock."

"So, does Deirdre take Sadie to school?" Brenna asked.

"She does. She picks her up too, along with Denny."

"What time is that?"

"She usually leaves at about ten minutes to three. Maybe you'd like to go with her and see Sadie's school?"

"Sure. Yeah. Good idea."

⌒

Brenna stood at the kitchen window at 2:45 p.m. She had a clear view of the Griffins' apartment above the garage and the driveway. Dennis's truck was parked there. Deirdre came down the stairs at 2:48 p.m., got into the truck, and headed out toward the highway. School pick-up time.

Brenna slipped out the kitchen door. Meg was resting upstairs. This was her opportunity.

She crossed the driveway and climbed the stairs above the garage. She was certain Dennis wasn't home, having seen him leaving the apartment earlier, but knocked just in case. When no one answered, she tried the knob and found the door unlocked. She crept silently through the living-dining room. She glanced into the small kitchen and checked both bedrooms and the bathroom. The house was unoccupied. She checked the time: 2:51 p.m.

She wasn't sure where to start looking but reckoned she didn't need to look in Denny's room. She started in the kitchen, opening drawers and cupboards, exploring the utility closet, then moved to the hall closet, checking coat pockets. She found nothing out of the ordinary. She stepped into the bathroom and opened all the drawers, which were filled with ordinary bathroom stuff. On to the master bedroom. The bedside alarm clock said it was 3:06 p.m. She'd better be quick. She opened the dresser doors and checked the shelf above the clothes hanging in the closet. She looked under the bed and found a dusty sock and a briefcase.

The briefcase interested her, and she slid it out from under the bed. It was locked. She stared at it for a while. It was engraved with the initials DEG—Dennis whatever-his-middle-name-was Griffin, she assumed. She looked up and locked eyes with Deirdre, who was standing in the doorway.

"You'll need to unlock it," Deirdre said, and walked to the bureau. She walked toward Brenna and handed Brenna a small key.

Brenna took it.

"Open it," Deirdre said and sat on the bed.

"What's in it?" Brenna asked. Deirdre didn't answer, and her calm manner was unsettling.

Brenna struggled to control her shaking hand and get the key into the lock. She peered inside and saw an odd collection of items: a tangle of dark hair, a lighter, two framed photos, a Post-it note with *slip #* and a series of numbers written on it, and a set of keys. She examined the photos and saw that they were from her wedding and the San Diego Crew Classic. She picked up the keys.

"Oh, that's interesting," Deirdre said. "May I see those keys?"

Brenna handed them up to her. She stood up from the floor and sat on the bed as well. She watched as Deirdre examined them. About five keys hung from a keyring on which hung a brass *S*.

"Huh," Deirdre said. "I think these are Sheila's keys."

"Who's Sheila?" Brenna asked.

"She's a friend of mine. I'm sure I've seen this keyring before. Yes, I've definitely seen this in Sheila's car and on her boat."

Brenna stared at the keys. "Her boat?"

Deirdre pointed to the Post-it. "Can I see that?"

Brenna handed her the note.

"Sheila wrote this. I forgot my wallet on her boat one time, and she gave me the code so I could go get it. And this other number is the slip number."

Brenna stood up abruptly. She needed to get out of there. "Where's Sadie?"

"She went to show your mom what they made in art class today."

"Well, I better . . . ," Brenna said and began moving toward the door.

"Wait," Deirdre said, and dropped Sheila's keys and the Post-it note back into the briefcase. She closed it and handed it to Brenna. The key was still in the lock. "Take it."

ᔧ

That evening, Brenna had asked to speak to Meg privately. They waited until Sadie had gone to bed and met in Jack's den.

Brenna had a briefcase with her. She opened it and handed Meg the framed photos that had been missing.

"What's this?" Meg said, looking from photos to briefcase.

"It's Dennis's. Deirdre said I should take it. He keeps it under his bed, locked. But Deirdre had the key." Brenna held up a lighter. "This is mine," she said. "And I'm pretty sure this is too." She pointed to a snarl of dark hair.

"These keys belong to Deirdre's friend, Sheila," Brenna continued. "She said the Post-it note has the code for the gate at the marina where Sheila and her husband keep their yacht and the slip number.

"I'm going to the sheriff with the briefcase and my suspicions," Brenna finally said.

"Suspicions of what? That Dennis took the yacht?"

"Yes; and used it to cause Peter's boat to flip."

Meg asked Brenna to wait a minute and left the room. She returned with two photos.

"Take these too," Meg said, handing them to Brenna.

CHAPTER TWENTY

Dennis was unloading the new snowblower he'd picked up in Reno the day before. It had been dark when he'd gotten back to Tahoe, and he'd been tired and hungry. Jack was arriving later that day, however, and Dennis wanted to get the snowblower out of the truck and into the garage. It was gray and cold. It might even snow.

He was wheeling the snowblower into the garage when he saw a sheriff's car coming up the driveway. As he exited the garage, he found two officers waiting for him outside. One of them held a plastic trash bag.

"Can I help you?"

"Are you Dennis Griffin?" one of them said.

"I am."

Dennis could see Deirdre watching them from the Rileys' kitchen window. *Why was she just standing there?* he thought.

"We were wondering if we might ask you a few questions."

"What about?"

"Just tying up a few loose ends regarding the death of Peter Anderson."

"Uh, yeah, sure. But I don't know how much help I'll be." Dennis glanced at the Rileys' kitchen window again, but Deirdre was no longer there.

"What's going on?" Denny's voice drifted down from the apartment's deck.

"Nothing to worry about," Dennis called up to him. "Just talking. Go get ready for school."

To the officers, Dennis said, "Do we need to do this right now? I mean, I really don't know much about what happened."

"We just have a few questions."

Dennis saw Deirdre hurrying past them with Sadie. She glanced at them, while Sadie fired off questions: "Who are those men? What do they want?"

Deirdre got Sadie into the truck and laid on the horn. Denny came running down the stairs and climbed into the truck. As they pulled away, Dennis noticed Deirdre staring straight ahead as she drove, while both kids looked out the window at them. Dennis wondered what was up with Deirdre. *Why hadn't she stopped to ask what was going on?*

"Mr. Griffin?" one of the officers said.

The two officers were Sheriff Tanner and Deputy Sorensen. Dennis had invited them up to the apartment, and they were sitting at the kitchen table. Sorensen reached into the plastic trash bag and pulled out a briefcase, which was inside a clear plastic bag. He handed it to Dennis.

"Do you recognize this?"

Dennis recognized it right away, even before he checked for his initials.

"Yes, it's mine. How did you get it?"

"How well do you know Sheila Harris?"

"Who?"

"Sheila Harris, a friend of your wife's," Tanner said.

"I guess Deirdre's mentioned her, but I've never met her."

"Do you recognize these keys?" the deputy asked him, sliding a set of keys in a plastic bag toward him.

Dennis looked at the keyring in the shape of an S with five keys. "No, I don't think so."

"You're sure?" the deputy prodded.

"Yeah, whose are they?"

The officers ignored him. Tanner consulted a small notebook. "What were you doing on the morning of August 19?" he asked.

"Uh. I don't know . . . Wait, that was the day Peter died?"

Tanner just looked at him, waiting.

Dennis remembered the day well. "In the morning, I was walking around, checking the property."

"Checking it for what?"

"People camping, people dumping stuff, broken fencing."

"Was anyone with you?"

"No."

"Did anyone see you?"

"I don't know. I mean, I might have told my wife where I'd be."

"So, your wife was home when you left to go walking around?"

"I think so."

"But nobody saw you walking around?"

"No. I don't know. Maybe."

"So, you weren't out on the lake?"

"I wasn't."

Both officers looked at him for a beat.

"Do you think I had something to do with Peter's drowning? I thought it was caused by a boat wake. At least that's what it said in the paper."

"As I said," Tanner answered. "We're just tying up loose ends."

"Have you ever been on Sheila Harris's boat?" Sorensen asked.

"My wife's friend?"

"That's right."

"No," Dennis answered. "Wait. Is this about Deirdre?"

"Is what about Deirdre?"

"I think she's been on the boat. Denny told me she knew how to drive it."

"Who's Denny?" the deputy asked.

"Her—our son. You think Deirdre was driving the boat that caused the wake?"

"Why would we think that?" Tanner said, giving Dennis a hard look.

Dennis tried to think back to the criminal law class he took at Yale. *What was it that made someone a suspect? Opportunity? Means? Something else?*

"I don't know. I guess if she knew how to drive her friend's boat and she borrowed it that morning . . ."

"Are you saying you think your wife caused the drowning?"

"I don't know," Dennis said. "Maybe accidentally?"

"Was she out boating with her friend that morning?" the deputy asked.

"I don't know. I don't remember what she was doing that day."

"Okay, Mr. Griffin, which is it? Was your wife home when you told her you were going to be out walking around the property? Or was she out boating?" asked the sheriff.

"I don't remember."

The deputy slid a small plastic bag across the table toward Dennis. "What's on this Post-it note?"

Dennis picked up the bag. "Slip #34. And some more numbers."

"Does that mean anything to you?" Tanner asked.

"No."

Tanner stood up and motioned to Sorenson.

"Excuse us for a minute," the sheriff said, and the two of them stepped out on the deck.

Dennis could see them through the window and could hear them talking in low tones, but he couldn't make out the words. His mind raced. *Was he a suspect? Was Deirdre?*

Motive! he thought suddenly. *Opportunity, means, and motive. But what would be Deirdre's motive to drown Peter?*

The door swung open, and the two officers returned to their seats at the table.

As if reading Dennis's thoughts, Tanner said, "Mr. Griffin, do you know of any reason why your wife would want to harm Peter Anderson?"

"Uh, no, not really. I'm not sure they knew each other very well. I mean, we work here. Peter came up with his family to visit, and she cooked meals and cleaned the house."

"But you yourself weren't just the hired help, right, Mr. Griffin?" Sorenson said, flipping through his little notebook.

"Meaning?"

"Weren't you friends with Peter Anderson and his wife, Brenna, in college?"

"We rowed together, yes."

"But wasn't it more than that? Didn't you date Brenna Anderson?"

"No, not exactly."

"Then, what exactly, Mr. Griffin?" said the sheriff, leaning toward him.

"We weren't dating. She was with Peter. We hung out sometimes, that's all. The three of us, I mean."

Both officers sat looking at him. Dennis wasn't sure how much to say. Definitely nothing about the night in San Diego—or the day in Redwood City.

"Deirdre thought something went on, I think. She kept asking me how well I knew Brenna," Dennis said.

"So, Deirdre was jealous of Brenna? Even though you say you two never dated?"

"I guess."

"Let me ask you, Mr. Griffin," said Sheriff Tanner, looking at him intently. "Do you think Deirdre wanted to harm Peter to hurt Brenna because she was jealous of what she thought went on between you two?"

Dennis laughed a little. "Hard to say. Jealous women do crazy things."

"And what about jealous men?" the sheriff said carefully. "Isn't true that you wanted to date Brenna, but she chose Peter over you?"

"No. I mean, yes. I was interested in her in college. I asked her out, but she turned me down. Said she was with Peter. End of story."

"You're sure about that?"

"What do you mean?"

Dennis's heart started to pound. *What did Brenna tell them?*

"Do I need a lawyer?"

"I don't know, Mr. Griffin. Do you?"

⌒

A week later, Dennis sat on the hard bunk in his cell. It was a small jail with only a handful of cells and a drunk tank. Most of the other cells were empty, but the tank was occupied. Turns out he did need a lawyer. But he didn't know any. Except for his father and the other lawyers at his father's firm. And he certainly wasn't going to call any of them.

A deputy appeared, unlocked Dennis's cell door, and told him he had a visitor. Dennis assumed it would be Deirdre. Finally. But when he was shown into a visiting room, he found Jack pacing the floor.

The deputy stood just inside the door. Jack turned to face Dennis. Dennis could see that he was struggling to control his temper. He leveled Dennis with a hard look and said, "Do not lie to me. Did you do this?"

Dennis looked directly into Jack's eyes and said, "No, sir, I did not."

⌒

Jack posted Dennis's bail and took him back to the house. He told Dennis to get cleaned up and come over to Jack's den at four. Dennis followed Jack's instructions to the letter. The apartment was empty, and he noticed his truck wasn't parked in the garage. It was Wednesday, Dennis thought, and he had no idea where Deirdre was. Denny's school maybe. He showered and put on clean jeans, a T-shirt, and a V-neck sweater—nicer clothes than the ones he worked in.

He went out on the deck and smoked a cigarette. It had snowed while Dennis had sat in jail, but the afternoon was sunny, and it had mostly melted away at lake level. A black SUV was now parked in the driveway.

At four, he walked over to the house and let himself in through the kitchen. No sign of Deirdre, Meg, Brenna, or either of the kids. He made his way to Jack's den and came face-to-face with his father. Another man was with him.

"I'll leave you to it, then," Jack said, and left the room.

"Sit," his father ordered.

Dennis sat down.

No one spoke for several seconds.

Finally, the other man said, "You may remember me, Dennis, from when you interned at the firm. I'm Joe Calloway."

"Nice to see you, sir."

Dennis hadn't seen his father in seven years. Zachary looked pretty much the same, aside from a bit more gray in his hair.

"How's Mom?"

"She's fine," Zachary answered testily. "You might have called. She cried for weeks after you left."

Dennis didn't say anything. He would call his mother, now that he'd been found.

"How did you find me?"

"My secretary saw an article about your arrest in the *L.A. Times*," Zachary said.

"The *L.A. Times?* Why would they run it?"

"Because you're my son, and I'm a partner at L.A.'s biggest law firm."

"So, what do you want? You here to save your firm's reputation?" Dennis said. He found, to his surprise, that his father no longer scared him. He was merely an aging, angry little man.

"In part, yes," Zachary said, his eyes cold. "But we're also here to represent you. You're going to hire us."

Dennis laughed. "Why the fuck would I do that?"

Zachary slammed his fist on the arm of his chair.

"How dare you speak to me in that way—"

"Look," Dennis said, turning to Joe Calloway. "No offense to you, sir. I'm sure you're a first-rate lawyer—"

"He's the best criminal defense attorney in the state," Zachary growled. "Joe and I got our investigator on this as soon as that article about you appeared in the paper. We are certain we can get the case dismissed."

"Don't you even want to know my side of it? Whether I did it?"

"It doesn't matter whether you did it—"

"If I may jump in here," Calloway said. Zachary nodded, looking away from Dennis in disgust. "Our investigator found out useful information on your wife, along with Brenna Anderson. We think the evidence against you is flimsy at best. And that one of them could have just as easily done it. We're sure we can get this dismissed, but just in case, we have plenty of dirt on them both."

"No," Dennis said.

"Do you want to be charged with this crime?" Zachary shouted.

"I didn't do it. It was probably just a freak accident. Why would Deirdre kill Peter? Why would Brenna?"

"Dennis," said Calloway, "all we'd have to do is enough to plant reasonable doubt in the minds of the jurors, but let's not get ahead of ourselves. It's unlikely to go that far."

Dennis stood up and looked at Zachary. "Let me make this as clear as I can. I don't care what happens to Deirdre; she's basically turned on me. But I will not let anyone drag Brenna into this. She . . ."

"Brenna is the mother of your child, isn't she?" Zachary said.

Dennis gaped at him. "How do you—"

"Never mind that. She disappeared the day her husband drowned. She was gone all day, according to her staff at the *Tribune*. She left your daughter with a babysitter for several hours. She had enough time to drive up here, drive a boat at her husband, and drive back to San Francisco."

"Why would she do that?"

"Any number of reasons," Calloway said. "She's an alcoholic. Maybe she was in a blackout. Maybe the marriage was falling apart. Maybe her husband found out you are the father of the child. Maybe he was abusing Brenna. Maybe she wanted him out of the way so she could be with you. Again, all we would need to do is raise the possibility that she did it. If it comes to that. Which it won't. You just need to sign this legal services agreement and let us help you make this go away."

Calloway pushed some papers across the coffee table, along with a pen.

Dennis stared out the window but made no move to sign.

"Consider this, Dennis," Zachary said. "We can keep certain facts about your relationship with Brenna from coming to light in court, under attorney-client privilege. Or we can walk out of here with no such restraints on what we might let slip to, say, the press or Jack Riley or . . ."

Dennis stared at his father, his hateful, awful father. Then, he picked up the pen and signed. His father had always had control and still did.

⌣

Dennis was back in the apartment when he heard a quiet knock on the door. When he opened it, Meg Riley was standing there.

"Do you have a minute?"

"Of course, come in."

"Actually, could you come out here? I know it's cold, but . . ."

"Yeah, sure." He grabbed a jacket from a hook by the door, but instead of putting it on, he gently draped it over Meg's shoulders. Meg looked surprised but quickly recovered.

"I just wanted to let you know that Deirdre and Denny are going to stay with us for a while," she said. "I wondered if you might leave the apartment for about half an hour while they come and get some of their things."

"Yeah. Sure. Whatever they need," Dennis said. He felt deflated.

"Thank you," Meg said, handing him his jacket. She turned for the stairs.

"Mrs. Riley?"

Meg turned back.

Dennis looked directly into her eyes and said, "I don't know what you must think of me, but I didn't do this. I didn't cause Peter's boat to flip."

"I met your father earlier today. He's . . . very angry with you."

"I've always been a disappointment to him."

"Really?" Meg said. "Even when you were at Stanford and Yale?"

"My whole life."

"That's awful. I can't imagine feeling that way about Brenna. I can't imagine a parent not being proud of their son, especially with all of your accomplishments—at least when you were younger . . . ," she trailed off.

"The last straw for him, I think, was when I didn't go back to Yale."

"But didn't he refuse to pay for law school after you didn't make the Olympic team?"

Dennis nodded, unsure how to respond. Of course, Jack would

have told her that. He'd almost forgotten about that story he'd made up.

"I guess that explains his comment. He said to his lawyer friend that maybe they should just pack it in and go back to L.A., that you weren't worth it," Meg said.

Dennis nodded. "That sounds about right."

"I've never had a very high opinion of you, Dennis," Meg continued. "I was one of the first to suspect you had something to do with Peter's drowning."

Dennis looked at the ground.

"And you've hurt Deirdre and Denny—I mean, physically. Haven't you?"

Dennis sighed. "I grabbed Denny and shook him once when he was in kindergarten, and he ran away from me. I never touched him again."

"And Deirdre?"

"I've grabbed her. More than once. In anger."

"How many times?"

"I don't know. Three, maybe."

"She's afraid of you," Meg said. It was not a question.

"I can lose control of my temper sometimes. I know that."

"She also knows that you don't love her."

"Has she said that?"

"No. But she can see—as can I—that you're in love with Brenna."

Dennis stared at Meg.

"I remember Peter and Brenna's wedding. You couldn't take your eyes off her then and you still can't. And Sadie. You love her too, don't you?"

CHAPTER TWENTY-ONE

Denny sat on one of the twin beds in the room at the Rileys' where they were going to stay "for a while." He was watching the apartment, of which he had a clear view from the bedroom window. *No one at school could ever find out he was sharing a room with his mother!* he thought, but he actually didn't mind that much.

He sat thinking about the numerous ways people could die. Some of them he heard from his friends at school, like people getting eaten by bears when they were standing in their own yards. Or people who fell into sinkholes that suddenly opened up. Others were from stories on the news Dennis watched. Like people who were driving and the accelerator pedal getting stuck cause the floor mat got bunched up under it and they crashed and burned.

Or like Sadie's dad . . .

Denny didn't like thinking about that, though, so he thought about his day instead.

He hadn't seen Dennis get arrested. He'd ditched school with Craig and Eddie. They'd gone down to the river and smoked and goofed around. He snuck back to school in the afternoon and hid in the bushes outside until his mom came to get him and Sadie. When they got home, he headed for the apartment, but his mom stopped him.

"Your dad got out of jail," she said.

"He's not my dad."

"Fine. Dennis is back home, and I think we should leave him alone for a while."

"Why's he out of jail?"

"Mr. Riley bailed him out," his mom said.

Sadie, who'd been listening to all of this, asked, "What's 'bailed him out' mean?"

Denny rolled his eyes. But he didn't know what it meant either.

"Paid money to get him out," his mom said.

"That sucks," Denny said and turned away.

"Go to the Rileys'! Not the apartment!" his mother said.

"Why?"

"We're staying there for a while."

"Oh, man!" Denny started toward the lake.

"Wait for me!" Sadie yelled. Denny began running, and Sadie gave chase.

Denny picked up the pace and looked over his shoulder to see Sadie give up. He sat on a log by the water and waited until his mother and Sadie had gone inside the house. After a few more minutes, he crept back toward the truck.

For a long time, Denny thought Dennis was his father. He had been only four years old when his mother married him. He'd loved Dennis for the first few years; he was the only father he'd ever known. Even after Dennis started yelling at him and his mother. Even after Dennis grabbed him and shook him. But earlier in the summer, Denny found out that he was also hurting his mother. That's when Denny got angry. It was also about the time he found out Dennis wasn't his real father.

He'd come home one afternoon and heard the shouting even as he climbed the stairs to the apartment—again. Dennis was yelling at his mother more and more lately. He stood outside the front door, listening.

"—don't know what you're so upset about!" his mother was saying, her voice trembling.

Then: "Let go of me! You're hurting me!"

Denny opened the door and saw that Dennis had a tight grip on his mother's left arm. She was wincing in pain.

"Hey, let go of her!" he yelled. Dennis released his mother's arm, brushed past Denny, and stomped out the front door.

A few days later, Denny was helping Dennis clean up some junk out near the highway. They had driven the truck over and were loading some old tires into the bed. It was a hot afternoon and Denny was sweating.

"How long is this going to take?" Denny asked.

"You got somewhere to be?" Dennis asked, looking amused.

"I was gonna go swimming with Eddie."

"Mmmm. Couple of hours, probably."

Denny sighed dramatically and said, "Oh man."

Dennis was suddenly in his face. "Hey, you know what? If it weren't for me, you wouldn't even have your friend Eddie. You wouldn't live here. You'd still live in the crappy house in Daly City with your whore of a mother and your crackhead grandmother. If I hadn't married your mother and treated you like a son, and taken this shit job—"

Dennis suddenly stopped his tirade. "The least you could do is help me out," he said quietly.

"What did you mean, 'treated me like a son'? Aren't I your son?"

Dennis turned away and said, "Yes, of course you're my son. Let's finish up here so you can go swimming."

Dennis let Denny drive back to the house as if to make up for what he'd said earlier. Denny made sure to leave the keys in the ignition, which Dennis usually did. Dennis never locked the truck either; there was no need. The Riley compound was far away from its neighbors and the highway, Dennis had said.

Now, outside the Rileys' guest bedroom window, Denny saw Dennis illuminated in the porch light of the apartment. Dennis descended the stairs, got in his truck, and drove away. Denny opened the window and leaned out into the cold air. *This was it!* He listened and waited for a fiery crash.

CHAPTER TWENTY-TWO

Deirdre woke up to a commotion coming from downstairs.

She got out of bed and made her way to the top of the stairs. Sheriff Tanner was in the front hallway. She stood and listened.

Jack was saying, "—back to jail? That is outrageous!"

The cop said, "Jack, his blood alcohol level was more than twice the legal limit."

"Sheriff Tanner?" Deirdre called as she descended the stairs. "What happened?"

Jack, Meg, and the sheriff looked up at her.

"Ma'am," Sheriff Tanner said, nodding to Deirdre. "Your husband ran his truck into a tree. He's got a concussion, maybe whiplash. You can probably see him tomorrow."

Deirdre shook her head slightly.

"He'll go back to jail once he's released from the hospital on the DUI and—"

"What about the hearing?" Jack asked.

The sheriff said, "That'll pro'bly be postponed a day or two, but we'll see."

Deirdre and Denny had moved back into the apartment. They were waiting for Sadie to meet them at the truck so Deirdre could drive them to school. A little snow had fallen over the weekend, and Sadie appeared wearing her fleece-lined boots and crunched along on the inch or two of accumulation.

"Grammeg said I can take ski lessons soon!" Sadie told Deirdre excitedly. Deirdre couldn't help but love Sadie, even though she could see before her the obvious possibility that Dennis was her biological father. The resemblance was hard to ignore.

"I think Santa might bring me skis for Christmas," Sadie said with glee.

Denny rolled his eyes and started to say, "Santa? No way *that's* gonna happen—"

"Denny! Get in the truck."

After delivering Sadie to her classroom, Deirdre saw Sheila, Sara, and Jen in the parking lot huddled together near Jen's truck. She approached and said, "We doin' coffee?"

All three turned, but no one spoke.

"What's going on?" Deirdre asked. Of course, Dennis had been in the local paper again for his DUI, his hospital stay, and his upcoming return to jail.

Sheila spoke first: "Sheriff Tanner called on Friday. Said he had a warrant to search our boat. The hubs called his buddy in the D.A.'s office and found out that they think your—what was it? Your neighbors' caretaker? Anyway, he *allegedly* used my keys to access our boat to wake Peter Anderson."

"Really? Why—"

"Skip the bullshit, Mrs. Griffin," Sheila said stonily.

Deirdre and Denny both used Deirdre's last name, Monroe.

"I . . ." Deirdre didn't know what to say.

"You what?" Jen said. "You lied to us?"

"It was you who took my keys the day we went hiking, wasn't it? And you gave them to your handyman hubby, right?"

"No, it wasn't like that. I did take your keys, but not to give to Dennis. I took them on an impulse. I thought I might need to get away." That was the truth. At least initially.

"From what?" Sara asked. "Get away from what?"

"From Dennis. He hits me. I was desperate. I took your keys and then I was too embarrassed to give them back to you."

Jen and Sara had relaxed their posture and were leaning toward her slightly.

"Oh, Dee—" Jen began.

Sheila wasn't quite there yet. "Why should we believe you, Deirdre? You've lied to us about everything."

"I don't know. I'm sorry I lied. I guess I didn't think you'd be friends with me if you knew I cooked and cleaned for the Rileys."

Silence all around.

"How did Dennis get hold of the keys?" Sheila finally asked.

"He must have found them in my jewelry box. Where I hid them."

"But how did he know the key to our boat was on there? How did he know which boat ours was? How did he know the marina code?"

"I kept the Post-it you gave me when I went to find my wallet. I came up with a crazy plan to drive your boat to the South Shore and then catch a bus to the Bay Area. I thought if I left from there, Dennis would have a harder time finding me. It was stupid, I know."

"Geez, Dee." Sara finally came toward her and put an arm around her shoulder.

Sheila looked skeptical but not quite as hostile.

"What did you tell the sheriff?" Deirdre asked her.

"What could I tell him? I said I lost my keys, but I didn't know someone had taken the boat. I let them into the marina and showed them where the boat was. Then they said they were seizing it as evidence in their investigation."

"Sheila. I'm sorry. I should have returned your keys."

Sheila considered her response for a minute. "Well, I guess Dennis going back to jail is a good thing for you, with the asshole hitting you and all. Come on, girls. I need coffee."

Deirdre hung back as they started walking. She wasn't sure of her status anymore.

Sheila turned around. "You coming, Dee?"

CHAPTER TWENTY-THREE

Dennis sat at the defense table with his father and Calloway, waiting for his preliminary hearing to start. He glanced around the courtroom. There were a few spectators, locals with time and curiosity. And Jack Riley was there too, seated just behind the defense table next to Dennis's father. Finally, the bailiff commanded all to rise, and the judge appeared through a side door and took his place on the bench.

The judge told all who were assembled that this was a preliminary hearing to determine whether the defendant would be charged with second-degree felony murder and that they would now hear from witnesses.

The prosecutor, an extremely tall and fierce-looking woman named Samantha Beckett, called Sheriff Tanner to the stand. Dennis wondered if she'd been a rower in college.

"Sheriff Tanner," Beckett said after Tanner was sworn in and introductory matters were completed, "what led you to begin your investigation into Peter Anderson's death?"

"My office received a call from an eyewitness who said he had seen—"

"Objection. Hearsay," Calloway said.

"Overruled," said the judge. "Counsel, this is a preliminary hearing, not a trial."

"Continue, Sheriff," said Beckett.

"I received a call from an eyewitness who said that on the morning of August 19 he'd seen a powerboat traveling toward a rowing boat. As the powerboat got closer to the rowing boat, he saw it veer away from the rowing boat, creating a wake of approximately three feet, which caused the rowing boat to capsize."

"And what about that phone call caused you to connect it to Peter Anderson's death?"

"The eyewitness said he had read about Mr. Anderson's drowning in the newspaper when he'd returned from vacation and that the reported timeframe of Mr. Anderson's drowning fit within the timeframe that he witnessed the powerboat waking the rowing boat, along with the area of the lake in which Mr. Anderson's boat and body were found."

"So, you began investigating at that time?"

"No, we didn't open our investigation until after Mr. Anderson's widow, Brenna Anderson, came into the office."

"Sheriff Tanner, why did Mrs. Anderson come to see you?"

"She offered evidence to support her belief that the defendant was responsible for Mr. Anderson's death."

"And what evidence was that?"

"A briefcase with the defendant's initials engraved in it, which contained a set of keys and a Post-it note. She also brought in two photographs."

Beckett produced all these items and asked the judge to enter them into evidence.

"And what was the significance of this evidence?"

"She said the keyring contained the key to a powerboat owned by Ms. Monroe's friend, Sheila Harris, and her husband. The Post-it listed the slip number of the Harrises' boat and the code to access the marina where it was moored."

"The Tahoe City Marina?"

"Yes."

"And the photos?"

"The photos show Mr. Anderson rowing out into the lake. In one, there appears to be a wooden object that Mrs. Anderson thinks is part of a rowboat that the defendant used to row to the marina."

Dennis reached for Calloway's legal pad and wrote: *I was NOT in the rowboat!!* He nudged Calloway to ensure that he saw the note.

Sheriff Tanner then testified that he had interviewed Dennis and that he did not have an alibi that could corroborate where he said he was on the morning of August 19. He said that he'd interviewed Deirdre and that she corroborated Brenna's claims.

He also testified that he had obtained a warrant to search Dennis's apartment and truck.

"And did you discover anything during your search?"

"Yes, we found a duffel bag that contained a pair of black insulated pants, a black ski parka with a hood, a black balaclava, and a pair of black ski goggles."

"Where did you find this?"

"In the back of the hall closet in the defendant's apartment."

Beckett produced all the items Tanner had listed, each in a clear plastic bag, and asked the judge to admit them into evidence.

When it was Calloway's turn to cross-examine the sheriff, he stood and said, "Sheriff Tanner, in August on Lake Tahoe, how many boats would you say are typically on the lake?"

"Hundreds."

"Boats of all sizes? Powerboats, sailboats, kayaks, rowing boats?"

"Yes."

"Just to recap, then, the evidence you have amassed to date is this: an eyewitness who saw a powerboat wake a rowing boat on a busy August morning on the lake, a set of keys, a Post-it note, a couple of photographs of someone in a rowing boat and some kind of wooden thing, and a set of black clothes, correct?"

"That's right."

"Were my client's fingerprints found on the keys?"

"No."

"How about the Harrises' powerboat?"

"No."

"Any other physical evidence that puts my client at the marina or on the boat? Shoe prints? Tire marks? Hairs? Fibers?"

"No."

"Did the eyewitness identify the man who'd capsized in the rowboat as Peter Anderson?"

"No."

"Do you have any eyewitnesses who saw Dennis rowing this alleged wooden rowboat toward the marina?"

"His wife said she saw him rowing away from shore in it."

"His wife."

"Yes."

Calloway paused, shaking his head.

"Did his wife, Ms. Monroe, tell you how she came into possession of the keys?"

"She said she had taken them from Ms. Harris because she feared that her husband was going to hurt her. She said she had thought she could use the Harrises' boat to get away and he'd be less able to follow her."

"Did she say how the keys ended up in my client's briefcase?"

"She said she had hidden them in her jewelry box and that she guesses he must have found them, taken them, and placed them in his briefcase, along with the Post-it note, until it was time to use them."

"This bag of black clothes. What size are the pants and jacket?"

"Large, if I recall correctly."

Calloway turned and indicated Dennis. "You've interviewed my client, and you can see him now. Doesn't he look more like an extra-large to you?"

"I can't say for sure."

"But you can see him sitting right there. Go ahead and stand up, Dennis."

Dennis got to his feet just as Beckett jumped to hers. "Objection! Asked and answered."

"Sit down, Mr. Griffin," said the judge. "Sustained. The witness answered the question. Move on, please."

"Sheriff, about the duffel bag that the clothes were in: was there anything distinguishing about the bag that indicated who it belonged to?"

"There was an identification tag, yes."

"And whose name was on the tag?"

"Deirdre Monroe."

At the break, Dennis said to Calloway, "What if I tried on the clothes? If they're too small, won't that help?"

"And if they fit?" Dennis's father, who was leaning forward from his seat behind the defense table, said with a sneer. "What if they fit?"

"Zachary's right. If they fit, it won't help you. Even if they don't fit, it doesn't make that much difference. You could have worn other clothes and gotten rid of them."

"Isn't that what I would have done anyway? If I had done it—"

"If you were smart," Zachary muttered.

"Listen," Calloway said. "There's no direct link between you and Peter's death. Don't worry. This is not going anywhere—"

The bailiff called for everyone to rise as the judge entered.

When the proceedings resumed, the prosecution called the eye-witness, Harvey Jones, to the stand. A man in his late forties or early fifties came forward and was sworn in. He was going prematurely bald and had a tan face and an athletic build.

"Good morning, Mr. Jones," Beckett said, and Jones gave her a nod. "You were out on the lake in your boat on the morning of August 19, is that correct?"

"Yes, ma'am."

"About what time was that?"

"I'd say around eight o'clock."

"Can you tell us where you were on the lake?"

"I was heading toward the West Shore from Dollar Point."

"So that would be south-southwest?"

"Yes."

"And what did you see when you were out on the lake that morning?"

"Well, not much until I passed Tahoe City. Then I saw a boat coming out of the marina."

"A powerboat?"

"Yes, that's right."

"And what happened next, Mr. Jones?"

"The boat picked up speed and was coming toward me. Not at me, but in the same direction I was going. I also saw what I thought was a kayaker going in the same direction but closer to shore."

"So, the supposed kayaker was also traveling south-southwest?"

"Yes."

"Thank you, Mr. Jones. Then what did you see?"

"As I got closer to the kayaker, I saw—and heard—the driver of the powerboat throttle up and turn toward shore. I tried chasing 'em down because I was afraid he didn't see the kayak."

"So, you tried getting the attention of the driver?"

"Yeah, I mean, it looked like he was heading right for the kayaker."

"Could you see the driver's face?"

"No, he was wearing a ski mask; black. He was dressed all in black."

"Then what happened?"

"I couldn't see exactly what happened, but the powerboat appeared to veer away from the kayaker and head south. It looked like the kayaker was in trouble, so I headed over that way. The boat had flipped over and there was a guy hanging on to it."

"Did you know the guy hanging on to the boat?"

Jones hesitated a minute. His eyes flicked toward Dennis very briefly. "No, ma'am."

"What did you do next?"

"I asked the guy if he was okay and if he needed help getting back in his kayak. He said it wasn't a kayak, it was a rowing shell. He said he was fine and that he'd be able to get back in just fine. He thanked me for checking on him."

"Then what did you do?"

"I continued down the West Shore. I mean, if I had known the guy wouldn't be able to get back in his boat, I would have stuck around." Jones looked around the room as if asking for forgiveness from them all.

"And from what you observed, Mr. Jones, would you say that the powerboat caused the rowing boat to flip over?"

"Oh yeah. Like I said, it was heading right at the guy. And when it turned toward the south, it had to have kicked up a huge wake. I didn't see it that well, as I said, but the speed it was going, it had to have been a three-foot wake."

"And that would be enough of a wake to flip the rowing boat?"

"Oh yeah, I would think so. When I got close to it, I saw how skinny it was, like less than a foot wide, maybe."

"Thank you, Mr. Jones. Nothing further, your honor."

"Mr. Calloway?" said the judge.

"Mr. Jones, when the prosecutor asked you if you knew the rower who had flipped, you looked at my client, Dennis Griffin. Can you tell us why you did that?"

"The guy looked kind of like him, that's all. But it wasn't him."

"You're sure about that?"

"Yes, it was a different guy."

"But you didn't know him?"

"No, sir."

"You didn't ask his name?"

"No," Mr. Jones said, looking somewhat sheepish.

"And he didn't volunteer his name?"

"No."

"So, you have no idea who the man was?"

"Well, when I read in the paper that a man was out rowing and drowned, I put two and two together, but—

"You referred to the driver of the power boat as 'he.' But you said the driver was wearing a ski mask. How do you know it was a man?"

"I guess I don't. I just assumed."

"Could it have been a woman?"

"Sure, I guess—"

"Thank you, Mr. Jones," Calloway said, and turned to the judge. "Nothing further, Your Honor."

"Ms. Beckett," said the judge. "Call your next witness."

"The People call Sheila Harris."

Sheila was sworn in, and Beckett, who remained seated, said, "Ms. Harris, can you tell the court how you know the defendant, Dennis Griffin."

"Well, I've never met him, but I'm friends with his wife, Deirdre Monroe. Our kids go to school together."

"And you and your husband own a yacht, is that right?"

"Yes."

"Where is it docked?"

"At the Tahoe City Marina."

"And has Ms. Monroe been aboard the yacht?"

"Yes—"

"When was that?"

"It was last June, just after school got out for the summer."

"Can you tell us about that day, when you and Ms. Monroe were on the yacht?"

"Sure, Deirdre and I—along with our two other friends—went out on the lake in the morning. We drove around a while, got some sun, and came back in the afternoon."

Beckett stood up.

"Ms. Harris, is there a locked gate at the marina?"

"Yes."

"And how do you access it? Do you have a key?"

"No, all the boat owners have a code to get in."

"And did Ms. Monroe have the code?"

"Yes. She lost her wallet, and I gave her the code so she could check to see if she'd lost it on the boat."

"Did you write it down for her?"

"Yes, on a Post-it note."

Beckett strode back to her table and picked up the plastic bag with a yellow piece of paper in it. She walked over to the witness stand and placed the bag in front of Sheila.

"Do you recognize this item?"

"Yes, it's the Post-it with the code and the slip number."

"Is this your writing?"

"Yes."

Beckett returned to her table and picked up the bag with the set of keys, which she carried over to the witness stand.

"Ms. Harris, do you recognize these?"

"Yes. They're my keys."

"How long have they been out of your possession?"

"Since last July. Deirdre and I and our two other friends went hiking. We had driven in my truck, and when we got back to the parking lot, I couldn't find them."

"And where had you last seen them?"

"I had put them in my backpack just before we started hiking."

"Did you ever find out what happened to them?"

"Deirdre took them while I was swimming."

"Ms. Harris, do you know how your keys ended up in the defendant's briefcase?" said Beckett.

"Objection. Calls for speculation," said Calloway.

"Sustained."

"Nothing further, Your Honor."

"Mr. Calloway," the judge asked. "Do you have any questions for this witness?"

"I do, Your Honor," Calloway said. "Ms. Harris, when and where did you meet Deirdre Monroe?"

"We met volunteering in our kids' classroom. Earlier this year."

"And what did she tell you about herself?"

"Um, she said her husband was a property manager and they had moved here from San Francisco. She also said she volunteered taking care of an elderly woman."

"Did she tell you the name of this elderly woman?"

"No."

"Did you ever go to her house?"

"No."

"Do you know where she lives?"

"I didn't before. I do now."

"But you said you didn't know Deirdre's husband. You never met him?"

"No."

"Ms. Harris," Calloway said, "can you tell us if, to your knowledge, Deirdre Monroe knew how to drive a powerboat?"

"Objection!" Beckett said with a look of outrage. "Relevance!"

"Sustained."

"Nothing further, Your Honor."

⌒

"The People call Deirdre Monroe," said Beckett.

The door at the back of the room opened, and Deirdre walked in. She was sworn in and took her seat in the witness box. She did not look at Dennis.

Beckett stood up and walked around the table to face Deirdre.

Beckett went through a whole series of questions about Deirdre's lost wallet and the marina code, about Sheila's keys and Deirdre's theft of them.

"Ms. Monroe, where were you on the morning of August 19?"

"I was in the kitchen at the Rileys'."

"And did you see Peter leaving for his row?"

"Yes, I saw Peter out the window. He went into the boathouse, got one of the rowing boats, and launched it off the dock."

"Did you see the defendant that morning?"

"Yes, a few minutes after Peter rowed away, I saw Dennis run down to the wooden rowboat. He got in it and rowed away in the same direction Peter had gone."

"She's lying," Dennis hissed at Calloway.

"How did the keys and the Post-it get into the defendant's briefcase?"

"Objection. Speculation," said Calloway.

"Sustained."

"I'll rephrase," said Beckett. "Ms. Monroe, where had you been keeping the Post-it note and Ms. Harris's keys?"

"In my jewelry box."

"And do you *know* how they got into your husband, the defendant's, briefcase?"

"No."

"Thank you, Ms. Monroe. Tell me about your husband's briefcase. When did you discover it?"

"I knew he kept it under the bed. I'd seen it before."

"Had you ever opened it prior to the day you discovered the keys and Post-it?"

"No."

"Did you know where the key was?"

"No."

"How did you open it then?"

"I looked for the key and found it in Dennis's drawer."

"And why did you decide you needed to look in the briefcase?"

"I became overwhelmed with the thought that Dennis had caused Peter Anderson's drowning. I decided I needed to look for some proof, other than seeing him row after Peter that morning. I was looking through his bureau drawers for something and that's when I found the key. I had a suspicion it would unlock the briefcase. And I was right."

"Why did you think your husband caused Peter's drowning?"

"Because . . ." Deirdre paused. "He's in love with Brenna. They used to date in college or maybe they had an affair—"

"What did you do after you opened the briefcase?"

"Once I saw what was in it—the keys and the Post-it—I gave the briefcase to Brenna."

"Thank you, Ms. Monroe. Your witness." Beckett returned to her seat.

Calloway stood.

"Ms. Monroe, did you tell Ms. Harris that your husband was a property manager?"

"Uh, I don't remember."

"Did you lead her to believe that you lived next door to the Rileys?"

"I don't remember."

"Did you ever tell Ms. Harris that you worked for the Rileys?"

"Well, sort of, I guess. I said I took care of a woman—"

"Did you tell Ms. Harris you took care of Mrs. Riley?"

"I don't think I ever said her name."

"Ms. Monroe, isn't it true that you lied to Ms. Harris about what your husband did and where you lived, and led her to believe you were volunteering your time taking care of an 'elderly woman'?"

"Objection! Asked and answered," said Beckett.

"Sustained. Move on, Mr. Calloway," the judge said.

"Were you and Brenna Anderson friends?"

"Uh, no. I mean I saw her when she came up for visits."

"Yet you gave her the briefcase?" Calloway looked at Deirdre with great skepticism.

"Well, I mean, it was her husband who had died. She should know what I saw and what I found."

"Interesting," Calloway said, pausing for a moment. "Did your husband ever say to you that he was in love with Brenna Anderson?"

"No, but I could see—"

"Thank you. Ms. Monroe, did you want to leave your husband?"

"Yes."

"Is that why you took Ms. Harris's keys? So, you could escape in the Harrises' boat?"

"Yes, until I realized it probably wasn't a good plan."

"Why is that?"

"Because I was afraid that he would come after me."

"But you knew how to drive the boat?"

"Yes."

"So, would you say that you had to think of another way to get out of your marriage, Ms. Monroe?"

"Objection!" Ms. Beckett jumped to her feet so violently that her chair fell over backward.

"Sustained."

Dennis looked at Deirdre, who appeared to be a little shocked at what had just transpired. He almost felt sorry for her. There was no way he was going to let Calloway go at Brenna like that.

"Ms. Monroe, did you put the Post-it note and Ms. Harris's keys in your husband's briefcase before giving it to Brenna Anderson?"

Beckett twitched. The judge held up a hand. "You may answer, Ms. Monroe."

"Of course not."

"Thank you, Ms. Monroe. No further questions."

CHAPTER TWENTY-FOUR

Brenna walked nervously to the stand and her hand shook as she was sworn in. She tried not to look at Dennis, but her eyes were drawn to him anyway. He looked thin. And tired. Jack was seated behind the defense table.

Beckett asked Brenna a series of questions that corroborated Deirdre's testimony regarding the briefcase and its contents. Brenna also provided additional details about the photos, saying that her mother had given them to her and said she had taken them the morning Peter died when she was out painting.

"Mrs. Anderson," said Beckett, "can you tell us how you and Dennis Griffin met?"

"We were at Stanford together: Dennis, myself, and my . . . Peter. We were all on the rowing team. Peter and Dennis were rowers, and I was a coxswain."

"I see. And what does a coxswain do?"

"Steers the boat and calls commands for the crew."

"Wasn't it true that Dennis wanted to date you?"

"Yes, he asked me out, but I was with Peter, so I turned him down."

"And what was his reaction?"

"He continued to try and insert himself into my life. He pretended to be Peter's friend and always seemed to be around. Then he started working at my parents' place here in Tahoe."

"Thank you, Mrs. Anderson. Your witness."

Calloway stood up.

"Mrs. Anderson, I'm very sorry for your loss. You and Peter Anderson were married in 1983, is that right?"

"Yes."

"Would you say you had a happy marriage?"

"Objection. Relevance," said Beckett.

"Sustained. Move on, Mr. Calloway."

"Isn't it true that you are an alcoholic?"

As expected, Beckett jumped to her feet and objected.

"I withdraw the question," Calloway said. "Mrs. Anderson. You testified that after my client asked you out and you turned him down that he pretended to be Peter's friend and"—Calloway consulted his notes—"always seemed to be around. Can you elaborate?"

Brenna glanced at Beckett. "Well, as I said, he got a job working for my father so that he would see me when I visited Tahoe."

"But wasn't he married when he came to Tahoe?"

"Well, yes."

"So, it is your testimony that this was one of the ways he tried to insert himself into your life?"

Brenna again looked to Beckett, who nodded slightly.

"Yes, I mean, why else would he work for my father?"

"Isn't it true that he met your father at your wedding? And that your father gave him a business card and asked him to stay in touch?"

"I'm not sure . . ."

"Weren't Dennis and Peter real friends?"

"I don't know. I think Dennis made Peter his friend to get close to me."

"I see. And do you and Dennis have much interaction when you visit Tahoe?"

"No, not really."

"How about Dennis and Peter?"

Brenna hesitated. "Uh, I mean, Peter and Dennis hung out

sometimes. They rowed together on the lake. Well, I should say, one would row a shell and the other would try and catch them in the rowboat. My dad would get in on that too. Sometimes they would go hiking, Peter and Dennis."

"So, Dennis and Peter did things together? Like friends?"

"I guess, but as I said, only because he wanted to get close to me," Brenna said.

"When did you and Peter start dating?"

"It was in the fall of 1981."

Calloway looked down at his legal pad. "Isn't it true that during the 1982 spring season, you, Peter, and Dennis traveled to San Diego for a regatta?"

"Yes," Brenna said, glancing at Dennis.

"And that, on the evening after the race, you went for a walk along the beach with Dennis? Just the two of you?"

"Yes." The color drained from her face.

"And that even though you were dating Peter you had sex with Dennis on the beach?"

"Objection! Relevance!" Beckett said.

Dennis grabbed Calloway's arm and hissed, "What are you doing?" Calloway shook him off and stood up.

"Mr. Calloway?" said the judge.

"Your Honor, I'm trying to establish the relationship between Mrs. Anderson and Mr. Griffin."

"I can see that, but for what purpose?"

"Ms. Beckett is trying to show motive for my client to have killed Peter Anderson because he was in love with Brenna Anderson, when in fact it was Mrs. Anderson who was obsessed with my client, not the other way around, and that she and Ms. Monroe are trying to set my client up for Mr. Anderson's death—"

"Your Honor, Ms. Monroe and Mrs. Anderson are not the defendants here," Beckett said.

The judge held up his hand. "I will allow this line of questioning, but only to a point. Objection overruled."

"Mrs. Anderson," said Calloway, walking around the defense table. "Isn't it true that you and my client had sex that night on the beach?"

"Yes," Brenna said quietly.

"I'm sorry, I didn't catch that. Can you repeat your answer?"

"Yes."

"And after your sexual encounter, did my client ask you out again?"

"No."

"Did he pursue a relationship with you beyond friendship?"

"No."

"And isn't true that you only married Mr. Anderson because my client didn't pursue any further romantic or sexual relationship with you?"

Brenna looked close to tears. Dennis could almost feel Jack's eyes behind him boring into his back.

Dennis stood up and yelled, "Stop!"

"Sit down!" Zachary hissed at him.

"Mr. Calloway," said the judge. "Please advise your client to refrain from this type of outburst. We'll recess for fifteen minutes." The judge exited the courtroom.

Calloway returned to the defense table. Beckett and Brenna walked by on their way out of the room.

"You don't need to put her through this. It's Deirdre who's trying to set me up, not Brenna. Put me on the stand, so I can explain," Dennis said to Calloway, as his eyes followed Brenna.

"Keep your voice down," Calloway whispered, taking a seat at the defense table. "That's a bad idea."

"Why?"

"We can control our side of the narrative," Calloway said quietly, "but we can't control Ms. Beckett's. I do not want her cross-examining you."

"Why not?"

Zachary snorted. "You'd think he didn't have a year of law school."

Dennis stood up and turned on his father. "What are you doing here anyway? Mr. Calloway is the one doing all the work. You don't need to be here. In fact, why don't you go home!"

Zachary slammed his hand on the table and stood up.

"Leave!" Dennis continued. "Go back to L.A. No one needs you here. You were never a father to me, and you aren't now. You straight-up lied that none of this information about me and Brenna would get out! Just tell the newspapers you've disowned me—"

"All right! All right!" Calloway said. "Let's all calm down." Calloway looked around the room. Only a handful of people remained, and they had turned their full attention to the scene at the defense table.

Zachary and Dennis stood staring at each other.

"Zach," Calloway said quietly. "Maybe it is best that you leave us to talk for a few minutes."

"Fine," Zachary said. He turned and exited the courtroom.

Calloway let out a deep breath and sat down. Dennis sat down too.

"Listen," Calloway whispered. "We have to keep the ball in our court. It's not a good idea for you to take the stand."

Calloway paused, waiting for Dennis to respond. Dennis slumped in his seat, suddenly too tired to argue. *What did it matter, anyway?*

When the proceedings resumed, Calloway said he had no more questions for Brenna, and she was excused. The last witness was Meg, and Beckett was questioning her about the photos she took.

"I took one of the photos of Peter rowing—the one where he's closer to shore, with the sun still low in the sky behind him," Meg said. "I was going to do a painting from that photo and give it to Peter at Christmas. But the other one. The one where the rower is further away? With the wood thing in the lower corner? I don't think I took that one. You see, I'd gone inside for more coffee right after I'd taken the other photo. I don't think I—no, I'm sure I didn't—take that second photo."

"But weren't you the one who told Brenna you'd taken the photos? And weren't you the one who gave the photos to Brenna to take to the sheriff?" Beckett looked annoyed.

"Yes, but I told her I wasn't sure if I'd taken both of them."

"Didn't you tell her that you thought the 'wood thing' in the corner was the rowboat?"

"Well, yes, I thought so at the time, but I'm not so sure now. In fact, I don't even think that's Peter in the second photo. I think it's Dennis. And it's not even the same day. There are differences between the two photos—the sun's position, the light, the clouds."

"Did you check the negatives to see if both photos were part of the same roll of film?"

"There were no negatives in the packet."

"Did you ask for the negatives when you picked up the photos after they were developed?"

"I didn't pick up the photos."

"Who did?"

"Deirdre did."

"Deirdre Monroe?"

"Yes."

"Your Honor," said Beckett. "We request to treat this witness as hostile."

Meg had taken the wind out of the prosecution's sails, according to Calloway. Calloway filed his motion to dismiss and felt certain that the judge would dismiss the case. Dennis wasn't so sure.

⌇

Back in his cell, Dennis lay on his bunk trying to read. A deputy approached and said Dennis had a visitor. "Your father."

Dennis sighed. He didn't have the energy.

"Tell him I'm asleep."

"Will do," the deputy said, and left.

Dennis gave up on reading. He thought about life with Zachary. He thought about his mother, whom he hadn't called yet. He thought about Jack, who had never believed he was guilty, but now probably hated him. He thought about Meg's testimony and how it could help him but hurt her relationship with Brenna. He thought about what would happen if he wasn't charged. He knew what would happen if he was. He thought about whether he would go back to work for Jack. And if Deirdre planned to leave him. He thought about Sadie. About how much she knew about what was going on. About whether she really was his daughter. And he thought about Denny and suddenly realized he missed him.

The next day, the judge dismissed his case for insufficient evidence to establish probable cause and proceed to trial. He told Dennis he was free to go. Calloway was smiling and shaking his hand. Dennis felt both relieved and disbelieving. *Was it really over?* he asked Calloway.

"Pretty much," Calloway said. "Although the judge did dismiss the case without prejudice. If new evidence arises, the case could be reopened. But I doubt that will happen."

He clapped Dennis on the back.

Great, Dennis thought. *Now I'll have this hanging over my head for the rest of my life.*

Dennis looked around for his father but didn't see him. He walked outside with Calloway and thanked him. It had been a while since he'd been outside, aside from some brief walks between jail and courtroom. It was cold and sunny. He didn't have sunglasses and squinted at the lake shimmering in the late morning. People drove by with skis on the tops of their cars, tire chains rattling and clunking.

Calloway asked him if he could drop him off somewhere, but Dennis said he'd be fine. He actually had no idea where to go. Calloway said goodbye and walked toward the parking lot.

Now what?

Jack pulled up in his truck, and Meg rolled the passenger-side window down. Jack jerked his thumb at the backseat, and Dennis climbed in.

CHAPTER TWENTY-FIVE

Jack never brought up the topic of Dennis and Brenna's past relationship. Nor did he treat Dennis any differently than he always
had. Dennis was surprised and grateful. He stayed in the guest room
at Jack and Meg's through the new year. Deirdre and Denny were still
in the apartment, but Meg said that Deirdre was going back to the
Bay Area—with Denny. Her friend Sheila was going to take them.
Dennis was not surprised. Deirdre had scarcely been over to the
house. She clearly didn't want to see him.

Once they left, Dennis would move into the apartment. The tentative plan was for him to stay on as caretaker and for Meg (at Jack's
insistence) to hire a house cleaner to come once a week. Meg was
going to stay in Tahoe permanently. Brenna and Sadie had returned
to Redwood City after Brenna had testified.

On the morning Deirdre and Denny were to leave, light snow was
falling, and Dennis was outside shoveling the walkway.

"Hey," said Denny's voice behind him.

Dennis turned and said, "Hey."

They stood not looking at each other for a minute.

"So, you're leaving today," Dennis said.

"Yep." Denny had gotten taller, Dennis noticed. He'd turn twelve
this year, but he looked more like fourteen.

"Guess I probably won't see you for a while," Dennis said. "I'm sorry about that and about a lot of other things. Whatever happens, I'll always think of you as my son."

"But I'm not," Denny said.

Dennis nodded slowly. "I'll still think of you that way."

"Whatever." Denny turned and started walking away.

"Hey, Denny. Give me a call sometime? Let me know how it's going?"

Denny thought for a minute. "Sure."

Denny turned away, and then suddenly turned back. "You know I tried to kill you," he said.

"Really? No, I didn't know that."

"Yeah, that night you drove your truck into the tree. I bunched up your floor mat so the gas pedal would stick. And before that, I tried to—"

A pickup truck came roaring up the driveway. *Must be Sheila*, Dennis thought.

"I better go," Denny said, and jogged back toward the apartment. Dennis made himself scarce as well.

Dennis stood in the kitchen, drinking coffee, and watched out the open window as Sheila helped Deirdre and Denny load their stuff into the back of her truck. She drove a new Toyota Tundra with an extended cab. *Nice ride*, Dennis thought.

Another vehicle was coming down the drive. A sheriff's truck. Sheriff Tanner and a deputy got out, approached the Tundra, and placed handcuffs on Deirdre. Sheila started shouting. Deirdre was focused on Denny, telling him to go upstairs, it was going to be okay. *What the hell?* Dennis thought and debated whether to go out there. Then he saw Jack heading for the group and decided to stay put.

The sheriff escorted Deirdre to the sheriff's truck and put her in the back. Sheila had followed and was still yelling, while the deputy attempted to calm her down. Jack went to Denny and said something to him. Denny went upstairs to the apartment.

Sheriff Tanner talked to Jack for a few minutes, then Jack returned to the house. Dennis heard the front door close, then saw the sheriff's truck turn around and head out to the highway.

"Ah, Dennis, there you are. Meg's waiting in my study. Please join us."

Dennis followed Jack through the dining room and down the hall. Meg was standing at the window looking out at the snow falling on the lake.

"Deirdre's been arrested for trying to frame you for Peter's death. Sheriff Tanner says they're charging her with lying to the sheriff and the court—"

"Oh my God," Meg asked. "What about Brenna? She went to the sheriff based on what Deirdre told her. Will they arrest her too?"

"Sheriff Tanner couldn't say for sure. But she will be questioned. I'm leaving tomorrow for the city."

Meg sunk into a chair. "What's going to happen to Denny?"

Jack looked at Dennis. Dennis nodded and headed for the door.

He found Denny in the apartment, watching TV with the sound off.

"Cops take her away?" Denny asked, eyes still on the screen. His face was tear stained.

"Yeah."

Dennis sat down in the armchair next to the sofa where Denny sat flipping channels with the remote. He settled on MTV.

"Guess we're not leaving town then."

"Guess not. At least not today," said Dennis.

They watched as members of a band drove down a dirt road in a car, one moving his mouth, probably singing, lip-synching, or whatever they did in music videos.

"You can stay here. With me," Dennis ventured. He wasn't sure how Denny was going to react to that idea. He wasn't sure about the idea himself.

Denny shrugged.

"It would just be until your mom comes back. Then maybe you'll leave for the Bay Area."

"She's not coming back," he said. He stood up and went into his room, slamming the door as he went.

CHAPTER TWENTY-SIX

Deirdre didn't come back. Dennis noticed that when Denny was home, he hurried to the window whenever he heard a car door. Deirdre was held for a few hours until Sheila posted her bail. Jack came up to the apartment to tell Dennis that he had gone to the jail to find out what was happening, but, by then, Deirdre was gone. He also said that Meg was going to go with him to Redwood City the next day to help Brenna with Sadie. Dennis wanted to ask if Sadie was all right, but he kept quiet. He wondered if Deirdre was going to show up at the apartment that day; she didn't, but she called.

"I'm staying at Sheila's until the arraignment," she said when Dennis answered. "Put Denny on."

Dennis knocked on Denny's door. "Denny, your mom's on the phone."

Denny opened it, his head down. Dennis could tell he'd been crying again.

"Mom? . . . Okay . . . Yeah, I'm okay . . ."

Jack and Dennis went out on the deck, giving Denny space to talk to Deirdre. Jack left soon after. A few minutes later, Denny opened the door and stepped out to the deck.

"She's at her friend's house. Mrs. Harris."

"I'll drive you over when you're ready," Dennis said.

Denny stood still, making no move to go back inside.

"She said I shouldn't come there. She said I should stay here," he said quietly.

As Denny spoke, Dennis realized that he wanted Denny to stay. They could work together on the property, Denny could continue at his school, see his friends, and sleep in his own room. He didn't know what was going to happen to Deirdre, but Dennis understood that he had the opportunity to do something useful: take care of his son.

Deirdre was charged with several counts: filing a false report, planting evidence, perjury, and suborning perjury. Dennis was surprised. He didn't think Deirdre had it in her. They stopped short of accusing her of Peter's murder, though; Dennis wondered if it was because there was no evidence to support the charge and it really had been an accident.

Dennis also wondered whether, if he had paid more attention to her, Deirdre would have done this. He should have tried harder with her. He felt bad for her, back in jail, waiting to be arraigned. He knew what that was like. Dennis knew he had failed her. She'd had a crappy life, and he hadn't made it any better. He thought about going to see her, but he didn't think she'd want to see him.

Jack and Meg returned from the Bay Area after spending a couple of weeks there. They asked Dennis to come over the morning after they got back. Denny was at school. He and Dennis had settled into their routines: Dennis let Denny bike to and from school by himself. He could hang out with friends after school, as long as he came home for dinner and homework. On weekends, he spent a few hours working with Dennis—shoveling snow, stacking wood, and making repairs. Dennis paid him a few dollars an hour.

Dennis went to Jack's study as instructed, and Meg poured him some coffee. Jack told Dennis that Brenna had been questioned by Placer County Sheriff's deputies in Auburn. Brenna had told them that she had gone to the sheriff because she had believed Dennis caused Peter's death. But she told them the truth: Deirdre hadn't found the briefcase; Brenna had. And that she had gone to the apartment to search for proof Dennis had done it and that Deirdre had found her there and given her the key to the briefcase. She agreed to sign a statement to that effect and testify at Deirdre's trial. So, she wasn't arrested.

But Deirdre's case never went to trial. She accepted a plea deal where she agreed to five years of supervised probation. Denny said she was going back to her mother's house in the Bay Area. Denny said that Deirdre wanted Denny to live with her, but she didn't want him to have to change schools. Dennis never heard from her directly. When Denny got his driver's license, Jack bought him a used Ford Bronco with four-wheel drive, which Denny drove to Daly City to stay with Deirdre some weekends and for longer visits during the summer.

Dennis did the best he could with Denny, and he thought Denny was turning out all right. Dennis knew Denny partied with his friends sometimes but hadn't gotten into any trouble. His friends planned to go to college and Denny said he wanted that too. Jack said he would pay for it. Denny had started running cross-country in middle school, and when he grew several inches right before high school, he also joined the basketball team. He kept his grades up so he could play sports. Denny also spent a lot of time with Jack, who offered advice and treated Denny like a grandson. Denny talked about majoring in computer science and working in the tech industry.

Overall, things were going well for Denny and him. Too well, in Dennis's opinion. He waited for the other shoe to drop. But it never did.

The day after she testified at Dennis's hearing, Brenna took Sadie back to the Bay Area, sold the Redwood City house, and moved them into an apartment in San Francisco.

Brenna had thought they might charge Deirdre with the murder. When they questioned Brenna, they'd even asked her if she thought Deirdre had done it. Brenna had answered honestly that she supposed it was possible, but she really didn't know. As time went on, she began to consider that maybe Deirdre *had* done it.

She was furious with her parents for a long time—with her father for taking Dennis's side and with her mother for seeming to cave to Jack's influence and backpedal about the photos at the hearing. But her parents had been there for Sadie through Brenna's interrogation, through the uncertainty of whether she'd have to testify at Deirdre's trial, throughout that whole time when Brenna was—yet again—unable to focus on her daughter. The stability of Meg and Jack was always a known quantity for Sadie. For this fact alone, Brenna's anger at them began to thaw with time.

Her AA sponsor, Abigail, had stood by her as well and always showed up when needed—for Brenna and Sadie both. As Brenna strung together years of sobriety, she was better able to build a relationship with Sadie. She started by just being there more, and then she made amends to her. She only wished she had talked to Jack first.

Sadie was in her room getting organized for the next day. She laid out the clothes she planned to wear to school, put her books and completed homework in her backpack, and packed her crew bag with the clothes she would need for rowing practice. Rowing was in her blood; her Grandpa Jack had told her when she was younger. Sadie had replied that she would never row; rowing had killed her dad.

But the summer after she turned fourteen, two of her friends wanted to join a junior team that rowed out of the nearby Bair Island

Aquatic Center. They talked Sadie into joining too. At the end of their novice year, Sadie's friends quit, but Sadie found that rowing really was in her blood and that she was good at it. So, she joined the varsity team. Rather than avoiding the sport, Sadie found rowing to be a way to honor her dad.

As she stuffed her spandex shorts and tank into a duffel bag, she heard a knock at her door.

"Sadie?" Her mother opened the door and poked her head in.

"Hey, Mom."

Brenna entered the room and said, "Can we talk?"

"Sure," Sadie said, placing the duffel next to her backpack. She sat on the bed and her mother sat next to her.

"What's up?" Sadie said when Brenna remained silent.

"I'm trying to think of how to start."

"Am I in trouble?"

Brenna turned to her and took her hand. "No, no. Nothing like that. It's just . . . you know how I go to AA to stay sober and work with Abigail."

Sadie nodded.

"Well, part of my recovery includes listing all of the people I have harmed and making amends—apologizing—to them."

Sadie nodded again.

"So, I want to make amends to you," Brenna said.

"Me? You haven't harmed me."

"I disagree. Maybe you were too young to remember, but I wasn't around much when you were younger. And I was drunk a lot."

"I don't remember you being drunk a lot," Sadie said. "But I guess I remember you not being around that much. Mrs. Nash took care of me a lot. And Dad. And Grammeg. But I didn't mind. And you were around sometimes."

Sadie was a little alarmed to see tears running down Brenna's face.

"Mom, it's okay. Really."

Brenna swiped at her tears and said, "You are so like your dad—and your grandmother. Kind, trusting, always seeing the good side of everything. That's why this is so hard for me to say."

"What is?"

Brenna took a deep breath and took both of Sadie's hands. Facing her, she said, "Your dad will always be your dad, and he loved you deeply. But . . . but . . ."

"What?" Sadie felt alarm growing within her.

"Your dad may not have been your biological father," Brenna blurted, looking away.

"What do you mean?"

Brenna shook her head, trying to compose herself.

"Mom?"

Brenna turned back to Sadie. "Your actual biological father may be Dennis."

Sadie stared at her mother. "Dennis? Mr. Griffin?"

"I'm sorry. I know this is hard to hear."

Sadie stood up and went to her window. She slid it open and took deep breaths.

"It's a possibility, not a certainty. And your dad—Peter—loved you more than anyone in the world—"

"Then why are you telling me this?" Sadie said. Her head was spinning, and she felt like the room was spinning too. She gripped the windowsill so as not to fall over.

"Because you have the right to know the truth. You also have the right to have him in your life if that's what you want."

"Well, you must be pretty sure he is my father then," Sadie said, and sat down in the chair by her desk, right on top of the school clothes she'd laid out for tomorrow.

"I'm sure enough. Although he's never taken a paternity test."

"So, was I born before you married Dad? Were you seeing both of them at the same time? Did Dad know that Dennis might be my father?" Sadie burst into tears. Brenna went to her and tried to hug her, but Sadie waved her off. "Actually, don't answer those questions. I don't want to know. And please, just leave."

"I'm sorry, Sadie," Brenna said, crying too now. But she did as Sadie asked and left the room.

⌒

A few days after her disastrous conversation with Sadie, Jack had called Brenna to say he was in town and invited her to lunch. Brenna spotted Jack at a table by the window overlooking the marina.

"Hey, Dad," she said, and sat down across from him.

"Sweetie. Good to see you." He stood to give her a hug.

Their waiter approached and asked for their drink orders.

"Just water, sparkling if you have it," Jack said. Brenna recognized the gesture as respect for her sobriety. They chitchatted about Sadie and her rowing and school news until the drinks came and the waiter took their food order.

"I want you to come back to the paper," Jack suddenly blurted. "You are a talented editor, and it's a shame for that to go to waste."

"Oh . . . thanks, Dad. I've been offered a job."

"As an editor?"

Brenna nodded.

"Where?"

"UC Berkeley. In the publications department."

"Well, congratulations! Their gain is our loss," Jack raised his glass to her.

"I'm coxing again, too, for a master's team at Lake Merritt."

"Well, that's great."

Jack reached across the table for Brenna's hand. Brenna waited a couple of beats before pulling hers away.

"Dad, there's something I need to tell you."

"What's that?"

"About a year after Peter and I got married, before he started working for you, Dennis showed up at the house in Redwood City."

Jack looked at her expectantly.

"Peter wasn't home. We got caught up. And then . . . uh, we slept together." She couldn't bring herself to say Dennis had assaulted her; Sadie could never know that. "Dennis might be Sadie's father."

Jack didn't say anything for a while.

"I told Sadie that Dennis might be her dad."

"Well," Jack finally said. Oddly, he didn't seem upset or angry. "Thank you for telling me. How did she react?"

"She was shocked, upset." Brenna looked away as her eyes filled with tears.

"Bren . . ." Jack reached for her hand. Brenna pulled it away.

"Sadie's always liked him, as you have," Brenna said with slight bitterness. "I guess both of you can't be completely wrong, but . . . don't you think it's odd that he ended up contacting you for the care-taker job? Don't you think it was to try to get to me?"

"Well, given what came out at Dennis's hearing and what you've just told me, I guess it's possible."

Brenna felt a wave of profound sadness as she looked out the window.

"You know, grief is a funny thing," Brenna said. "My AA sponsor, Abigail, has helped me understand that my drinking made it impossible to fully grieve for Peter after his death. It seems that I'm doing it now."

Jack reached for her hand again, but Brenna again pulled it away as she composed herself. She turned back to Jack.

"How can you be so sure that Dennis didn't kill Peter?"

"I just know."

"Dad, that's not good enough."

"Brenna, I can't get into this. You just have to trust me."

"I can't just trust you. I need to know. I told Sadie it was her choice

if she wanted him in her life. I have to know that wasn't a mistake."
Brenna's voice shook and she looked away again, taking deep breaths.

"I see. Okay, Brenna. I saw someone driving away in Dennis's
truck the morning Peter died. It wasn't Dennis."

"Was it Deirdre? She drove Dennis's truck all the time."

"No, I don't think it was Deirdre."

"Who was it then?"

Brenna had thought long and hard about what her father had said
next. *It wasn't possible. Was it?*

Over and over, she replayed images in her mind—of Deirdre
calmly finding her in the apartment with Dennis's briefcase and the
way she had all the answers about the Post-it note and the keys; of the
ambiguous photographs of Peter—or Dennis—rowing away from the
shore; of Jack's description of the driver of Dennis's truck heading
out on the morning Peter drowned.

If what her father suspected was true, Deirdre hadn't set Dennis
up out of anger or fear for herself; she'd done it to protect her child.
But it seemed pretty far-fetched. And Jack had said he wasn't certain
who was driving the truck.

CHAPTER TWENTY-SEVEN

Dennis sat at a table in the bar, waiting for Gina. They'd gone out a couple of times. She was thirty-five-ish with ashy-blond hair. She worked at the True Value in town, and Dennis got to know her when he picked up things for his work at the Rileys'. He was nearing forty and had come to the realization that he'd been the Rileys' caretaker and handyman for almost fifteen years. Denny had just finished his senior year of high school. He'd be leaving for college in just a couple of months.

These realizations had prompted Dennis to apply to law school in Sacramento. He made the four-hour round-trip commute for his classes three days a week. He didn't mind the drive so much. But he knew when it started snowing it might not be so easy. He'd made friends with a guy who said Dennis could stay at his place in Sac during the week if he needed to. He'd figure that out when the time came.

Jack was fully supportive of Dennis's return to law school, even though it meant that Dennis was working fewer hours on the property. Denny picked up some of the slack, and Jack paid him directly. Dennis was interested in criminal law, sparked by his experience in jail and at his hearing. Despite it being a miserable experience, he'd found the process interesting. He had an idea he might become a public defender.

"Hey, you," Gina said, and gave him a quick kiss before sitting across from him.

"Hey," Dennis said, and smiled at her. She was nice. He'd dated other nice women. All of them asked him about his getting arrested and set up—by his *own* wife—for something he didn't do. The injustice! He wondered if they only asked him out to get the details not mentioned in the paper. Not that it mattered. None of them interested him enough for him to keep seeing them. Sadly, he thought, not even Gina. He suddenly wished he were home, watching a movie.

"How was your week?" Gina asked. Her drink had arrived, and she lit a cigarette. They were in a locals' bar on the Truckee River. A few tourists ventured in, but most went elsewhere.

Dennis liked Tahoe well enough but was ready to move on. He planned to look for a job in the Bay Area when he graduated from law school. Denny had been accepted to Cal State East Bay in Hayward, so Dennis thought maybe he'd settle nearby. For the first time in a long time—maybe ever—he was looking forward to something.

He and Gina had drinks, ate nachos, and threw some darts. She invited him back to her apartment, but he begged off, saying he had to study.

"It's Friday night, Dennis," she complained. She looked offended and more than a little annoyed, but he just wasn't into it. That was probably the last he'd see of her.

Brenna and Sadie arrived in Tahoe two days before Thanksgiving.

Dennis needed to go to the hardware store. He decided to drive out to Truckee, rather than go to the True Value in town. Gina had left him several progressively angry voicemails, but Dennis hadn't called her back yet. He planned to but didn't want to run into her first.

As he descended the stairs from the apartment, he saw Sadie and Denny next to Denny's truck, talking. Sadie laughed at something Denny said. Denny was light years away from the sulky, scared kid who'd bullied his classmates and tormented Sadie. Sadie was tall and willowy with blond hair and blue eyes, and with Brenna's face and outgoing nature. It hurt Dennis to look at her. He tried to turn and head quietly back up the stairs.

He heard Denny say, "Catch you later, then!" before he got in his truck and left.

Then he heard Sadie say, "Mr. Griffin?"

Dennis stopped mid-step and turned. She was looking up at him.

"Miss Sadie," Dennis said, and bowed like he'd done when she was a child.

Sadie laughed. "You remember! I haven't seen you in years."

"Yeah, I guess I haven't been around much when you've been up."

"I guess," Sadie said, giving him a strange, knowing look. "Or maybe you were avoiding us."

"Maybe I was. I didn't think your mom would want to see me."

"You know, I never thought you caused my dad's death. You were his friend. I remember when you and my dad and sometimes Denny would go on hikes. My mom wouldn't let me go, and I was so jealous."

Dennis was afraid to speak. Tears were welling up in his eyes, and he didn't trust his voice.

"I think it was just a very sad accident, what happened to my dad," Sadie continued, looking away from Dennis as if to not embarrass him. "My mom and I have talked about it. She said at first she thought you had done it, but Grandpa Jack never believed it. Grammeg thought you did it too, at first, but then she changed her mind. Mom was really mad at both of them for a long time, but she says she now understands that you didn't kill my dad."

Dennis could only stare at Sadie. "So," he finally said, "she's doing okay?"

"She's good," Sadie said. "You know, she hasn't had a drink in years. She goes to AA and meets with her sponsor. Her name's Abigail, and she's super cool. She's kinda like my aunt."

Sadie looked past Dennis at the lake. After a few moments, she met his eyes and said, "You know, my mom and I have gotten pretty close over the past few years. It's been just the two of us. And . . ."

Dennis waited. Sadie clearly had something she needed to say.

"We talk a lot about stuff. She told me something recently. She said my dad loved me very much, but that maybe he wasn't really my dad. Maybe you are."

"She told you that?"

"As part of her, um, getting sober, she makes these amends to people. Kind of like apologies for things she did in the past that hurt them. She said I had a right to know about you. It totally freaked me out. At first, I couldn't understand why she would tell me, but then I understood. I don't have a dad anymore . . . so she said if I wanted to have a relationship with you, it was my choice."

"Wow, okay," Dennis said. His head was spinning.

"She said my dad, Peter, will always be my dad, but . . ." Her voice broke and she trailed off, composing herself. "I'm not sure how to do this."

"Me neither."

"Denny and I are gonna hang out later, so maybe I'll start with that," Sadie said, "Now that he might be my big brother. He always kinda acted like he was anyway when we were kids."

"We can all take it slow."

"That sounds good," Sadie agreed. "You know, when I was little, you were, like, my third favorite adult. First, my dad, then Grammeg, then you."

Sadie smiled and turned around to head back to the house.

Dennis stood halfway up the stairs, trying to wrap his head around what had just happened.

PART THREE
2003–2007

CHAPTER TWENTY-EIGHT

Dennis stood in the back of the crowd at the outdoor stadium. When Sadie's name was called, she teetered across the stage on impossibly high heels to accept her high school diploma, as friends and family applauded and cheered. Sadie was tall and lean and headed to Stanford to major in environmental studies and row on the women's lightweight team. Dennis knew Brenna, Jack, and Meg were somewhere up in the front rows of chairs on the grass, but he couldn't see them.

After Sadie left the stage, Dennis headed for the parking lot. He drove onto the 101, then to the Bay Bridge toward his office in Oakland. Traffic was backing up, but he expected to just beat the worst of the Friday afternoon gridlock. He had some files to pick up to work on over the weekend. He and a law school classmate had opened a criminal defense firm. One of his clients had a hearing Monday. He knew he'd have to be quick to make it home before Denny arrived from Hayward. The two of them would take the BART into the city for the Giants game.

Sadie sometimes met them for baseball games and burgers after. Sadie wasn't meeting them tonight, of course. After dinner with the family, she had plans to celebrate with her friends. Sadie had known Dennis was there somewhere; Denny would have been too if he hadn't had a final exam.

⌐〜

Denny let himself into Dennis's apartment with his key. Dennis wasn't home yet. He grabbed a beer from the fridge and settled in on the couch to wait. He pulled out his cell phone and pushed the button to speed-dial his mother.

"Mom? How are you?

"I'm okay. How did your exam go?"

"Fine, I think."

"Good. That's good," Deirdre said.

"You sound tired."

"Yeah. Long day at work." His mom was waitressing out in Pacifica.

"How's Gramma?"

"She's okay. Chemo yesterday, so she didn't get out of bed today. You going to the game tonight?"

"Yeah, just waiting for Dennis. He went to Sadie's graduation today."

"Oh?"

"Yeah, but he said he was going to stand in the back and leave right after he saw her get her diploma."

"Well. I'm happy for Sadie. Please tell her congratulations next time you speak to her."

"Will do."

Denny heard a key turn in the lock and the front door opened.

Mom, he mouthed to Dennis, who nodded and dumped a stack of files on the dining table.

"Gotta go, Mom. I'll see you tomorrow?"

"I get off at three."

"See you then."

⌐〜

Brenna and Abigail sat in a booth away from the other customers at the coffee shop. They examined a piece of notebook paper on which was a list of names. Some of the names had checkmarks next to them, including Sadie's at the top of the page.

"You're making good progress, Bren," Abigail said, and took a sip of coffee.

Brenna nodded, then shook her head.

"What?"

"What if I don't think I'll ever be able to make one of the amends?" Brenna asked.

Abigail pulled a book out of her bag, flipped to a page, and pointed. "Read it."

"I've read it."

"Read it again."

Brenna took the book and sighed. "Step nine. 'Make direct amends to such people wherever possible, except when to do so would injure them or others.'"

Abigail nodded. "It says, 'wherever possible' and when to do so won't injure anyone."

Brenna picked up a pen and circled the name *Dennis* on the list.

Brenna wadded the paper up into a ball in frustration. The two sat in silence for a minute, drinking their coffee. A server came by and refilled their cups. Brenna unwadded the list and smoothed it out on the table.

"I haven't been totally honest with you, Abigail."

"About you and Dennis?"

"No, no. I told you everything about that." Brenna hesitated. "About Peter's murder. I've known for a while that Dennis didn't do it—and I also know who did it."

"Who?"

"I can't tell you."

"Okay. You don't have to tell me," Abigail said. "But you do have to resolve this in a way that allows you to move on, because this is tearing you up. And Brenna . . ." Abigail reached across the table for Brenna's hand. "I'm afraid for your sobriety."

Deirdre sat at a booth in the back of the dining room, counting her tips. Denny slid into the seat across from her.

"Hey!" she said.

"How are you?"

"I'm $103 richer," Deirdre said, stuffing the money into her purse.

The restaurant was on a cliff overlooking the ocean and the money was good, even during the lunch shift.

"Do you want to go for a walk?"

Deirdre's feet and back ached, but she nodded. "Sure."

They went outside and wound their way down a dirt path to the beach. It was cool and foggy, typical of the summer weather on this part of the coast, but Deirdre took off her shoes and let the sand massage her tired feet.

"I'm not sure how much longer your gramma's gonna last," Deirdre said. "The doctor's recommending hospice."

Denny nodded.

"I need to call Alana and Tommy. To have them come see her."

"Sorry, Mom." Denny put an arm around her shoulder.

"Thanks, honey. She'll soon be at peace."

They walked in silence for a few minutes.

"Do you ever think of getting back together with Dennis?" Denny asked.

"What?" Deirdre stopped to look at him. "Why would I do that?"

Denny shrugged. "I just worry about you. Maybe after Gramma . . . goes . . . you could come and live with me, and we could all three of us hang out. Doug's moving out next week, so you could have his room."

"Oh, honey, that's a nice idea, but you don't want your old mom around cramping your style."

"Sure, I do," Denny said, smiling. "But in all seriousness. What you did for me. I can never repay that—"

"You have nothing to repay. I'd do it again, in a second."

"I think Dennis feels bad about all that happened, and if he knew why you did what you did—"

"No, he can never know. It's water under the bridge. It's done," Deirdre said vehemently. "It was a terrible accident, as far as anyone needs to know."

"Okay. But Dennis is different now. He doesn't get mad anymore. He's . . . I guess he's happy. But he's alone. And so are you."

"I appreciate your concern. But it's over between Dennis and me. We've started divorce proceedings. And I'm not alone. I have you."

CHAPTER TWENTY-NINE

Dennis walked rapidly away from the courthouse, trying to calm down. He was stunned by what had just happened. And still angry. And mortified. He didn't know what had come over him. He had never lost his shit like that in court before.

His client had been accused of raping a woman at a party. It had been the first sexual assault case his firm had taken on, and Dennis guessed it must have struck a nerve with him, given that Brenna had accused him of the same crime. Dennis's alibi witness, a friend of his client, was supposed to testify that his client had not even been at the party at the time of the attack and that his client had been in a bar with the witness.

Dennis called the witness to the stand and began questioning him. At first, everything went as expected.

"What time did you and my client leave the party?"

"About 10:45."

"Now we've heard testimony from the prosecution that the alleged assault took place around 1:05 a.m. on November 8, 2003, at the party in Jack London Square." Dennis looked at the jury to make sure they were paying attention to the timeline. "Mr. Grant, what was the location of the bar where you and my client were drinking that night—or early that morning, rather?"

"It was a few blocks from where the party was," answered Mr. Grant. He was in his mid-twenties and prone to smirking. Dennis could only think *frat boy* when he looked at him.

"And how did you get from the party to the bar?"

"We walked," Frat Boy said, glancing at the judge.

"How long was the walk?"

"About five or ten minutes."

"So, you got there just before 11."

"Yes, sir."

"And what time did you and my client leave the bar?"

"Well, I didn't leave until after last call, but Shane—your client— left earlier."

This was not what Frat Boy had told Dennis yesterday.

"Last call was, what, 1:45?"

"Thereabouts."

"And what time did Shane leave the bar?"

"He left around 12:30."

"And you're sure about this?"

"Yes, sir, I am sure," he said, nodding with what looked like mock solemnity.

Dennis's blood was beginning to boil. This smug little shit was his clients' only chance at acquittal. Why was he changing his story?

"You're sure you didn't leave together, sometime between 1:45 and 2:00?"

"Objection. Asked and answered," said the prosecutor.

"Objection sustained. Move on, counselor."

Frat Boy actually winked at Dennis. His face was turned away from the jury, and Dennis received the message as clearly as if the witness had shown him his middle finger. Dennis had no other witnesses. No one else—the other party guests, the bartender, the servers—remembered anything or would admit to remembering anything. Next to him, he heard his client mutter, "Lying fuck."

His head buzzed and the next thing he knew Dennis was picking up his thick trial binder from the defense table and throwing it at the witness stand.

⌐

After the judge recessed until Monday morning and called Dennis into his chambers where he proceeded to admonish him, Dennis left hurriedly and began walking away from downtown in the general direction of his apartment. He'd been too angry to speak to his client but promised a meeting at the jail later that day.

When he reached the path that circled Lake Merritt, he stepped off onto the grass and looked out at the lake. It was a Friday afternoon, and the lake was full of rowing shells. It looked like there was a regatta going on.

How was he going to tell his law partner about what had happened today?

Dennis started walking along the path along the lake. Crews rowed by on the buoyed racecourse. As one shell passed in the lane nearest him, Dennis could hear the coxswains say, "In two, up two! That's one and two, you're on!"

He was immediately reminded of Brenna. Dennis followed the path around the north side of the lake and came upon boat trailers and tents and folding chairs and rowers, lots of rowers.

"Heads up!" people yelled as they passed him carrying shells of all sizes to and from the lake. It might be better if he were hit in the head, Dennis thought. *Why did I lose it like that?* he kept asking himself. This case had bothered him from the beginning. Throughout the trial, he couldn't help but picture Brenna and hear her voice. *"No, we can't."*

His client wasn't quite as smirky and slick as the witness—his client's supposed friend. His client was scared, and he may even have been guilty. *But why had Frat Boy turned on him? Why had he changed his story?*

"Dennis? Is that you?" Dennis was snapped back to the present, just as someone yelled, "Heads up!" and the stern of a boat barely missed his right ear.

The voice came from behind him, and he looked around to find Dave, his coxswain from the V-8 at Head of the Charles.

"I thought that was you!" Dave said as they shook hands. "Man, how many years has it been?"

"I don't know. A lot. How are you?"

"I'm good," Dave said, leading the way to a grassy spot away from the path and the fray. Dave was wearing a polo shirt that said Lake Merritt Rowing Club. "I'm coaching masters if you can believe that. It's fun!"

"No shit," Dennis said. "So that's your job?"

"No, no. I work at Oracle. This is just a side hustle."

Dennis nodded.

"And you?" Dave asked. "What are you doing these days?"

"I'm a criminal defense attorney. At least I think I still am."

"What do you mean?"

"Nothing. So, this is a pretty big regatta."

"Yep, it's a lot of work. Our club puts it on, and I should get back to it. Great to see you!" They shook hands again and Dave started away, then turned back, "Hey, we're short a coach, you know. For the masters competitive program. You interested?"

"I haven't done any coaching."

"Aaah, I'd take issue with that. You were always telling me and everyone else what to do!" Dave laughed. "But seriously, think about it," he said, handing Dennis a business card. "Give me a call. You know, we've got a coxswain from the old days helping us out too."

"Oh, yeah?" Something about Dave's last statement made Dennis's ears perk up.

"Yep! Brenna Riley, er, Anderson." Dave made a telephone gesture with his hand and hurried off.

෴

The sun was coming up as Brenna drove across the Bay Bridge. The competitive masters team rowed early, five o'clock. Traffic wasn't too bad at this hour, so it worked for her to cox in the mornings, then head to work. The drive home was miserable, but she was getting used to it. Books on tape helped.

Brenna parked her car near the boathouse. Plenty of spaces at that hour of the morning. It was still August, but a chill was in the air and Brenna pulled on her splash jacket and made sure her gloves were in a pocket. She loved being back on the water. For ninety minutes, she could focus only on the tasks at hand: steering the eight-person shell, calling drills, making technical comments. Their coach, Margaret, had left on maternity leave and Dave had been coaching the practices for a couple of weeks. But he was head coach and had a lot on his plate, so he was looking for someone to take over Margaret's position while she was away. He'd asked Brenna if she was interested in coaching, but she said she was content with coxing.

Brenna locked the car and walked toward the building, waving to the others heading in the same direction. This and her job demanded her full attention. It was when she was engaged in neither of them that her mind circled back again and again: Peter, Sadie, Deirdre, Denny. And Dennis, always Dennis. She knew he lived and worked in Oakland, but, thankfully, she hadn't run into him anywhere.

෴

The boathouse was abuzz with dozens of conversations, people warming up on the mats and the rowing machines, and blaring music. Brenna went into the boat bay to get her cox box and headset. She heard a cheer go up from the other room and, when she came back in, noticed the music was off and Dave was speaking.

"I know it's been hard putting up with me since Margaret

left"—laughter and catcalls erupted—"so I'm happy to introduce our new competitive masters coach. He rowed at Stanford, and I was his coxswain." A murmur went through the assembled group of rowers, and Brenna wondered, *Who was this new coach?* Had to be someone she knew. Due to Brenna's short stature—and Dave's—she could only see the top of Dave's head.

"He also made a run at the Olympic team in the single—when was that? 1984?"

Brenna's ears began to ring, and her stomach lurched. *No. No, no.*

"So put your hands together for our new coach, Dennis Griffin. Stand up, man."

To her horror, Brenna saw Dennis's face rise above the heads of the rowers, who broke into applause.

"Thanks, thanks," Dennis began, but Brenna didn't hear the rest of whatever he said because she turned and ran.

౼

She stood outside, leaning against the building, taking deep breaths, hoping this was just a bad dream and that she would wake up soon. The door opened, and Deb, one of the other coxswains, came out.

"Hey, Bren, the new coach wants to talk to us . . . Are you okay?"

Brenna forced herself to nod and say, "Yeah. I just felt a little dizzy for a minute. Forgot to eat something this morning."

"Yeah, you look kinda pale. Here." Deb reached into a pocket and extracted a granola bar. She held it out to Brenna, who shook her head.

"I'm okay. Much better now," Brenna said, while her head spun.

"Take it. Eat it. We can't have you passing out in the boat."

౼

Dennis surveyed the crews while Dave drove the coaching launch. Dave wouldn't be there after this morning but said he wanted to attend Dennis's first practice and show him around. There wasn't much to it, Dennis thought: standard boathouse, small lake with enough space for a 1,000-meter racecourse, and three eights full of masters rowers ranging in age from late twenties to upper forties.

Dave had suggested mixed lineups of men and women so the boats would stay together. Dennis had had a short meeting with the coxswains, including Brenna—who wouldn't meet his eyes—at which he said he wanted them to call a standard warm-up, then go into some pause drills, where he wanted the rowers to stop at different positions of the stroke: legs straight with arms extended or at the halfway point. Then he wanted them to row continuously, rotating through six rowers with one pair keeping the boat steady, then transition to all eight rowers with some power pieces. Dennis told them he wouldn't do a lot of coaching that day, mostly just observing.

As Dennis and Dave motored along behind the shells, Dave said, "Well, I'd say you have a pretty good idea how to go about this."

Dennis tried to focus on assessing the rowers, whose abilities spanned pretty good to marginal, in his opinion, but his eyes kept landing on Brenna, who was the most experienced coxswain. The woman steering the boat to Brenna's starboard kept trying to veer into Brenna's boat, but each time, Brenna would call, "Deb! Watch your point!" while never missing a beat with her commands to her crew. *Just like the old days*, Dennis thought.

After practice, Dennis caught Brenna just as she was unlocking her car.

"Hey, Brenna!" he said, with a big, friendly smile. "Great job out there. You haven't lost your touch."

Brenna stared up at him. He looked pretty much the same as the last time she'd seen him up close—which was . . . when? At his hearing, she decided, more than a decade ago. She'd rarely gone to Tahoe while he was still up there, and when she was there, she'd seen him only from a distance. He seemed to understand that they shouldn't interact and stayed away from the house.

But now, here he was, front and center, finding another way to intrude on her life. He was a little more weathered, a little thinner, but still the same. She tried to control her pounding heart, which she was sure he could hear, but to no avail.

"So, I hope this isn't too weird. I ran into Dave the other day, and he talked to me about coaching. I only just called him back last night, and, well, he said to come on down."

Brenna didn't know what to say, so she said nothing.

"Okay, well, I hope you enjoy the rest of your day. Good to see you." Dennis turned away.

Brenna found her voice. "I'm probably going to quit coxing here. Just so you know."

Dennis stopped and turned back to her. "Because of me?"

Brenna didn't answer.

"Oh shit," Dennis said. "No, please don't do that. You're the best coxswain on the team. The others, well, they need more mileage."

Brenna looked at the ground.

"Listen. I promise to keep things strictly professional. I know I treated you badly in the past. I really do know that." Brenna heard his voice breaking. "I really am sorry for everything."

Brenna lifted her head. To her shock, his ice-blue eyes were full of tears, as if he really was sorry.

"I'm sorry," Dennis said again, clearly trying to pull himself together. "Look, what if we just give it a couple of weeks and see if it works. If not, *I'll* quit."

Brenna felt herself getting sucked back in. She felt it physically and fought to stop it. He continued to look at her with those icy eyes, thawed with what appeared to be the depth of his sorrow.

Then she heard herself say, "Okay. Two weeks."

CHAPTER THIRTY

Dennis had been true to his word. He was nothing but professional at practice. The rowers loved him. He had gruffness about him, like he expected more, much more, from his rowers. But he also made them believe they were capable of more and circled back to praise improvements. The adult rowers were every bit as competitive as juniors or collegiate rowers, and Dennis seemed to be able to get the best out of them.

"He's going to make us fast. I know it," gushed Janet, the stroke of Brenna's boat that day. Janet gazed somewhat dreamily at the coaching launch that was approaching the group of shells. Brenna had heard the whisperings: many of the women—and maybe some of the men—had a coach crush.

When Dennis's two-week "probation period" was up, he asked Brenna to stay after practice a minute, if she had the time.

"Well?" he asked with great earnestness. "How'd I do?"

Brenna couldn't help but laugh. His anxiousness reminded her of their days in the Stanford freshman eight when he'd be having a self-effacing day and he'd ask her how he'd done in the stroke seat.

"You passed," she said with a sigh.

"Really?" he lit up. "That's great! Really great."

They smiled at each other for a bit, until Dennis said, "I know it's probably hard for you to believe, but I'm not the same person I was in college—and right after the trials. I was young and stupid and messed up. I know I hurt you. I just hope we can maybe be friends someday."

"We'll see," Brenna said.

Driving away, she wondered if maybe he had changed. It was possible, wasn't it? She wasn't ready to dive into friendship with him, but he was (probably) Sadie's father. He was in Sadie's life, and now Brenna's, too.

Her dad had said he didn't know for sure whom he'd seen that day in Dennis's truck. The sun had been in his eyes. He was probably mistaken when he said it wasn't Deirdre. Brenna told herself it was probably just Deirdre, driving Denny to school. *Or maybe she was letting Denny drive. That would make the most sense. Maybe no one had meant to kill Peter; it was just an accident.*

Brenna knew that if she told this to herself enough times, she'd start to believe it.

⌒

During their phone conversation that evening, Abigail was not convinced.

"Oh, Bren, I don't think this is a good idea. You're playing with fire."

"Only for a couple of hours three days a week," Brenna tried to joke. "But seriously, I love coxing there. I can't let him drive me away."

"You can find another club, can't you? Aren't there a bunch of rowing clubs in the Bay Area?"

"Yes. But Lake Merritt's convenient to work, and I've made friends there. It's like I've found a home. Sadie's so busy at school; I'm tired of just going to work and coming home and being alone."

"Well, tell him to quit then."

"I'll be careful. I promise. I will never forget what he did to me, no matter how many times he apologizes."

"I'm going to hold you to that. Being careful and never forgetting how dangerous he is. He may not have killed your husband, but he straight-up raped you. Plain and simple. And he's found a way back into your life."

"He was already in my life—as Sadie's probable father."

"Right, but you never saw him. And I think that was a good thing," Abigail said. "Have you reconsidered asking him to take a paternity test?"

"I'd rather just believe Peter's her father."

"But you'd know for sure."

"I don't want to know for sure. Regardless, I'm confident he would never, ever hurt Sadie."

"I don't know where this confidence comes from, Brenna," Abigail said gravely. "But please keep me posted. One false move on his part and I'll . . . well, I'm not sure what I'll do. I'll have to think about that."

Brenna laughed. "Well, whatever you decide you'll do, I'm glad you're in my corner."

Dennis was in his office after a meeting with his law partner, Andy. They had weathered Dennis's outburst, paid the fine imposed by the court, and decided to move on.

"Every attorney loses it sometimes. Maybe not so, uh, overtly, but don't sweat it, man," Andy had said.

Dennis had been profoundly relieved. He'd had to do a lot of explaining about being wrongfully accused of Peter's murder, even with the dismissal, when he applied for his license to practice law. He feared further repercussions if something like throwing his trial notebook at a witness occurred again. He supposed Frat Boy could file a complaint with the bar association, but he'd deal with that if it happened.

It was late Tuesday afternoon, and Dennis packed up some files and headed out into the late summer warmth. The light in Oakland captured him. Sometimes the sun's rays filtered through the fog that so often shrouded San Francisco during the summer, creating a kind of glow that had a calming effect on him.

Dennis decided to skip the bus and walk the couple of miles to his apartment. Denny was due to come over in an hour, and if Dennis wasn't home, Denny had a key to let himself in. They were headed into the city for the Giants game. The team was on track to win the National League West title.

As he passed by Lake Merritt, he saw the junior crews practicing. He pulled out his phone and speed-dialed Sadie.

"Hey, I'm about to head to the ballpark," Sadie said.

"Great! I'm halfway home. Say, could you text me your mom's number? I need to ask her something before tomorrow's practice."

"Uh, sure, but maybe I should call her first? Not sure she wants you to have her number."

"Oh, right. No, it's okay. She wrote her number down for me, but I left it at the office."

"Oh, okay then. I'll text you, and I'll see you guys soon."

As Dennis ended the call, his phone buzzed with Sadie's text.

Dennis punched in the number.

"Brenna Anderson," Brenna said.

"Oh hey, it's Dennis. Hope you don't mind that I'm calling you. Dave gave me a roster of all the masters' contact numbers."

"Oh. Yeah. What's up?"

"I wondered if we might meet sometime this week to talk about the fall racing season. Since I'm new to all this, Dave suggested that I tap into your wisdom."

"Really. You know, we do have a team captain—George Goldman. He's the one you should talk to about regatta stuff."

"Oh, Dave didn't mention him. That's fine. I'll give him a call. Thanks—"

"No, wait. If Dave said you should talk to me, then that's fine."

"Great! Can you grab coffee after practice tomorrow?"

Denny let himself into Dennis's apartment. He went immediately to the kitchen and downed a beer. Then he grabbed another one and went into the bathroom. He reached into his pocket for his gram vial and hit that a couple of times. The drug flowed into his system immediately and his brain seemed to come into focus. The beer would finish the job of clearing his head.

As he exited the bathroom, Dennis came through the front door.

"Hey, hey!" Dennis said, cheerfully. "There's the college senior. Next week, right?"

"Yeah, classes start on Monday."

Dennis pulled him into a hug and clapped him on the back.

"You're in a good mood," Denny said. In fact, Dennis's mood had improved considerably over the past few days, Denny thought. Not that he'd been in a bad mood before—well, except for that court thing.

"Sun's out. Ballgame's happening. There's beer." Dennis headed for the kitchen and returned with a beer. "I'll just chug this and we'll head out. Sadie called and confirmed that she's coming."

"Okay, I'll just hit the head once more," Denny said, raising his empty beer bottle. Once in the bathroom, Denny reached for his vial again.

Dennis and Brenna sat in a coffee shop a few blocks away from the boathouse. Dennis had a list of the fall regattas—head races—he'd put together, and he and Brenna were checking off the ones the team usually attended.

"Okay, Head of the Port. Check. What about Head of the Charles?" Dennis said.

"We sent a women's four last year, but it didn't place in the top half and requalify."

"Did you cox it?"

"No."

"Well, that's why it didn't qualify," Dennis said.

Brenna couldn't help but laugh. "I don't think so. They borrowed a local cox who knew the course."

"Whatever. Let's think about entering a couple of boats in the lottery, then. We don't have much time. The entry deadline is September 1. I'll make an announcement at practice tomorrow and post a sign-up sheet."

Dennis checked his list. "Looks like that covers it. Thanks so much for your help. I really appreciate it."

Brenna drained the last of her coffee. "Well, I didn't do much."

"You did though. Just having a sounding board helps me think things through."

"You're welcome, then. Listen, there's something else I wanted to talk to you about. But it's a little awkward, so I'm not sure how to start."

"What's the topic?"

"Well, Denny, actually. How's he doing?"

"He's good. He goes back to school next week. His final year."

"Sadie says he's doing well too. She went to the game with you last night, didn't she?"

"She did." Dennis stifled a yawn. "Stayed out a little late. Have to get used to getting up this early. We went for burgers after."

"And Denny, I mean, do he and Sadie hang out a lot?"

"Not that much, really," said Dennis. "Mostly when we go to the games."

"Oh, I see. Well, that helps. Thanks."

"Why do you ask?"

"I was just curious. Sadie doesn't talk much about him—or you for that matter. I think she thinks it upsets me."

"And does it? Upset you?"

Brenna smiled thinly. "It did. After I told her about you probably being her father, I said it was her choice if she wanted to see you, but that I didn't want to see you. And I don't know Denny very well. I remember him as an angry, mean little kid."

"He was. But he's grown up. He's a good kid, so don't worry. And I would never let anything happen to Sadie. I hope you know that."

"Okay," Brenna said. "This is just new and kind of weird, being around you and all. I just worry about Sadie. She's so trusting and . . . well, never mind."

"Did you tell her about, um, how she came about?" Dennis asked.

"Do you mean how she may have been conceived?" Brenna said, her voice lowering a little. She looked extremely uncomfortable. "No, I didn't. And she didn't ask. I don't think she wants any details—I mean, she hasn't asked me for any. Has she asked you about it?"

"No."

"Good." Brenna looked at him for a couple of beats, as if she wanted to say something more. But she said only, "I have to get to work. I'll see you at practice."

Dennis watched her hurry away and kicked himself for asking her about Sadie's potential conception. He felt like he'd made a lot of progress with her, and he hoped he hadn't caused her to retreat again.

Dennis was on his way to West Sacramento to watch Sadie row. His thoughts kept returning to Brenna. He knew he shouldn't spend so much time with her. But he couldn't stop himself. He'd enlisted her as sort of an assistant coach, seeking her advice, asking if she thought the practice went well, who she thought was the better stroke—Phil or Sean—and initiating weekly coffee meetings to discuss regatta details. Brenna seemed willing to help, so what was the harm? It was just about rowing, that's all they discussed. Neither of them had brought up anything personal—not about Denny, Sadie, or any topic other than rowing. That is, until the other day when she'd asked him about Denny. He hoped again that he hadn't blown it with his question about Sadie's conception.

He pulled into the parking lot at the venue. Stanford was scrimmaging UC Davis. He walked past the crews readying their shells toward the group of friends and parents at the water's edge. Some of the boats were already racing, and he hoped he hadn't missed Sadie's races.

He asked the woman standing next to him if the lightweight women had raced yet.

"No," she said. She was about his age, attractive, and dressed in a UC Davis sweatshirt and well-fitting jeans. "You here watching your girlfriend?"

Dennis laughed. "No, my daughter. You?"

"My son," she said, giving him an appraising look. "You don't look old enough to have a college-age daughter."

"Well, you don't look old enough to have a college-age son," Dennis said, although she actually did when the sun hit her full in the face.

"Dennis! You made it!" Sadie said, hurrying toward him. "I thought I saw you walking by!"

"Hey! Of course, I made it," he said, hugging her.

"We're launching in about five minutes, so keep your eyes peeled for us."

"No need. You'll be out in front."

"Ha! I hope so! See you after!" Sadie jogged back toward the boathouse.

"I'd say good luck, but you won't need it!" he called after her.

The UC Davis mom had observed this interaction. "What a beautiful girl," she said. "She looks just like you, too. Did you row in college?"

"I did. At Stanford, in fact. Well, it was nice talking to you."

Dennis moved away to a better viewing point. He could sense she was ready to pounce and wasn't into it. He was here for Sadie.

CHAPTER THIRTY-ONE

On the day before Thanksgiving, Sadie, who was on a short break from school, accompanied Brenna to her masters practice. They planned to leave for Tahoe right afterward for the long weekend. Sadie wanted to watch her mom cox and asked Dennis if she could ride along in the coaching launch.

"You sure you don't want to stroke my women's eight? They could learn a lot from you." Dennis had started attending Sadie's regattas whenever he could—now that he and Brenna were on more comfortable terms. Sadie appreciated having him there. She still didn't quite think of him as her dad—more like an uncle.

"No, but thanks," Sadie said, laughing.

Dennis had the crews do steady state pieces, up and down the lake and the side channel. Now that the fall regatta season was over, he told Sadie, it was time to relax, work on tech, and focus on fitness—until after the holidays when training for the spring season would begin.

Dennis didn't say much during the practice, only occasionally calling reminders to individual rowers about catch timing, level hands, and other technical details.

"What do you think of the women's boat? I'm thinking of entering them in the San Diego Crew Classic," Dennis asked her.

"They look good," Sadie said. "Their catches are together. You might switch three and five, though. You need more power in the stern."

Dennis surveyed the two women Sadie had referenced. "You know, you're right. You have a good eye."

"Like my mom," Sadie said proudly. "She's such a good coxswain."

"The best," Dennis agreed. "I felt bad that the women didn't get their four in for Head of the Charles. San Diego might make up for that."

"I'll be there!" Sadie said. "Whether I'm rowing or not."

"You'll be rowing."

At the end of practice, Dennis dropped Sadie off on the dock and left to put the launch away. As he walked to the boathouse, he saw Sadie and Brenna heading for the parking lot.

"Hey!" he called.

"Thanks again for the ride-along," Sadie called, waving.

Dennis jogged toward them. "You're welcome. And Happy Thanksgiving." He pulled Sadie in for a quick hug. "Brenna, can I talk to you for a second?"

"I'll wait in the car, Mom," Sadie said, and Brenna passed her the car keys.

Once Sadie was out of earshot, Dennis said, "I thought we were going to coffee. To talk about winter training."

"Oh, right, sorry. I forgot."

Dennis felt his pulse quicken. "You forgot?"

"Yeah, sorry. Can we do it Monday? We're heading for Tahoe."

"Tahoe? For the whole weekend?" Dennis said. He tried to hide his irritation. "I was going to work on a plan this weekend, and I need your input."

"I'm sure you'll be fine without it," Brenna said, laughing a little nervously.

Dennis felt the anger enveloping him. *She was blowing him off. They had a meeting. And she was blowing him off!*

He took a couple of deep breaths and said, "Enjoy your Thanksgiving, Brenna," in a way that sounded like he'd just told her to go fuck herself and walked away.

"Hey! What's wrong with you?" Brenna called, but he kept walking and thought: *What is wrong with me? Why am I reacting this way?*

He knew he was being unreasonable. And ridiculous. But he couldn't stop the anger from coursing through him like a rogue wave.

Denny spent Thanksgiving with Deirdre, his grandmother, and his aunts and uncles in Daly City. The house was crowded, with Deirdre and her sister Alana in the kitchen preparing the food and everyone else in front of the living room TV watching football. His grandmother was propped up on the sofa, her chemo-ravaged body wrapped in blankets. She wore a turban-like covering on her balding head.

"Denny, honey. Would you please turn up the heat a little," she asked periodically. Although the house was hot and stuffy, Denny obliged each time; his grandmother was wasting away and always cold. But she was hanging on.

During a commercial break, Denny poked his head into the kitchen. "Need help?"

"No!" his mother and aunt shouted at once. Alana was elbows-deep in a large, cooked turkey scooping stuffing out into a bowl.

Denny withdrew his head from the doorway.

"But thanks for asking, sweetheart!" his mother called after him.

The house was alcohol-free out of respect for his grandmother and for his Uncle Tommy, who was in recovery. Tommy had met his wife, Ada, in rehab, and they sat in chairs next to each other and held hands like the newlyweds they were.

Denny knew that his Uncle Rob, Alana's husband, had a cooler of beer out back, so Denny headed that way. Rob was already out there, chugging on a beer.

"My man, Denny," Rob said, and handed him a cold one.

"Thanks, Unc," Denny said. He liked Rob. Rob was easygoing in contrast to Alana's type A control-freakiness. In fact, through the open kitchen window, he could hear Alana scolding his mother: "Deirdre, no, that's not how . . . Let me do that!"

"So, dude," Rob said, "how's life treating you?"

"Can't complain. Just school, work. My humdrum life."

"What kind of work you doing?"

"I got a bartending gig near campus." Denny didn't mention his other gig, which he'd taken over when one of his coworkers quit.

"Right on," Rob said. "Well, gonna head back in. You coming?"

"Yeah, right behind you."

Denny ducked into the downstairs bathroom before joining the others. He pulled out his gram vial and packed each nostril, sniffed mightily, then headed back in to watch the rest of the game.

After dinner, he helped clear the table. Deirdre and Alana were ordered to sit down, while Denny, Rob, and Ada cleaned up and served the pumpkin pie. Denny handed his mother a plate and Deirdre patted the seat on the sofa beside her. His grandmother had gone to bed.

"Go get your dessert and come sit with me," Deirdre said.

"I'm good," Denny said, and sat down. He felt sort of creepy and crawly sitting where his grandmother had been propped up. Sick people weirded him out.

Deirdre took his face in her hands and stared into his eyes.

"Are you okay? You hardly ate anything, and you look like you've lost weight."

"Yeah, Mom. I'm good," he said, gently removing her hands. "Just

on the final stretch of the grind. I'm taking a full load so I can graduate on time."

"You're not working too much, are you?"

"Nah, just two or three nights a week."

"Okay," Deirdre said, looking into his eyes again. "You're a grown
man, so I trust you're taking care of yourself."

"I am. But I should head home. Dennis might stop by later."

"Okay, honey. But take some leftovers."

"Will do. Thanks for dinner, Mom."

Denny grabbed a container of leftovers that Alana—who couldn't
sit still—had assembled, and said his goodbyes.

He got a beer for the road from the cooler and headed for his
truck. He didn't head for home, however; he drove to the bar to meet
his supplier.

CHAPTER THIRTY-TWO

The team was in full training mode for the spring racing season, particularly the women's eight that was headed to the San Diego Crew Classic in early April. Dennis had scheduled mandatory extra practices for the women who wanted to be in the boat. Twelve women were competing for the available eight seats through weekly ergometer scores, along with regular on-water seat racing—a process in which rowers would switch seats in different boats to see who made it go faster. Dennis enlisted Brenna's help with analyzing the erg times and the seat-racing results, and they had regular weekly meetings, sometimes twice a week.

Brenna had been a little guarded since the incident right before Thanksgiving when he'd gotten so angry that she'd forgotten their meeting. But Dennis had been on his best behavior: professional, good-humored, and appropriate. *Maybe he was just having a bad day*, she thought. She almost began to look forward to the meetings, to going over the data and helping him make decisions, even though she knew some of the rowers were talking.

It had started when she and Dennis were at their usual coffee shop after practice one Saturday, and a group of masters rowers came in. There were a few raised eyebrows and whisperings as they waved and stopped by the table to chat. But, Brenna thought, it was clear what they were doing. All they had to do was look at the yellow legal pad pages with Dennis's seat-racing notes that were spread out over the tabletop.

Still, at the next practice, Janet, who would probably stroke the San
Diego boat, came up to Brenna in the erg room and said, "Sooooo,
you're sure spending a lot of time with Coach D. I heard you two were
getting cozy over coffee the other day."

"Cozy talking about seat racing."

"Mmm-hmmm," Janet said, with a sly smile.

Brenna wasn't too concerned. She knew it was just idle chatter.
There always had to be some drama. *As the Boathouse Turns*, Brenna
thought.

"I also heard a rumor that you and Coach D dated back in college," Janet said.

"What?" Brenna felt her face redden. "Where'd you hear that?"

"Oh, just here and there."

"Well, we didn't," Brenna said, more harshly than she'd intended.
Janet held up her palms. "Okay, okay."

In late February, Dennis announced he was going to run one more
2,000-meter erg test before posting the final San Diego line-up at
the end of the week. That way the boat would have all of March to
practice together. On test day, Brenna walked around the erg room
and kept an eye on their numbers. If she saw someone flagging, she'd
shout encouragement over the blaring music.

Dennis walked around too, but he was silent and frowning.
Brenna knew it would not be easy for him to cut four women who
had worked so hard to make the boat. He'd told her often that it
was going to be a hard day when he announced the crew. But the
erg scores and seat-racing provided solid data, which the rowers
couldn't dispute.

After each rower completed their test and collapsed, breathing
hard, over their knees, Brenna checked each machine's monitor and
wrote down their overall times and 500-meter split times. Once

finished, she handed the list to Dennis, who was telling the women to walk it off, then Brenna would lead stretching.

As the rowers drifted back inside and gathered on the mats, Dennis said, "Go ahead and stretch on your own. Brenna, I need to see you."

He motioned for her to follow him outside.

"I'm looking at these numbers, and one of them is clearly wrong," Dennis said.

"Which one?"

Dennis pointed at the sheet of paper he held, on which Brenna had listed the erg times.

"Oh shoot. You're right. Looks like I wrote it down wrong."

"Oh shoot," Dennis said mockingly. "Looks like you fucked up."

Brenna's stomach lurched. "Are you really mad about this? I'll just go and find the machine she was on and get the correct time."

"Do you remember which erg she was on?" Dennis asked, with what appeared to be barely contained fury.

"I'll find it!" Brenna said, her heart hammering. "I'll look at all of them if I have to!"

"You do that! This process is hard enough on these women without you screwing things up!" Dennis shouted.

Brenna stared at him. "You know, you can just find someone else to cox in San Diego. It's not like I'm looking forward to going back there. If Sadie weren't rowing, I wouldn't be going at all!"

Brenna turned around and headed back toward the door.

"Brenna, wait!" she heard Dennis call after her. She kept walking. He didn't follow her.

When she entered the room, the twelve women were quietly stretching. Some wouldn't meet her eye, but others gave her sympathetic looks. They'd obviously heard that delightful exchange.

Finding the correct erg time made her late for work. As she sat at yet another red light, her cell phone buzzed. It was Dennis. She let it go to voicemail and focused on getting to her office. It wasn't until lunchtime that she remembered the call. Looking at her phone, she noticed two additional missed calls from Dennis. Sighing heavily, she pressed the voicemail button.

"Hey, Bren. I'm sorry I yelled at you. And thanks for making the correction. I really am sorry. I'm just stressed about having to disappoint those four women. But I shouldn't take it out on you. Call me back when you have a chance."

Brenna erased the message, put the phone in her desk drawer, and headed outside to eat her lunch. It was a beautiful day, the late winter sun starting to emit the warmth of spring. The day's brightness gave her the courage to promise herself she would withdraw her name from the Crew Classic, even quit the team if necessary. They had other coxswains who could go to San Diego. She really didn't want to go—especially with Dennis, of all people.

Then she remembered Sadie. She was stroking one of the Stanford lightweight boats and was excited that they'd both be competing in the same regatta. Brenna decided that she'd have to make up a work issue to get out of watching Sadie row.

Denny was working behind the bar on a busy Friday night. The noise was deafening: people talking over each other and the live bluegrass band, the cocktail servers yelling out orders, customers at the bar trying to get Denny's and the other bartenders' attention. It was just the way Denny liked it, loud and chaotic.

He pointed to the guy signaling him with five fingers raised. Denny pulled him a draft beer. But he knew the guy wanted more than beer. Denny reached under the bar into a bank bag and fingered a half-gram packet. With a practiced hand, he plucked a coaster from the stack and placed it in front of the guy with the packet underneath. He put the beer on top of the coaster.

The guy laid a ten on the bar, but Denny knew there was a fifty underneath and snatched it up quickly.

"Keep the change, man!" the guy yelled, and Denny gave him a thank-you nod.

This same type of exchange happened several times throughout Denny's shift. Not including his tips from his alcohol-only patrons, Denny cleared close to a grand that night.

After closing down the bar, he walked out to the parking lot with his coworkers, one of whom invited him to a little "after-party."

"Sure, see you there," Denny said.

Once inside his truck, his ears rang in the sudden silence. He laid his head against the headrest and closed his eyes for a couple of minutes. He often joined the after-party, which usually featured beer, tequila, pool, darts, and drugs until the sun rose. But tonight, he was tired. He started up his truck and headed for home.

It was nearly three o'clock when he pulled into his parking space. He understood that he was walking a razor-thin line between keeping it together and losing it. But so far, he was staying atop the tightrope. He dreaded his college graduation. Once he had more time on his hands, who knew where his brain would take him? The feeling that he should go to the cops and confess his crimes was growing and threatening to overwhelm him.

Changing his mind, he pulled out his vial, partook of some of its contents, backed out of his parking space, and headed for the party.

Denny was still asleep when his phone started ringing. It was close to two o'clock Saturday afternoon. He fumbled for his phone.

"Yeah," he croaked into it. His head hurt. He hadn't gotten home until after seven that morning.

"Denny? It's Mom."

"Oh, hey, Mom. What's up?" Denny tried to sound normal. He reached for the bottle of ibuprofen on the night table and dry-swallowed three tablets.

"Are you okay?"

"Yeah, yeah. Just walked in the door. Out for a run." He marveled at how easy the lies came; it had become second nature.

"Oh, well that's good. That you're getting outside and exercising . . ."

Denny began picking clothes off the floor and rummaging through pockets, searching for his vial. He had the phone tucked under his chin, and his mom was still talking, but he couldn't hear her very well.

"Hey, Mom," he interrupted. He found his vial, but it was empty. He started searching for the bank bag in which he was pretty sure there were at least a couple more grams. "I gotta get in the shower. Is there something you need?"

"I'm just . . . I'm worried about you. You don't eat much when you come over, you're too thin."

"Yeah, I'm trying to get into shape. I might run a marathon this spring," he said, finally spying the bank bag on his dresser.

"Denny. Your eyes are always dilated. Remember that I grew up with an addict. You're doing coke, aren't you." It wasn't a question.

Denny stopped midway to the dresser. "Sometimes. Just so I have more energy for studying and everything."

"You're not doing anything worse, are you?"

"Worse?"

"Crack? Heroin?"

"No, Mom. No way," Denny said. And that was the truth.

"Please tell me you're being careful."

"I'm being careful, Mom. I really need to go. I start work soon. I'll call you in a few days." Denny ended the call and lunged for the bank bag. Thankfully, three small packets of white powder were inside.

CHAPTER THIRTY-THREE

Brenna steeled herself and punched Dennis's number into her cell phone. It buzzed twice and Dennis's voice came on the line. "Brenna?"

"Yeah, it's me. Listen, I need to let you know that I'm pulling out of the San Diego race. I'm sure you can get Deb or Jasper up to speed over the next five weeks."

Silence.

"Hello?" Brenna said.

"Yeah, I'm here and I heard you," Dennis said wearily. "Look, please don't quit. I know I am the world's biggest asshole. I had no right to yell at you the way I did. I don't know why I made such a big deal about such a ridiculously small mistake. It's not like I don't already know who's going to be in the boat."

Brenna sighed.

"Please. Can you accept my apology? I promise to do better."

Brenna sighed again. She felt her resolve weaken. Why was she considering changing her mind? Why couldn't she be strong?

"Brenna?"

"Okay, fine. I don't want to let the boat down, and I do want to see Sadie row."

"Really? So, you'll cox the race?" He sounded so hopeful.

"Yes," she said, mentally flogging herself. She should just quit the team and stay the hell out of Oakland altogether, as Abigail had advised. But she couldn't do it. She couldn't walk away.

"Thank you, Brenna. Thank you," he said, and she ended the call with his gratitude echoing in her head.

⌒

Abigail was not happy to hear the news that Brenna hadn't pulled out of the regatta.

"You know, people can be addicted to other people," she said on the phone that evening. "I think that may be why you can't stay away from each other."

"What do you mean?" Brenna said.

"Just think about it. After all that has happened between you two, you're seeing him three to four times a week—even more now that you're preparing for San Diego."

"Yeah, I know. But he's the one that keeps finding ways to be in my life."

"But you're letting it happen."

"Well, maybe I am, but I already said I'd go to San Diego. I don't have to hang out with him. The women's eight is renting a house near the racecourse. Dennis is staying with some of the coaches from other teams. We're sharing a trailer with Bair Island, and Dennis is driving down with their coach. I probably won't even see him that much. When I'm not racing, I'll be watching Sadie race."

"You're a grown adult. I'm not your mom. But just be careful, okay?"

"I promise."

⌒

As the plane descended into San Diego, Brenna knew she'd be careful. She was already on high alert. Just the sight of Mission Bay and SeaWorld brought up memories of the long-ago Stanford eight and the night on the beach with Dennis—*Stop!* she ordered herself and began stuffing her book and water bottle into her bag and readying for landing.

The women jumped into three taxicabs reminding Brenna of the night she'd cabbed back from Old Town with Dennis and whatever that guy's name was who kept yelling "Whooooo!" out the window. And then they'd arrived back at the hotel, and Dennis said he was going for a walk, and—*Stop!* she commanded herself again.

As the taxi pulled up in front of the rental house, Brenna resolved to make new and different San Diego memories.

As she settled into her room, her cell phone rang. It was Sadie, letting her know that her plane had landed and that her team was heading to the hotel—the same one the Stanford team had stayed in all those years before. But Brenna wasn't going to think about that. Sadie would be busy all weekend with her own racing, but they ended the call saying they'd try to meet for coffee at some point.

On Friday morning, Brenna and the other women walked down to the race venue. They found Dennis at the trailer, and he handed them wristbands indicating that they were competitors and gave Brenna a packet with their bow numbers, a race schedule, and information about the coaches' and coxswains' meeting. Brenna thanked him, but didn't look him in the eye, and hurried away to help the rowers take their boat off the trailer for rigging.

Dennis called a short meeting before the crew went out for a practice row.

"I want you to do your pre-race warm-up and then row the course. I don't want you to row the whole thing at full pressure, but I do want steady-state with a start and power twenties at the 500-, 1,000-, and 1,500-meter marks. You can walk through your sprint but make it quick and light.

"The wind is coming up, and that's a good thing. It'll give you the chance to practice managing it. After you cross the 1,000-meter mark, get ready for that wind to come through the channel opening and hit you hard on the port side. Brenna knows what I mean and may call for starboard power if she needs to."

Brenna nodded without looking at him.

"Okay, that's it. Have a good practice."

"Hands-on!" Brenna commanded, indicating that the rowers should prepare to lift the boat before Dennis could think of something he needed to say to her privately.

Sadie's first race was Saturday morning: the collegiate lightweight heats. Sadie's boat rowed to an easy win in their heat as Brenna and her boatmates watched and cheered on the beach. Brenna hadn't seen Dennis yet, but she was sure he was somewhere watching too.

After Brenna met Sadie's boat as it landed and gave her a big hug, the Lake Merritt group decided to walk toward Pacific Beach and find a coffee shop. Their first race, the women's club heat, wasn't until later that afternoon.

As they turned from the beach, they ran into Dennis.

"Hey! How's everyone today?"

"Good!" "Great!" "We're getting coffee. Wanna come with?" several of the rowers replied at once.

"Brenna, wait a second," Dennis said. She reluctantly turned around. "How proud of Sadie are you right now?"

"The proudest! Absolutely!" Brenna said, relieved at the topic of conversation. "Glad you were watching too."

"She's amazing," Dennis said.

They stood and smiled at each other for a bit.

"Are you going with them to get coffee?" Dennis asked. The rest of the women had stopped a few paces ahead upon realizing that Brenna and Dennis hadn't started walking yet.

"Yes. You coming?"

"I don't want coffee. I wanted to talk to you a bit about the course," Dennis said.

"Well, I mean, the race isn't for hours. There's plenty of time for us to talk later, isn't there?"

"You guys coming?" Monica, the bow-seat, called back to them.

"Yes!" Brenna said and started walking toward the group.

"I don't see why you have to go with them," Dennis said, suddenly grumpy and petulant.

"I want to go. You don't have to."

Dennis gave her a withering look and turned to walk the other way.

"What was that all about?" Janet said when Brenna caught up.

"Nothing. Just stuff about the race."

"Mmmmm-hmmm," Janet said with that aggravating sly smile.

Their heat did not go well. Nerves combined with a brutal crosswind were their undoing. The club race was also very competitive, with the top teams fielding their best lineups. Just before the sprint, the four-seat's oar hit a wave, and she crabbed, which meant her oar blade got stuck under the water and the handle flew over her head. She managed to wrestle it back into position without Brenna having to stop the boat, but the damage was done. They got fifth, which meant they wouldn't race in the final. But they still had their masters–age group race the following day.

Dennis was waiting when they landed at the beach, and he, Brenna, and the crew were solemn as the rowers carried the boat back to their spot near the trailer.

"Okay, well, you all looked pretty nervous, but now you've gotten that out of your system, right?" Dennis said when they gathered. He didn't appear to be angry but was clearly disappointed for them. "Nice job recovering from the crab, Barb. Let's shake this one off and move on to tomorrow's race. Your sprint looked strong, so let's pick it up from there in the morning. Okay? Go and get some rest."

Brenna hurried away with her teammates and didn't look back.

Dennis sat at the hotel bar drinking a beer. He blamed himself for the boat's bad result. He didn't know what was wrong with him. One minute, he and Brenna were celebrating Sadie's success and the next he was pouting about her wanting to go with her boatmates to get coffee. He knew how important it was for a crew to bond, particularly on race day. And he'd ruined it, he felt sure.

He knew, when he was being honest with himself, that Brenna was trying to pull away from him, which was the exact opposite of what he wanted to happen. He could see that she was trying to keep him at arm's length, and, worse, that she was a little afraid of him. And that infuriated him.

He slapped a five-dollar bill on the bar and took the elevator up to his room. He paced up and down for a minute or so. He had to talk to her, to iron things out.

He picked up the phone and dialed Brenna's cell number. The call went straight to voicemail. Dennis yanked the cord out of the wall and threw the phone across the room. It flew through the open bathroom door and clattered and skidded across the tile floor until it hit the base of the shower.

Brenna's boat raced in the masters' women's "B"–age group race the next morning and took the bronze medal. They'd had calmer water and nerves and were able to race effectively. At the post-race meeting, Dennis said how proud he was of them, but Brenna thought he looked a little subdued. Then she asked herself why she even cared about Dennis's state of mind.

Once they had their boat secured on the trailer, the rowers wanted to celebrate with a nice lunch at a nearby resort. They invited Dennis, but he said he was going to catch up with a friend for lunch.

The women walked to the resort, some of them complaining that Coach D didn't seem all that happy for them. Brenna stayed out of the conversation.

Most of Brenna's boatmates were back at the rental house packing up when Sadie raced in her boat's final. Brenna stood by herself on the beach as the crews came charging down the course. She didn't see Dennis anywhere, but the crowds were thick on the shore, with the college teams cheering for their lightweight women.

When they crossed the 1,500-meter mark, Brenna realized that the Stanford lights were in the lead—by quite a lot. Sadie kept a strong, steady rhythm and then upped the stroke rate for their sprint. They flew across the line well ahead of the other boats.

After making her way down to the beach landing and hugging her ecstatic daughter, Brenna returned to the house and called a cab to take her to the airport.

Brenna's flight was delayed, so she decided to grab a bite to eat at a bar and grill near her gate. She was tired but also thrilled with their race that day. Janet had been rock-solid in the stroke seat, setting a powerful cadence for the women behind her. It was like night and day between Saturday's disappointing race and today's podium finish.

She sat at the bar, ordered a diet coke and a chicken Caesar salad, and found her mind wandering to Dennis's behavior the day before. She could only describe it as whining. He'd seemed intent on separating her from the group.

Brenna took a bite of salad and thought: *But that's what he'd been doing since he started coaching at Lake Merritt—always trying to get me alone, needing my advice, wanting to run things by me, seeking my approval.*

And I've been letting it happen, until yesterday. And when I didn't do what he wanted, he didn't like it.

Brenna felt a sense of dread washing over her as she realized that one of them would have to leave the rowing club.

A man sat down next to her at the bar. She glanced at him and—to her complete dismay—it was Dennis.

"Hey, hey," he said, all sunshine and smiles. "Awesome job today. And Sadie! She was unbelievable."

Brenna nodded, wanting to bolt but feeling rooted to the spot. Dennis ordered a beer.

"What are you doing here?" she finally asked. "Aren't you driving back with the trailer?"

"No, one of the Oakland Strokes coaches is riding back with Ted. I've got a flight in an hour. What flight are you on?"

"Alaska. It was supposed to leave"—she glanced at her watch—"well, now. But it's delayed."

"I'm on Southwest. Too bad we're not flying together."

"Yeah. Too bad," she said flatly.

Dennis downed his beer and signaled for another. "Do you want another Diet Coke?"

"No thanks."

"Is it hard? Sitting at a bar and not drinking?"

She thought for a minute. "No, I guess I don't think much about it anymore. It was at first."

"You're very strong," Dennis said.

"Not really. I just play it out in my head. If I have a drink, then that will lead to another and another. I can't stop once I start. Then, I'd probably miss my flight, and I'd have a horrible hangover tomorrow. So, I'd have a drink to chase it away. I wouldn't be able to focus on my job. I'd probably get fired. Sadie would be disappointed in me, we'd lose our apartment, she'd have to drop out of school, and on it goes."

"Wow," Dennis said. "That's a lot going on in your head."

Brenna finished her salad and asked for the check.

"What time's your flight?" Dennis asked.

"Not sure yet. I should go and check at the gate. No one's lining up yet—"

Just then, an announcement came over the loudspeaker that Alaska flight 238 to San Francisco would be delayed until 6:30 p.m., another hour away.

"Is that your flight?" Dennis asked.

"Yep."

"Mine leaves around the same time."

Brenna nodded. She tried to think of some reason to leave the bar, but she knew he would talk her into staying. She could say that she needed to use the ladies' room. He couldn't argue with that.

Dennis started on his third beer, turned to her, and said, "So, I was wondering. Peter's been gone for a while. Are you seeing anyone?"

"No. Why?"

"Just curious. I mean, I'm no longer married to Deirdre. We're both single."

Brenna stood up.

"Wait. I'm sorry. I just . . . I think about you and Sadie. I could take a paternity test, and then we would really know if I am her father—"

"No, I don't think that's a good idea. I need to go," Brenna said, picking up her bag. She walked out of the bar and headed toward the ladies' room. She'd hide there until her flight was called if need be.

"Brenna!"

She heard him calling to her, but she didn't turn around. The worst part was that she wanted to turn around. She was still attracted to him, and that was what scared her most of all.

But by the time her plane landed in San Francisco, she was angry and knew what she had to do.

CHAPTER THIRTY-FOUR

"**W**ouldn't it be easier to find another rowing club?" Abigail asked on the phone the next day.

Brenna was in her office, editing the proofs for the campus alumni magazine when Abigail called to find out how the weekend went. It was technically her lunch hour, but she had planned to work through lunch since she'd missed two days during the previous week.

"Hang on a second." Brenna went to shut her office door.

"Yes, it probably would," she said, answering Abigail's question. "But I need to do something, or he'll never leave me alone. I just don't know if I have the courage to do it in person."

"You could send him an email."

"Maybe. Or I could call him," Brenna said. "Yes, that's what I'll do. I'll call him. And I'm going to do it tonight before I lose my nerve."

"Okay, but please call me afterward. I'm not sure this is a good plan; it could backfire somehow."

"It's the only way. I need to get myself and Sadie free of him. I never should have told Sadie he might be her father. Her relationship with him is just inviting him into my life again."

On her drive home, Brenna thought about what to say to Dennis. She didn't want him to force her out of Lake Merritt, but she might have to leave. It wasn't about the rowing club or even about him repeatedly finding a way into her life—and destroying whatever happiness she had found. She finally had to admit to herself that she still wanted him. And that was the scariest thing of all.

She hoped that he would agree to leave—both the club and her life—but she had to play it very carefully.

～

"Brenna?" he picked up right away.

"Yeah, hey, Dennis. Um, do you have a couple of minutes to talk?"

"Of course. What's up?"

Brenna hesitated, trying to get her heart rate under control. "I think it would be better if we don't spend so much time together. I think you should ask our captain to help you with the regatta stuff."

Dennis didn't respond.

"I just . . . I feel that in our current relationship as coach and coxswain, our interactions have become more personal than I am comfortable with."

More silence.

"Dennis? Are you there?" She felt like she might hyperventilate.

"I'm here," he finally said. "So, you think our meetings have been personal? All we've talked about was rowing. Maybe you're projecting your own feelings onto me?"

He sounded calm and spoke in a reasonable tone. It unnerved her. He knew. He could see inside of her.

"Well, last night in the airport. I felt the conversation was inappropriate—if I was seeing someone, that you were single, that you would take a paternity test."

"Brenna, I'm sorry you misunderstood. I was only asking because I care about you. As a friend. I just wanted you to know that I understand it's hard to be alone. And the paternity test? I was just offering. I have no doubt I'm Sadie's father, but I didn't know how you felt about it. I, personally, don't need a test to continue my relationship with Sadie.

"Again, I'm sorry. I'll do a better job of keeping things professional from here on out."

Brenna was floored. This was not how it was supposed to go. He was supposed to become upset—or angry. Say that he loved her, and they needed to be together. Give her an opening to threaten to tell Dave he was harassing her. Then he was supposed to say he would quit coaching the team.

She began to doubt herself. He *had* only come to coach at Lake Merritt because she was there, right? He *had* been suggesting that they start seeing each other, hadn't he? *But what if both those things were only true in her head?*

~

The next morning at practice, Dennis was jovial and made a big announcement to the team about the women's bronze medal in San Diego. He made jokes during the row and praised everyone.

But about halfway through the session, he began criticizing Brenna's steering.

"Watch your point, Brenna! You almost cut the other boat off!"

Brenna gaped at him. She had not! The other coxswain had veered toward her.

"Stay on the shoreline, Brenna! Don't veer out into the middle!"

Brenna couldn't believe what he was saying. She was nowhere near the middle.

"I need you to focus, Brenna! I said twenty hard strokes, not ten!"

He did not! she thought, frazzled and angry.

After practice, she escaped to her car as soon as possible. Driving to work, she expected her phone to buzz, as it usually did, with an apology from Dennis. But her phone remained silent, except for a voicemail alert from Abigail, whom she'd neglected to call after her phone call with Dennis.

⌒

Sadie knocked on Denny's door again. Still no answer. That was odd. She checked her watch again. They'd agreed that Sadie would pick Denny up and meet Dennis at the ballpark in Oakland for the A's game.

Sadie knocked again. She heard a muffled thump from inside.

"Denny?" she called. She tried the door handle, but it was locked.

"Shit!" she heard coming from the other side of the door, which suddenly flew open.

Denny stood there, his hair sticking up in all directions, his eyes bloodshot, his clothes looking as if he'd slept in them.

"Hey! Oh, man, what time is it? I must have fallen asleep. Worked late last night. Come in!"

Sadie entered the apartment, dark with the shades drawn. But she could see it was a mess: clothes and shoes strewn about the floor, empty beer bottles on the coffee table and side table. It smelled like old beer and other unpleasant things she couldn't quite identify. She didn't even want to look in the kitchen.

"What time is it?" Denny asked again, rubbing his eyes.

"It's ten after four. We should leave pretty soon."

"Right! Lemme just jump in the shower. I'll be five minutes. Here . . ." Denny indicated an armchair and removed a pile of magazines and socks from it to the floor. "I'll be quick."

Denny disappeared into the bathroom. Sadie looked at the chair. It had what looked like grease stains all over it, and she didn't want to sit on it. She heard the water start up in the bathroom. The TV was on, but the sound was off. A man in a suit was pointing to a weather map. Sadie found the remote and shut it off.

Then she heard a crash from the bathroom. She rushed to the door and knocked on it. "Denny? Are you okay?"

"Yeah."

A couple of minutes later, Denny came out wearing an old flannel bathrobe. His hair was wet, and he was holding on to his head.

"You okay?"

"Yeah, I just slipped and fell. I'm fine." But she could see a red bump forming on his head when Denny dropped his hands to the arms of the filthy chair and sat down.

Sadie took a tentative step toward him. "That looks like it hurts."

Denny looked up at her, and she saw remnants of white powder below his right nostril. Sadie didn't do drugs, but she'd been to a lot of parties where people did. She knew what she was seeing.

"Hey," she said, sitting on a corner of the coffee table and facing him. "What's going on with you?"

Denny buried his face in his hands. For one shocking moment, she thought he was crying. He shook his head and looked at her. His eyes were dilated, but dry—and full of misery.

"I'm sorry. I'm making us late for the first pitch," He started to stand up, but his legs seemed to refuse to support him, and he flopped back into the chair.

"Never mind the game. I'll text Dennis that we'll be late. You need to eat something. Do you have any food?"

Sadie stood up before he could answer, steeled herself, and went into the kitchen. Surprisingly, it wasn't that bad. Almost as if he never came in here. She opened the refrigerator and saw lots of beer, but not much else. She checked the cupboards and found a box of crackers and a jar of peanut butter. She took them and a butter knife out to the living room.

"I don't think I'm up for going to the game," Denny said. "But you should go. Think I'm coming down with something. Don't want you to get sick too."

Sadie turned on a lamp, which caused Denny to wince and squint for a moment. She spread peanut butter on a cracker and handed it to Denny. He ate one, then sprang to his feet and lurched to the bathroom. She could hear him throwing up and fought the urge to run out the front door. Instead, she went to the window, raised the shade, and opened it. Fresh air, fragrant with flowers, wafted in.

She pulled out her phone and texted Dennis: *Denny sick. Not coming.*

The bathroom door opened, and Denny emerged. He headed for the couch this time and collapsed onto it.

"Sorry," he muttered.

Sadie's phone buzzed with a text from Dennis. *Should I come?*

Nah. I got it. Enjoy game.

Sadie went into the kitchen, found a glass, and filled it with water. She carried it out to Denny, and he sipped at it tentatively.

"Thanks," he said. "Really, I'll be okay. Just a bug. You should take off."

"It's not a bug. You're hungover. Seriously hungover."

Denny didn't say anything, just sat there slumped on the couch.

Sadie braved the stained chair and settled in. "Talk to me, Denny."

"Okay, yeah. I partied kinda hard after work last night," he said defensively. "No big deal. Now that I'm done with school, I'm just livin' life a little."

"So you drank all these beers last night?" Sadie swept her hand, indicating all the empty bottles.

"No. Yes. I mean, not last night. Those are just from this week. I don't have much time to clean."

"Clearly," Sadie said.

"What're you? My mom?" he said wearily.

"No, I'm your friend. I want to help."

"Well, you can't. And there's no need. I'm fine."

Sadie's phone buzzed again. Dennis. *On my way.*

"Is that Dennis?"

"Yeah, I said you were sick. He's worried. He's coming over."

"Great!" Denny said in exasperation.

They sat in silence for a minute. Sadie picked up the box of crackers and handed him one, sans peanut butter, but he waved her off.

"Look, I'm sorry," he said. "I get that you wanna help. But you can't. It's too fucked up. *I'm* too fucked up."

Now, she did see tears welling up in his eyes.

"I've done some fucked-up things. And I can't stop thinking about them. And all the trouble I've caused."

"What things?"

"Things I did when I was a kid." He picked up a shirt and blew his nose.

"Well, you were a little asshole. I'll give you that," Sadie said.

Denny tried to smile but produced a grimace.

"But seriously. Can you tell me about it?"

Denny shook his head. "I can't tell anyone," he said quietly; so quietly, she barely heard him.

Sadie nodded. "Okay, but I'm here for you, bro."

She stood up, found an empty grocery bag in the kitchen, and began collecting the beer bottles. She wiped off the coffee table with a paper towel. Over his objections, she started picking up Denny's clothes from the floor, until the front door opened, and Dennis walked in.

Denny groaned. "You didn't need to come. I'm fine."

"It's no fun going to the game alone. We'll order pizza and watch it on TV," Dennis said, and walked directly to the kitchen. He returned with three beers. He offered one to Sadie, but she shook her head. He tossed another to Denny, who considered it a moment, then cracked it open and took a slug.

Sadie waited for Denny to bolt for the bathroom again, but he didn't. His stomach appeared to accept the hair of the dog.

Dennis sat in the stained chair and looked at Denny. "What happened to your head?"

CHAPTER THIRTY-FIVE

Brenna stood at her station, which featured hearty red wines. The rowing club held a wine-tasting event in the summer to raise money for new equipment. Brenna and some of the other rowers had volunteered to pour. Abigail had viewed this event as yet another reason Brenna should find a new club, but Brenna had assured her that she would be fine. With so many years of sobriety under her belt, Brenna wasn't worried.

Her teammates and the friends and relatives they'd invited stopped by her table to chat and taste. As instructed, Brenna poured two fingers of wine into their glasses. She spotted Dennis as he entered the room and busied herself with opening another bottle of Syrah. She recognized it as a wine she'd drunk with Peter. *Maybe this was a mistake. Maybe I should call Abigail. Or say I'm not feeling well and leave.*

She tried not to watch Dennis making his way around the room but kept glancing up to monitor his progress. The event room was filling up and, as the tasting progressed, getting progressively louder—and warmer. Brenna opened the window near her table a little wider.

Dennis was at the rosé table now. A group of rowers had gathered around him and were having a jolly old time.

At Brenna's table, people extended their glasses and Brenna poured them samples from the bottles they pointed at. People were talking to her, but she couldn't hear them very well. She nodded and smiled.

Jasper, one of the other coxswains, sidled up to her. "Hey, you need a hand here? Maybe you need a break to try some wine yourself?"

"Nope. Not me. Haven't sampled wine in many, many years."

"No kidding. What do you drink?"

"Coffee. Diet Coke."

"No, I mean alcohol."

"No alcohol."

"No alcohol?"

"No alcohol."

"You know, you're at a *wine tasting*," Jasper said in mock disbelief. "Let me know if you need a break."

Dennis was now standing about eight feet away from her. He was flanked by three women, and they were all smiling and laughing. One of them, a long-legged, dark-haired mediocre rower named Cynthia, who, it was widely known, had a big crush on Dennis, was hanging all over him in her tight dress. She kept touching his shoulder or forearm and leaving her hand there until Brenna saw with satisfaction Dennis casually shrugging her off.

Suddenly, Dennis caught her eye—caught her watching him, actually. Brenna hastily turned away and, in the process, knocked over one of the open bottles of Cabernet. Thankfully, it was almost empty, but it crashed to the floor. It didn't break but instead rolled into the middle of the room, dribbling red wine as it went, and stopped to rest against Dennis's foot.

Dennis picked it up and walked toward her, as several people cluck-clucked and grabbed napkins to wipe up the spill.

"I believe you dropped this," Dennis said, handing her the bottle.

"Thanks."

Dennis surveyed her for a second. "You look nice. I like that shirt. Can I try some of that?"

He pointed randomly at a bottle.

"Sure," Brenna said, and tried, unsuccessfully, to stop her hand from shaking as she poured.

He took a taste, shrugged, and said, "Thanks."

And he walked away into the crowd.

Brenna's shift was finally over an hour or so later. As she walked out into the dusky evening to her car, she saw something that made her stop short and stare. In the next row over, Dennis was holding the passenger side door of his car open, and Cynthia was getting in.

She thought Dennis had looked over at her, but she wasn't sure. She felt her face redden, along with a surge of irrational and annoying jealousy as she got into her car. Worse, she felt like following them or going back inside and pouring herself at least six fingers of wine. But she forced herself to drive home.

Over the next several days, Brenna couldn't stop thinking about Dennis and Cynthia. She truly thought she was losing her mind. Why did she care if Dennis was pursuing or dating or sleeping with Cynthia? Why couldn't she turn off the image in her head of Cynthia getting into his car? She had told Dennis that she didn't want his personal attention. Obviously, he had moved on. *Why did this bother her so much?*

Not able to focus on work one day, Brenna decided to go out for a walk at lunchtime. It was a sunny, warm day and people were filling the outdoor tables at the restaurants on Shattuck Avenue—including, Brenna noticed with a start—Dennis and Cynthia. She started to turn around before they saw her, but . . .

"Brenna!" Dennis called. He even stood up and waved to her. "Come join us!"

Joining them, she thought, was the last thing she wanted to do. But her feet were propelling her toward them. *I'll tell them I have to get to a meeting,* she thought. But her curiosity was getting the better of her. What were they doing in Berkeley so close to her office? Were they really dating?

Dennis asked the guy at the next table if a chair was available. He nodded, and Dennis slid it over for Brenna. She sat.

"You had lunch yet? We just ordered." Dennis flagged down a server and asked for another water and menu.

Cynthia did not look thrilled with Brenna's making them a threesome.

"Oh, actually, I brought my lunch today," Brenna said. "It's back at the office. I just wanted to get out for some air."

The waiter brought her menu and water. "Can I bring you anything to drink?"

"She'll have a Diet Coke," Dennis said. Then, to Cynthia, he said, "Brenna works near here in the communications office."

How does he know that? Brenna thought. But maybe she'd mentioned it. Or Sadie had.

"Cynthia's a grad student in archaeology," Dennis continued, looking at Cynthia, who nodded. He turned back to Brenna. "Did you know that?"

"I didn't," Brenna said. She took a sip of water and started to get up. "You know, I don't want to intrude on your . . . uh, date. I should get back."

"Nice to see you," Cynthia said, suddenly cheerful.

"Aw, you have time, don't you?" Dennis said. "Stay. Hang out. Look, here's your drink."

"Ready to order?" the waiter asked.

"Just this," Brenna said, gesturing at her Diet Coke.

The waiter snatched up her menu.

"You know, Brenna helps me a lot at the club," Dennis was saying to Cynthia. "She's really like an assistant coach."

"I'm aware," Cynthia said, not trying to hide her displeasure. "Everyone's aware."

"Oh yeah?" Dennis said, head swiveling between the two of them.

"Sure. We all know how much time you spend together—alone, out to coffee, whatever," Cynthia said.

"A lot to talk about," Dennis said, seeming to deliberately ignore Cynthia's sour tone. "I'm glad everyone understands how much Brenna does for the club."

"I really do need to go," Brenna said, glancing at her watch. "Got a meeting in ten minutes."

She made her escape quickly, forgetting to pay for her drink. *Oh well*, she thought. *He ordered it. He could pay for it.*

She made a beeline for her office; confident she had her answer. They were dating. Cynthia's jealousy said it all. Brenna was both relieved and hurt. She tried to focus on the relief side of her emotions: now maybe he'd leave her alone, stop asking her to help him. Now she needed to figure out how to get Sadie to spend less time with him.

When she got back to her office, she called Sadie and invited her to dinner that weekend.

⤚

Since running into Dennis and Cynthia in Berkeley, Dennis had essentially ignored Brenna at every practice that week. He coached the rowers in her boat but didn't direct any comments at her whatsoever. He no longer asked for her help with club matters.

One morning, when they returned to shore, Dave was standing near the docks. After Brenna's crew had put their boat away, Dave approached her and asked if she had time for a chat.

They went into the coach's office, and Dave shut the door. He looked uncomfortable as he took a seat across the table from her.

"I have to get to work, as I'm sure you do, too, so I'll get right to the point. There's been a complaint."

"A complaint? About me?"

"I'm afraid so, Bren," Dave was having trouble looking her in the eye. "Look, I know you and Dennis have known each other for a long time. I know you were with Peter, but there were rumors . . . And there seems to be again."

"This is about Dennis?" Brenna felt suddenly too warm in the small, airless room.

"Yes. Someone told me that you've been hitting on him, that you told him you wanted to date him in an airport bar in San Diego."

Brenna could only gape at Dave.

"The person says it's making everyone uncomfortable and that they feel that it's interfering with his coaching—"

"And you believe this shit?"

Dave looked miserable. "I don't know. I just needed to let you know what was said and ask that you not, uh, pursue Dennis anymore. If in fact, you are."

"Listen, Dave . . . ," Brenna began. *But what would she say? That it was the other way around? That he had something going with Cynthia now (whom she was 100 percent sure had lodged the complaint)? That he had sexually assaulted her, and they might even have a child together?*

"We really don't encourage coach-athlete relationships, anyway," Dave added lamely.

Brenna laughed bitterly. "Fine, Dave. Consider the situation resolved."

She stood up, walked out the door, and never went back.

CHAPTER THIRTY-SIX

Sadie and Brenna sat outside on the little balcony at the apartment eating dinner. The sun was still warm, but the air had a hint of crispness to it. Fall was fast approaching. Sadie had been working at an outdoor boating camp for city kids over the summer but would soon begin crew practices at Stanford and classes a week or two later.

"I feel like I haven't seen you much at all this summer," Brenna said.

"I know! It was so busy. I'm glad to have a week to myself now that camp has ended."

Sadie dug into her pasta primavera that Brenna had made. She'd recently decided to become a vegan and appreciated her mom's effort at accommodating her, even if the pasta didn't have much flavor to it.

"Good, Mom," Sadie said, indicating her plate.

"Really? Without butter and cream, I was sure it would be a little bland."

"Nah, it's delicious."

Inside, the phone began ringing.

"Do you need to get that?"

Brenna shook her head. "They'll leave a message if it's important."

After a couple more rings the answering machine clicked on. Dennis's voice poured out of the small speaker.

"Hey, Brenna. Just trying to reach you again. Just hoping to talk to you about why you quit the club. Call me back, please."

"You quit the club?" Sadie asked. "Why?"

"Uh. Well, I guess that's a topic related to something I wanted to talk to you about."

"Oh?" Sadie noticed that her mother's demeanor had changed rapidly since the phone message had played. The sun was still shining, but it felt to Sadie like a dark cloud had spread across the sky.

"First, I quit the club because Dennis was making me uncomfortable."

"How?"

"I wanted to keep things strictly business. Coach and coxswain. But he wanted things a little more . . . personal."

"Huh. He told me he had a new girlfriend. A rower at the club," Sadie said.

"Did he?" Brenna said, her voice suddenly tense. "How often do you see Dennis?"

"I mean, not that much. We mostly just meet for baseball games. He calls sometimes just to see how I'm doing. He comes to watch me row."

"And Denny?"

"Games mostly. He doesn't call me. Unless we have plans for me to pick him up for a game in Oakland." Sadie stopped, remembering the last time when Denny had been so hungover, and Dennis had come over to watch the game on TV. Denny had continued drinking beer and disappearing into the bathroom and appeared to experience a remarkable recovery, as Dennis, who was clearly onto him, had remarked.

"Why do you ask?" Sadie said.

"This is complicated, but I'll try to explain," Brenna said, taking a deep breath. "When I was first working the steps and getting sober, my brain was really messed up. I'm sure you remember. And I made amends to you and told you about Dennis and that I was okay with you having a relationship with Dennis."

Sadie nodded. "That was when you told me about him maybe being my dad."

"Right. But I'm regretting telling you that I was okay with you having a relationship with him. It seemed fine for a while, but I see now that it was a mistake."

"What do you mean?"

"I mean," said Brenna. She paused, seeming to struggle for the right words. "I don't know if he is actually your father or not. But what I do know is that he has inserted himself into our family in an apparent attempt to get to me."

Sadie started to feel bad for her mom, who seemed to be exaggerating her importance in Dennis's life. He rarely mentioned her to Sadie.

"I don't know what happened between you two, you know, around the time I was . . . conceived," Sadie said carefully. "I haven't wanted to know, actually, because you were married to Dad at the time, so you obviously cheated on him—"

Brenna started to say something, but Sadie held up a hand. "I'm not judging. You made a mistake, but you and Dad worked it out. I don't want to know the details. But I guess I am wondering why you never found out for sure whether he's my father. Like with a paternity test?"

"I think about that a lot, actually," Brenna said. "I guess I don't want to know. If there's still a chance it's not true—and there is—I'd rather just keep that hope alive."

"Okay, I get it."

They sat in silence for a minute, watching the sun lower between the downtown skyscrapers.

"I would like to ask you not to spend time with Dennis anymore," Brenna said finally. "I don't want to make you uncomfortable, but there are things you should know, things that will help you understand the reason I am asking this."

⌒

After Sadie arrived home and threw up in the bathroom, she called her grandmother. She burst into tears upon hearing her grandmother's voice.

"Grammeg, I need to talk to you," Sadie said between sobs.

"Sadie! What is it? Has something happened?"

"I'm fine," Sadie said. "Everyone's fine. I mean no one's been in an accident, no one's sick." *Except maybe my mother*, Sadie thought. She tried to stop crying, but she wanted to be in Tahoe, with Meg, who had been the only constant in her young life, along with Jack.

"My mom told me some stuff tonight," Sadie said. "About Dennis and Denny. And I don't know what to think. I'm afraid she's drinking again and may be delusional, Grammeg."

"Oh, Sadie. How can I help?"

"I need a reality check." Sadie wasn't crying anymore, but she was angry.

"Okay. Shoot and I'll do my best."

"She said that Dennis showed up at her house one day—after she and Dad got married—and that he had raped her. And that's why he might be my father."

"Oh, dear. She said that?"

"Do you believe that's what happened?"

"I don't know, honey. My understanding was that it was consensual."

"That's what I always thought. Were they having an affair?"

"No, I didn't get that impression. He had shown up out of the blue. They hadn't seen each other for a year or so."

"But my dad never knew?"

"No, not to my knowledge, sweetheart."

"Okay," Sadie said quietly. After a pause, she said, "Mom told me that Dennis has been kind of stalking her ever since the . . . whatever it was. She said he got the job in Tahoe so that he'd be able to see her. And that he started coaching at her rowing club for the same reason. She also said that's the reason he wants to have a relationship with me, to get information about her."

"I see. Well, there may be some truth there. I think Dennis has always been in love with your mother. But I also think he loves you."

"Did my mom ever tell you about how it was with them in college?"

"No, not much. We haven't had a relationship where she confides in me," Meg said. Sadie couldn't help but notice the sadness in Meg's voice.

"She wants me to stop seeing Dennis and Denny. They've been nothing but nice to me, and Dennis hardly ever brings Mom up. Maybe he's not in love with her anymore."

"Why does she want you to stop seeing Denny? He's been rather an innocent bystander."

"Except for what grandpa may have seen."

"What do you mean?"

"Mom said that he told her he saw someone driving away in Dennis's truck on the morning my dad drowned. And that he thinks it might have been Denny, but he wasn't sure."

Meg was silent.

"He didn't tell you that?"

"No, sweetheart. He didn't."

"Maybe because he wasn't sure? Denny's messed up, and he said he did some horrible things when he was younger, but I thought he meant being a bully and getting into trouble at school. But Mom said Grandpa thinks he might have taken Dennis's truck and driven to the marina. That he had the keys to his mom's friend's boat. And took that too. And . . ." Sadie stopped. "That seems like a pretty out-there scenario, don't you think?"

"Of course, darling. Denny was just a boy," Meg said, but she didn't say it with much confidence.

After she hung up, Sadie tried to organize her thoughts. On the plus side, her mom probably hadn't been raped, and if Dennis had been trying to find ways to get into her mom's life, it was because he loved them; her and her mom. On the minus side, Denny had said he'd done bad things when he was younger. Did that include swamping her dad's rowing shell? And why would he do that? It made no sense.

Also on the minus side was the fact that Sadie had purged again. She'd managed to stop over the summer, but the stress of staying under the 130-pound limit to remain eligible to row lightweight had built as the fall racing season approached. A lot of the girls were either not eating much or purging to make weight. Most of them said they had stopped having their periods. Sadie's had come back in the summer, but she'd missed the last couple of cycles. But among the lightweight rowers, the lack of menstruation was like a badge of honor.

CHAPTER THIRTY-SEVEN

Brenna paced up and down the length of her living room. Sadie had been so upset, and she hadn't committed either way regarding Brenna's request that she stop spending time with Dennis and Denny. Brenna was white-knuckling it through a compulsion to walk down to the corner liquor store for a bottle of vodka. *What good was being sober if everything you touched turned to shit?* She rationalized. Sadie was angry with her; Dennis had found someone else; she didn't have a rowing club and the social life that went with it anymore; she was having trouble concentrating at her job and her supervisor had commented on her careless work the other day. She knew she should call Abigail, but she hadn't, even though Abigail had left several phone messages. And that was the worst sign of all.

Fuck it, she thought, grabbed her wallet, and headed out the door.

As Brenna approached her apartment building, she saw Dennis peering at the tenant directory and pushing a button on the console. She did an about-face, but not quickly enough.

"Brenna!"

She turned around slowly as he jogged toward her.

"Just stopped by to see you," he said.

"Why? What are you doing here?"

"I was worried. You haven't returned my calls. And neither has Sadie."

"You know," Brenna said, "Most people would *take the fucking hint!*"

She was practically shrieking, and passersby were glancing their way.

"Can we go inside? To your place and talk?"

"No, you just need to leave!"

"Are you drunk? Is that a bottle in that bag?"

"Neither of those questions is any of your business," Brenna hissed.

"Is that why you quit the club? Because you're drinking again? Or because of Cynthia?"

"I quit the club to get away from you! And, yes, because of Cynthia!"

"We're not dating. She wants to, but I told her it was against club policy. The truth is, I only made it look like I was seeing her to make you jealous."

Brenna felt laughter bubbling up, and it exploded out of her. Dennis stared as she guffawed loudly, then pulled herself together.

"I didn't quit because I was jealous, you narcissistic jerk. I quit because you told Cynthia that I was hitting on you, and she complained to Dave! Anyway, that's beside the point, which is this: you need to leave us alone. We don't want you in our lives."

"Sadie feels that way too?"

"I don't know. But if she's not returning your calls, as you say, she probably does. I told her, you know, how she may have been conceived. Of course, she's very upset."

"You told her?" Dennis shook his head. "I think it might be time for me to get a paternity test."

"Oh, hell no! That's exactly what time it is *not!*" Brenna knew she was causing a scene, and pedestrians were staring or hurrying past, but she didn't care in the least. All of her pent-up rage was pouring out of her—and it was liberating.

"Sadie has a right to know who her father is. This isn't just about you."

Brenna stopped short and stared at him. She hadn't thought of that. He was right, actually. *Now, who was the narcissist?*

"Brenna, I know I've caused you a lot of pain. I do love you, but I get that you don't want me in your life. But please, please don't turn Sadie against me. She and Denny are the best things in my life."

"Well, I don't want her hanging out with Denny anymore either," Brenna said. She felt herself deflate, her anger dissipating into the air.

"Why not?"

"It doesn't matter."

"Tell me. Please."

Brenna took a deep breath. "Fine. My dad told me that on the morning Peter died, he saw Denny driving away in your truck—at least he thought it was Denny. And that the timing fit for Denny to have driven to the marina, taken Deirdre's friend's boat, and waked Peter."

Dennis thought about this for a few seconds. "I guess it's possible. He could have found the marina code and the keys. I taught him to drive my truck and driving a boat isn't that different."

Brenna watched him as he thought some more. It was almost a relief that he knew. She'd been keeping it secret for so long and trying to convince herself it couldn't be true.

"But," Dennis finally said. "Why would he want to go after Peter?"

"I've thought about that, and I have a theory. Maybe he thought it was you out there rowing, not Peter."

"Holy shit." Dennis looked stunned. Brenna almost felt bad for him.

"Did Deirdre know?"

"If she did, then she tried to frame you to protect him."

As Dennis rode the BART back to Oakland, he mulled everything over in his mind. *What if Denny thought it was me out rowing that day?* It made sense, actually. Denny had told Dennis years ago that he'd tried to kill him. He had mentioned bunching up the floor mat in the truck. Dennis thought back. He thought he'd remembered it being bunched up, but he'd smoothed it out. It hadn't caused him to hit the tree. He'd hit the tree because he'd been drunk.

He remembered something else about the day Denny had told him he'd tried to kill him. Denny was about to say something else when Deirdre's friend came driving up. Maybe it was that he'd tried to kill him by waking him down in the powerboat.

These thoughts almost eclipsed the fact that Brenna had agreed with him: Sadie had a right to know who her father was. She said she'd try talking to Sadie and see if she'd consent to the paternity test. Dennis was positive he was Sadie's father; he wasn't worried that the test would indicate otherwise. But he was worried about Denny. If what Jack and Brenna thought was true, it was no wonder Denny was drinking so much. The weight of what he had been carrying around for more than a decade had to be crushing him.

The bar had been busy for a Sunday night, but people were starting to filter out to get ready for their Mondays or whatever. Denny was jonesing for a line and a shot but just as he was about to ask the manager if he could announce last call two guys came in. One stood by the door talking on his phone, and the other headed for the bar.

"Evenin'," Denny said. "What can I get you?"

"How's it going?" The man held up five fingers, and said, "Whatever you have on tap." He looked kind of familiar, like he'd been in the bar before. He was probably a little older than Denny. Maybe he'd seen him on campus.

Denny reached under the bar for the bank bag, stuck his hand inside, and felt for a half gram. It had gotten so he didn't have to look anymore to know how much coke was in each packet. His supply was getting low, but his supplier hadn't shown up for their last meeting. Denny didn't know how to get a hold of him or even what his name was.

He palmed the packet, picked up a coaster with the fingers on the same hand, maneuvered the packet under the coaster, and set it down on the bar in front of the guy.

"Beer comin' right up," Denny said, and turned away to pull the pint. As he turned back and delivered the guy's beer, the guy showed him his badge.

"Fuck," Denny muttered. He thought briefly about running, but the man by the door who'd been on the phone was still standing by the door. He locked eyes with Denny and pushed his flannel shirt aside a little to show Denny his gun. And the undercover cop whom Denny had just served was walking behind the bar toward Denny, handcuffs at the ready.

Deirdre was asleep when the bedside phone began to ring. She fumbled for the receiver and said "Yeah" into it.

"Deirdre, it's Dennis."

Deirdre sat bolt upright, suddenly quite awake.

"Sorry to call so late, but Denny's been arrested. I thought you should know."

"Arrested? Oh, God. I knew this would happen someday. I just didn't want to believe it."

"Wait. You knew about this?"

Deirdre hesitated. "Yes. I tried to deflect the attention away from him, but I guess they didn't let it go."

"You *knew* he was dealing out of the bar?"

"What?" Deirdre was confused. "What are you talking about?"

"What are *you* talking about?"

"Peter's death. I knew Denny did it, but I made him promise never to speak of it. And I tried to get the cops to think you did it. I was willing to say I did it if it came to it."

"Well, this isn't about that," Dennis said impatiently. "Denny's been arrested for selling cocaine out of the bar where he works. He called me to represent him. He's at the jail in Hayward. I'm heading there now."

Deirdre hung up, threw on some clothes, walked out to her mother's car, and drove toward the Oakland Bay Bridge. Her mother was in hospice now, hanging on longer than anyone had thought possible.

She got to the jail around two thirty, but they wouldn't let her see Denny. They couldn't—or wouldn't—even tell her what was happening with his case or if Dennis had been in to see him. They told her to come back at one that afternoon when visiting hours began.

Deirdre drove home and tried to sleep. She tossed and turned until she finally got up around five o'clock and called in sick to work. She made coffee and wondered how she would make it until the afternoon. She had to see Denny before he did something rash like confessing to Peter's murder. She tried calling Dennis, but her calls went straight to voicemail.

CHAPTER THIRTY-EIGHT

Brenna woke up feeling extremely grateful that she hadn't drunk the vodka she'd bought the night before. After Dennis left, she had every intention of opening it. In fact, she did open it and got a glass tumbler from the kitchen, with every intention of drinking it. She poured four fingers into the tumbler and went so far as to pick the glass up. But something made her hand stop when the glass was midway to her mouth. She held it there for a while as the potential consequences began to play in her head like a movie: She'd drink the first glass, then pour and drink another, then another. At that point, she'd be drunk enough to lose track of how much she was drinking. She'd probably call Sadie and do some blubbering, which would further alienate her daughter. She'd finish the bottle and most likely stagger downstairs to pick up another one. At some point, she would pass out, probably on the living room sofa, but maybe the floor. She'd wake up late. Having missed a couple of hours of work, there would be voicemails from her boss. She was already skimming thin ice at work, so she would possibly be fired. She'd have to borrow money from her dad or move in with her parents because she wouldn't be able to pay rent.

And nothing would change with Dennis. So, what was the point? A few hours of oblivion?

She had set the glass down on the coffee table, sighed loudly, and rested her head in her hands. Finally, she stood up, took the tumbler back into the kitchen, and poured the vodka from the glass and the bottle down the sink.

She called Abigail and told her the entire tale of the previous night's events, and they'd agreed to rendezvous at a meeting after work.

Brenna spent the day trying to focus on her work and, for the most part, she succeeded. Every time her thoughts drifted to Dennis, Sadie, or anything other than work, she willed herself to recommit to her assigned tasks. At the end of the day, she'd done more work than she had in the last week and left the office ready to start anew in AA. She would listen to Abigail and take her advice.

"He's like a drug," Abigail had said. "Or a bottle of vodka. And you know that there's only one way to quit him. The same way you quit drinking. Complete abstinence. There are no half measures."

Brenna knew Abigail was right. She knew it meant getting Sadie away from Dennis too, regardless of what the paternity test showed. As long as Dennis was in Sadie's life, he'd find ways to get to Brenna.

She needed to make Sadie understand that if she wanted to find out who her father really was, that was her choice, but that she strongly encouraged Sadie to end her relationship with him. This was not going to be easy. First, she had to get Sadie to trust her again.

Deirdre finally got in to see Denny that afternoon. An officer escorted her to a visiting room, where Denny was waiting.

"Hey, Mom," Denny said dejectedly. "Sorry about this."

"Are you all right?" Deirdre said quietly, glancing at the officer, who was standing by the door.

"Ma'am, just knock if you're done early. I'll be outside," she said, and exited the room.

"Are you okay?" Deirdre asked again.

"Yeah. Dennis thinks he can get me a deal."

"And then they'd let you out?"

Denny shrugged. "I guess."

"When Dennis called, I thought you had . . ."

"Confessed?" Denny finished for her.

"Shhhhhh," Deirdre whispered, glancing around wildly. "They might be listening."

Denny shrugged again but lowered his voice. "I've been thinking about it."

"No, Denny—"

"It's tearing me up, Mom," he whispered furiously. "Every time I see Sadie, I think about what I did. I drove the boat straight at him, and when I saw his face, saw that it wasn't Dennis, I swerved away. But it was too late." Denny said. His face showed such anguish it took Deirdre's breath away. "I can't live with this anymore, Mom."

"I'm so sorry. I'm so sorry I married Dennis and got you into this mess—"

"I know—"

"But what good would it do to bring this all up again?" Deirdre said. "It won't change anything. It won't make Sadie's life any better. It might even make it worse."

"But at least she would know what happened."

"Just think about it—"

The door opened, and the officer stuck her head in. "Time's almost up, ma'am."

Deirdre gave her a wave of acknowledgment, and the officer closed the door again.

"Just think about it," Deirdre said again.

"It's not just Sadie. It's you too. You went to jail to protect me. How can I ever repay that?"

"Denny, listen. You can repay me by having a good life, by not going to prison—"

The door opened. Deirdre stood up. The officer chose to look away as Deirdre hugged Denny and whispered. "Think about it."

Brenna left several messages for Sadie to no avail. Sadie's silence created a big hole filled with anxiety in Brenna's heart, but she was determined to stay sober and give Sadie space. Brenna went to work each day and tried to limit herself from checking her cell phone for voicemails to once an hour. After work, she headed to an AA meeting, then went home and checked her messages on her home machine.

Finally, one day, there was a message from Sadie. "Mom. I'm sorry I haven't called you back. I just needed some time. We've also been training really hard for Head of the Charles. I'm pretty exhausted.

"I appreciate what you said in one of your messages about the paternity test—about understanding that it's just not about you, but also me. I guess I do want to know who my father is. I won't tell you the results if you don't want to know. I'll call Dennis and we'll figure it out.

"Maybe we can talk soon. I'll let you know when I'm free. Love you, Mom."

As the message clicked off, Brenna realized she was crying—partly out of relief, and partly out of a feeling that she didn't deserve Sadie. Sadie was everything that was good and kind and forgiving. *Had Brenna ever been like that? Before she went to Stanford? Before she met Dennis?* How could someone like Sadie have been conceived under such aggressive—even violent—circumstances? *Maybe she wasn't,* Brenna thought with a spark of hope. *Maybe she's Peter's after all.*

The sunny, autumn weather had shifted seemingly overnight, and as the family gathered outside for the burial, cold rain was falling. Denny stood next to Deirdre, with his aunt Alana on the other side.

He was fresh out of rehab and feeling pretty raw. His grandmother's casket was lowered into the ground, and each family member scooped a shovel full of dirt into the grave.

Denny realized how much like his grandmother he had turned out to be. He was afraid that thirty days of rehab was not a guarantee against relapsing. He also understood how lucky he was. Dennis managed to negotiate a plea bargain in which Denny would pay a $20,000 fine (which Dennis paid), along with the stint in rehab. No jail time. No naming names. According to Dennis, the cops had hoped that Denny could provide the name of his supplier, which would lead them to the larger distribution operation. But Denny didn't know his name. The bar manager had set it up where they'd meet at the bar and exchange product for money, and that was their only interaction.

Dennis had found out that they'd arrested the bar manager as well, and that he had apparently caved and given them the supplier's name. Because it was Denny's first offense and his part in the operation was small-time, the prosecutors had gone easy on him. Also, Denny's polygraph had indicated he really didn't know anything, so consequently, there was no point in holding him.

Denny had kept quiet about Peter.

⌒

After the family gathering at what was now Deirdre's house, Denny borrowed what was now Deirdre's car and drove down the peninsula toward Stanford. It was a big boat of a car, an ancient Buick that smelled like decades of old cigarettes, but it still ran.

Denny had given notice at his apartment and had moved in with Deirdre. In part, this was because he worried about her living alone, but also because he needed to save money so he could pay back the $20,000 fine Dennis had covered. Dennis had insisted that payback was not necessary, but Denny had insisted that it was. Now all Denny needed was a job.

After a few wrong turns and a hunt for a parking space big enough for the Buick, Denny arrived at the coffee shop a few minutes late. Sadie was seated at a small table outside.

"Hey. Thanks for meeting me. Sorry I'm late," Denny said. "I'm gonna go grab a coffee. Want anything? More coffee?"

Sadie shook her head.

Denny stood in line, dreading what he was about to do. But it had to be done. He couldn't live with the secret anymore. Deirdre had tried to talk him out of it. Sadie could turn him in, she warned, but Denny was adamant that this was a risk he was willing to take.

He ordered coffee, black, and returned to the table. It was warmer down here in Palo Alto, and the sun was trying to break through the clouds.

"How was rehab?" Sadie said as Denny took the chair across from her.

"Uh. It was good, I guess. Better than jail. I met some decent folks, and I now have 'tools' to stay clean and sober."

"You look kinda, um, shaky," Sadie said.

"Yeah, I guess that's a word for it. Just weird being back out in the world. I have a sponsor, and I have to go to meetings and get sign-off from the court, but . . . I just hope it works."

Denny looked down at his coffee and took a sip.

"I didn't ask you to meet me just to shoot the shit. There's something I need to tell you." He looked back up at her and suddenly noticed how thin she was. Like she might blow away in just the slightest breeze.

Sadie took a drink of her coffee and then asked, "What's up?"

"It was me!" Denny blurted. "I caused your dad to fall out of his boat and drown. I swear I didn't mean to."

"So, it's true." Sadie said it almost as if she were talking to herself.

"You already knew?"

"Not for sure, but my grandfather told my mom that he thought he saw you driving away in Dennis's truck that morning, early enough to have done it."

Sadie was strangely calm, as if they were discussing the weather. But then the sky clouded over and so did her face. "But what I don't understand is why. Why would you do that?"

"Because I thought it was Dennis. At the time, I hated him. He was abusing my mom." Denny said. "Why aren't you freaking out?" he added, almost accusingly.

"I don't know," Sadie said in that weirdly serene voice, and then she suddenly lost consciousness, slipped out of her chair, and fell to the ground.

After the ambulance drove off toward the hospital, Denny hurried to the car and headed there himself. He'd called Dennis and asked him to call Brenna. Denny arrived at the emergency department before anyone else did. He checked on Sadie at the nurses' desk and was told that Sadie was resting and that a doctor would be in to check her out soon.

Denny sat down in the waiting area. He was worried about Sadie, but his mind also ruminated over Jack seeing him driving Dennis's truck on the day Peter drowned. Presumably, Jack had told Meg, Meg had told Sadie, and Sadie had told Brenna . . . As if on cue, Brenna rushed in and made a beeline for the nurses' desk. Denny watched her talking to the nurse; she was clearly agitated and gesturing wildly with her hands. Denny thought: that means at least four people could potentially turn him in for the murder. The nurse at the desk pointed to Denny and Brenna whipped around, apparently seeing him for the first time.

Brenna charged toward him, yelling, "What did you do to her, you little shit?"

Denny recoiled in his chair. Suddenly, Dennis appeared behind Brenna and embraced her, pinning her arms to her side.

Brenna looked outraged and yelled, "Let go of me!" while strug-gling against Dennis's arms. Denny took that opportunity to head for the door. He could text Dennis for updates. Best to make himself scarce for the time being.

Others in the waiting room were watching Dennis and Brenna struggle with great interest as Denny made his retreat, and he saw a security guard rushing toward them. He didn't stick around to see what happened next.

⌒

"Folks, you need to calm down," the security guard said as he approached Dennis and Brenna.

Brenna immediately stopped trying to free herself and Dennis let her go.

"Sorry, officer, she's just upset. Her daughter was just brought in," Dennis said.

"I'm sorry to hear that, ma'am, but if you'd just take a seat."

Brenna nodded and sat down. She put her head in her hands and stayed that way for a minute or two. Dennis sat down and waited.

Brenna took a deep, sighing breath and raised her head.

"Did they tell you anything?" Dennis said, nodding at the nurses' desk.

"Just that she's resting, and that a doctor would take a look at her." Dennis nodded again.

"Then the nurse said Denny had been with her when she passed out. I saw him sitting there and just lost it."

"Denny said on the phone he doesn't know what happened. They were sitting at a café, and she just passed out."

Brenna didn't respond.

"I'm going to go get you some coffee. I'll be right back."

Brenna waved him away. She couldn't care less about coffee.

⌐∽

An hour later, or maybe two—Brenna had lost track of time—a nurse walked into the waiting room and called out, "Who's here for Sadie Anderson?"

Brenna popped up from her seat and the nurse walked toward her and Dennis. Brenna had almost forgotten that Dennis was there, she'd been so preoccupied with her thoughts and trying to keep herself from panicking.

"I'm her mother," Brenna said.

The nurse glanced at Dennis, who remained silent.

"Is Sadie all right?"

"She will be. She's dehydrated and malnourished," the nurse said.

"Malnourished?" Brenna said.

"Yes. I talked to her a bit, and she told me she's been purging—"

"Purging? What do you mean?"

"She makes herself throw up after eating. To keep from gaining weight."

"Oh God," Brenna said, and collapsed into her chair.

The nurse sat down next to her.

"It's called bulimia," she said. "It's an eating disorder."

"Oh, man," Dennis said. "I've heard it's pretty common among lightweight rowers, with the pressure to make weight. I never thought Sadie would fall into it."

The nurse nodded. "Unfortunately, any sport with weight requirements can lead to an eating disorder."

"Can you help her?" Brenna asked.

"Yes, we're rehydrating her and trying to get some calories into her. The doctor would like to admit her for a few days, and she has consented. When she's feeling better and has gained a couple of pounds, the doctor will talk to her about further treatment."

"What kind of treatment?"

"Most likely therapy."

"Can I see her?"

"Yes, as soon as she's settled into her room. Someone will come for you."

⌒

After the nurse left them, Dennis got up to stretch his legs.

"Just going outside for some air," he said to Brenna, who ignored him. "Let me know if they come get us to see her."

Brenna waved him away, as she had before.

When Dennis walked out into the early evening, he saw Denny seated on a bench just outside the door.

"Hey, I didn't know you were out here. I thought you were texting me from home."

"Anything new?" Denny asked.

"They're admitting her for a few days. We can see her soon."

"What's wrong with her?"

"Eating disorder. She's making herself throw up to make weight."

"Jesus. I noticed just today that she looked really thin." Denny paused, then said, "I told her what I did, you know. I thought I had upset her so much she passed out. And maybe I did. You know, put her over the edge. But she didn't act upset. I guess because she already kind of knew. Everyone does, it seems. Maybe even you."

"Told her what? What do I know?" But Dennis was pretty sure he already knew.

"That I killed Peter."

"Because you thought he was me."

"So, you do know."

"Rumor has it," Dennis said, trying to smile.

"Look, Dennis—"

"It's all right, Denny. I was an asshole a lot of the time. You were just a kid. A kid who'd not had an easy time of it."

"I guess," Denny said. "But you changed. After you got out of jail. After that, it was like you actually were my father. And you've been taking care of me ever since."

Dennis didn't know what to say. He felt in danger of choking up. He looked away to pull himself together. When he turned back, he managed a shaky smile.

"I almost told the cops when I was in jail that I had done it, but my mom talked me out of it. She said it wouldn't help Sadie or change anything."

"Your mom's right," Dennis said. "What happened, happened. It's over."

"But I felt that Sadie had the right to know the truth. I didn't know everyone already suspected me. One of them, probably Brenna, will turn me in."

Dennis thought about that for a bit. "I guess it's possible, but I don't think she will."

"But you don't know that for sure," Denny said wearily.

"No, but I wouldn't worry about it."

When Dennis returned to the waiting room, Brenna was gone—gone to see Sadie, and the bitch hadn't even come to get him.

CHAPTER THIRTY-NINE

Sadie had missed the last part of the fall racing season but recovered in time for the spring regattas. While people said they were glad to see her back at the boathouse, there was an undercurrent among some of the girls. They eyed her a little warily, she thought, particularly the ones who she knew purged or starved, especially during the few days before weigh-ins. Sadie couldn't blame them for feeling uneasy. The coaches asked Sadie perfunctory questions about her health and recovery, but it was widely known that they generally looked the other way.

She'd learned a lot about her eating disorder during her recovery and therapy sessions. Purging was all about feeling a loss of control and trying to regain it, the therapist said. In Sadie's case, the therapist helped her understand that her mother's alcoholism and inconsistent presence in her life, her father's death, and her "tale of two fathers" all contributed to Sadie's feelings of losing control and were compounded by the pressure of collegiate lightweight rowing.

Sadie had put on weight during her time away from the boathouse. Thanksgiving and Christmas had been challenging, but she'd managed not to escape to the bathroom after meals. She didn't know what she currently weighed, having thrown away her scale on her therapist's advice, but she figured she would start training again and her weight would stabilize. She hadn't ever been in danger of not making weight, her therapist had helped her realize. She naturally weighed about 127. But when one of the other rowers had told her about purging, she had thought it was good insurance for staying in the boat.

Brenna looked at the cell phone in her hand for a long time. Ever since Sadie's trip to the emergency room the previous fall, she'd been formulating a plan. Now it was time to execute.

She hesitated another minute. She'd shared the plan with Abigail, who didn't think it was a good idea at all. She thought it would certainly backfire, just as Brenna's previous plan had. But Brenna was determined.

Finally, she took a deep breath and pushed the send button.

Dennis picked up right away.

"Brenna?" he said. "Is Sadie okay?"

"Yes, she's fine."

"I guess you must have heard that we got the paternity test result back—"

"Yes, I did hear that, but I told Sadie I don't want to know the result, so I would appreciate it if you wouldn't tell me."

"I know," Dennis said. "She told me you don't want to know. I wasn't planning to tell you."

"Thank you."

"Is there something you need?"

Brenna took another deep breath. "Yes, there is. I need you to leave us alone. I need you out of our lives—mine and Sadie's."

Silence on Dennis's end.

"Dennis, did you hear me?"

"I heard you," he said, and she could hear the irritation in his voice. She told herself to stand firm, no matter what he said. "You know, Bren. I've loved you for so many years. I really have. But I'm starting to think maybe you're just not worth it." He paused as if collecting himself. "Sadie is, though. Worth it."

"What are you saying?"

"I'm saying," he said, the anger in his voice still sounding evident but tightly controlled, "that Sadie is an adult. It's not up to you to tell me to get out of her life. If she wants to tell me that, then I would respect it. But she hasn't. And I don't think she will."

"That's true, she is an adult," Brenna said, her voice shaking slightly. She hoped he couldn't tell. "But she is still my child. Whether you are her father or not is immaterial. You are not good for her regardless."

"That's for her to decide!" Dennis shouted.

His outburst caused Brenna to feel a sense of justification and gave her the courage to continue. "I called to make a deal with you," she said. "You disappear from our lives. You don't contact us anymore, and I won't turn Denny in for Peter's murder."

To Brenna's complete shock, Dennis started laughing. He laughed for a while, then sobered up and said, "First of all, he didn't mean to kill him. He thought it was me! Second, Denny was eleven years old. There is no way he'd be prosecuted."

"But you don't know that for sure," Brenna said, slightly shaken. "Sadie said he's still torn up about it. That he wants to confess. That will carry some weight with the judge, I think."

"I'll tell you what. I will stay away from you. That I can promise. But Sadie can decide for herself. I don't think she's going to look too favorably on this phone call."

Brenna hadn't thought of that. Of course, he would tell her about the call. She tried to predict Sadie's reaction and realized that Sadie would certainly not appreciate Brenna's threat to turn Denny in.

"Isn't it enough that you've ruined my life? Do you have to hurt Sadie too?"

"I have no intention of hurting Sadie," Dennis said, and ended the call.

Brenna stared at her phone again before throwing it across the room.

After a while, she retrieved it—still intact—and called her father.

～

It was weigh-in day, and Sadie was a nervous wreck. She hadn't taken off enough weight, she was sure of it. Her clothes still fit more snugly, and she felt heavy. She'd hardly eaten at all the last couple of days.

When she arrived at the boathouse that Friday afternoon, the lightweights were starting to line up at the scale. There was a lot of nervous chatter, but Sadie was too anxious to join in. Her friend Steph laid a hand on her shoulder and said, "Don't worry, you're going to make weight."

Sadie gave her a thin smile. Then it was her turn.

"Anderson," said the assistant coach. Sadie stepped onto the scale, her heart hammering in her chest.

"131.9," the assistant coach announced to the other coach, who wrote the number down.

Sadie's heart sank, and she walked quickly toward the locker room. She still had a chance to lose 1.9 pounds, though, before the official race weigh-in the following morning. Her stomach was so empty that it felt like it was eating itself, gnawing away at her insides. She loved rowing and being on the team, but she wasn't sure she could keep doing this. She tried to tell herself that she could row openweight, but she knew she'd have to get a lot bigger and stronger. Sadie's tall, slim build meant she would struggle to remain a lightweight but not quite have the muscle or power to row openweight.

Steph caught up with her. She held out a Red Vine, and Sadie recoiled as if it was a snake.

"You need some energy. Eat it and come with me."

Sadie did as she was told, telling herself that Steph was a year ahead of Sadie, and she knew the tricks of the trade. In the locker room, Steph told her to put on whatever layers she had, then she handed Sadie a pair of sweats, a fleece jacket, and a ski hat, and said, "Put these on too."

The team was warming up with a three-mile run. Sadie trundled alongside Steph in her bulky layers of clothing. Girls cast sympathetic glances as they passed, particularly the ones who had gone on "sweat runs" themselves. Sadie remembered seeing other girls bundled up and feeling bad for them.

She soon became uncomfortable and lightheaded under the spring sun. The run was doing what it was supposed to do: sweat was running down her face, down her legs, everywhere. When they got back to the boathouse, she stripped off the clothes as fast as she could and splashed water on her face over and over.

"You'll do that again tomorrow before the weigh-in," Steph said, handing her the pack of Red Vines. "If you feel like you're going to pass out, just eat one of these."

Sadie accepted the packet. "Thanks, Steph. This totally sucks."

"You'll be fine."

Sadie wasn't sure that was true. She felt awful during the afternoon row, but she managed to stay upright. She made weight the next day and was allowed to race, but at what price? she asked herself. *What am I doing to myself?*

She realized she had to start eating again to maintain her energy. Shortly after that, she resumed purging. At therapy, she lied and said everything was fine, just fine.

Brenna hadn't talked to Sadie that much since she'd gone back to school. Whenever Brenna called, Sadie said she was fine, studying a lot, training hard, feeling good. A few days ago, they'd spoken on the phone, and Sadie had mentioned that they were preparing for the Pacific Coast Rowing Championships, which their coaches fully expected them to win.

Sadie had been moved from stroke to the two-seat. Rather than feeling demoted, she was relieved. Stroking the boat put a lot of pressure on her; she'd rather just get in the zone and follow.

"Have you talked to Dennis much?" Brenna asked.

"Some. He calls from time to time. Like you do. I haven't had time to see him or Denny lately."

Brenna tried not to seethe. Dennis was still calling her. Of course, he hadn't agreed to stop contacting Sadie. Brenna's plan had back-fired, as Abigail had predicted. Dennis had been true to his word and hadn't tried to contact Brenna at all; she had hoped, obviously erroneously, that he would cut ties with Sadie as well.

"Once you're done with the season, let's find a time for you to come over for dinner—or better yet, spend the weekend."

No sooner had Brenna hung up with Sadie than her phone buzzed. Jack.

"Hey, Dad."

"Hi, sweetheart. Listen, I just heard back from my friend's friend at the environmental research center. They have a job doing water-quality monitoring starting in June, and he said it sounds like Sadie would have a good shot at getting it."

"Really? That's great, Dad. Thank you. Can you email me who Sadie should contact and I'll let her know? Or maybe you should call Sadie directly. Just say you heard of this opportunity and thought she'd be interested."

"So, you haven't told her your thoughts on getting her out of the Bay Area?"

"No, not yet. I don't know if I will. Maybe the job will intrigue her enough that she'll apply, and I won't have to tell her."

"Look, Bren. I'm sorry about everything that's happened with

Dennis. I know I am partly responsible. I still keep in touch with him—and Denny. I also understand why you don't want anything to do with him, but you do know that Sadie has the right to make her own choices."

"Dad, I don't want to get into this with you again. You know I don't feel the same way you do about him. I think he's dangerous. And that he's not good for Sadie. Even if you don't agree, please respect my feelings."

"All right, sweetheart. It's not that we would mind in the least having Sadie up here this summer."

Brenna stood on the shore of Lake Natoma, waiting for Sadie's race to start. She scanned the crowd for Dennis and, thankfully, didn't see him anywhere. She felt sure he was there, though, somewhere. And why wouldn't he be? He often attended Sadie's regattas.

The crowd began to buzz and focus their attention up the lake. The women's lightweight eights final was underway. As they closed in on the halfway mark of the 2,000-meter course, the Stanford contingent began cheering. Sadie's boat was out in front. At one thousand five hundred meters, they had increased their lead by about one hundred fifty meters. They were going to win it, Brenna thought excitedly, feeling so happy for Sadie, especially after the year she'd had—

But suddenly, the Stanford boat slowed a bit, then slowed a lot. Something was wrong. The bow pair had stopped rowing.

"Oh my God," a girl next to her said. "It looks like she passed out."

Brenna looked on with horror; it was the rower in the two-seat the girl was talking about. Sadie was in two-seat and was slumped over her oar. The rower behind her in the bow was holding on to Sadie to keep her from falling out of the boat as the remaining six rowers tried gamely to stay in the race. But the rest of the field passed, and Stanford crossed the line last.

An official's launch buzzed out to the Stanford shell, and they off-loaded Sadie. Brenna watched all this unfold as she pushed her way through the onlookers toward the finish area dock.

∽

Brenna rode in the ambulance with Sadie to the UC Davis Medical Center in Sacramento. She had regained consciousness but was pale and exhausted. Brenna held her hand the entire way. After they took Sadie into the ER, Brenna went into the waiting area. Dennis was sitting in a chair, head in his hands. He must have been at the race, she thought. She stood and looked at him for a while until he lifted his head and saw her. He immediately stood up and came to her, pulling her into an embrace.

Brenna was so stunned that she just let it happen.

He broke away and said, "Is she conscious?"

"Yes, she came to in the ambulance. She looked so weak and so pale, though."

"That fucking lightweight rowing culture," Dennis said, angrily. "Make weight at all costs."

"So, you were at the race?"

"Actually, I was in the launch that picked her up out of the boat. I volunteered to direct traffic at the finish area. I couldn't believe it when I saw her hunched over in her seat."

"Well, thank you for getting to her so quickly."

∽

Brenna and Dennis sat side by side, waiting. Brenna's thoughts were a jumbled mess of sickening worry about Sadie, wondering if she was wrong about Dennis and had judged him too harshly. He seemed genuinely worried about Sadie. Then she thought about how he'd treated her, as he repeatedly tried to worm his way into her life. Round and round it went.

As if reading her thoughts, he suddenly turned to her, and said, "Bren, look. I'm sorry for everything that's happened between us. I really am. I'm no good at relationships. I just mess everything up. Do you think we can start over, you and me?"

His ice-blue eyes tried to meet hers, but she was reluctant to look at him. More conflicting feelings whirled: *He is taking advantage of me at this time of crisis, he really does love me, I am attracted to him, maybe I even love him too, he is a manipulator, he knows how to work the situation—*

"Bren?" he prodded.

"This isn't the time or place for this," Brenna said. She got up and went to sit on the other side of the room. He didn't follow her.

⬿

Hours later, Brenna and Dennis got in to see Sadie after she'd been settled into her room. Brenna had called her parents, and they were on their way down from Tahoe. Again, Sadie had been admitted and was hooked up to fluids and nutrition lines. She was again severely malnourished, and the doctor told them her metabolism had gone haywire as a result of her purging and starving.

Brenna avoided looking at Dennis and focused all of her attention on Sadie.

⬿

Sadie was sitting up in her hospital bed. There was some kind of talk show on the TV, but she wasn't paying much attention to it. They'd finally unhooked her from the IV, and she was able to drink and eat on her own. She didn't feel much like eating, but she was extremely thirsty, so the nurses kept bringing her water and juice.

Thankfully, the rowing season was over; otherwise, she probably would have quit. She was so done with obsessing about her weight. It was a losing battle and one she wasn't going to fight anymore. She wondered if she could get strong enough to row with the openweights in the fall, but she wasn't sure she even had the energy.

Her grandfather had called earlier that day to see how she was doing. He and Grammeg had been here for a few days but had gone back to Tahoe when it was clear that Sadie was on the mend. Jack had mentioned that he'd heard about a summer job at the UC Davis Tahoe Environmental Research Center, doing water-quality monitoring, and had thought Sadie might be interested in applying. Sadie picked up the sheet of paper on which she'd written the contact name and address for sending her resume. Maybe that would be a good move. Get out of here for the summer and focus on something else besides rowing.

She sensed someone watching her and looked up. Denny was standing in the doorway.

"Hey, big bro," Sadie said, smiling. "Good to see ya."

"You're really glad to see me?"

"Of course! Get your ass in here."

Denny came in and pulled up a chair. "Been waiting for you to finally wake up. We haven't really talked since the last time you were in the hospital."

"That's true. It was a busy spring. School, rowing. I'm quitting lightweight, you know."

"Good, glad to hear it. You're way too thin."

Sadie looked at him. "Denny, I'm not mad at you. I know it was an accident. I just needed a while to process. You were like, what, eleven years old?"

For an uncomfortable moment, Denny looked as if he might burst into tears.

"Thanks, Sadie," he said. Sadie saw him trying to pull himself together. "I don't know if I'll ever forgive myself, but hearing you say that . . . well, it means a lot." Denny looked away and swiped at his eyes. Sadie reached for the tissue box on her tray table and handed him a wad.

"You know," he said, turning to her. "We're not really related. You do know that, right?"

Sadie looked at him. His face looked drawn, and his tone had taken on an odd, almost desperate, quality.

"Of course!" Sadie said. "But it's fun to pretend, isn't it?"

A nurse bustled in with Jello and chocolate pudding in little plastic containers.

"Whoever you are," she said to Denny, "you can stay if you encourage her to eat." She winked at Sadie and turned to the bedside tray to check Sadie's water and juice supply. Denny pointed at the Jello, and Sadie pulled the top off and began to eat.

"Mmm," Sadie said, smacking her lips.

Denny pointed to the sheet of paper on her lap with the Tahoe job information. "What's that?"

Denny was on the phone when he heard a knock on his bedroom door. Knowing it was his mom, he called, "Come in!"

"Okay, I'll talk to you soon, then," Denny said into his phone, then clicked off.

"Sorry, didn't know you were on a call."

"It's okay. We were done talking." Denny tossed his phone aside and moved his feet so Deirdre could sit on the foot of the bed.

"You all right?" Deirdre asked.

"Yeah. Fine. How was work?"

"Great!" Deirdre said.

"Really?" Denny asked. His mom looked happy. Really happy.

"The lunch prep cook gave his notice today, and Matt, the kitchen manager, said he'd try you out for the job!"

"Prep? I've never done prep."

"Sure, you have. It's mostly just chopping stuff up for the line. You cut plenty of limes and lemon twists behind the bar." She handed Denny a business card. "Matt says to give him a call tomorrow."

"He's going to want my employment history. References. I can't ask my last manager. He's in jail anyway," Denny said despondently.

"You don't need them. Matt says he'll try you out. No questions asked."

"'Matt,' huh." Denny looked at his mom. She looked less beaten down than usual, pretty, even radiant. "Something going on with you and this guy?"

Deirdre colored a little. "He asked me out, and—"

"Wait, no! You're not going to date your boss just to get me a job. I'm applying for jobs every day. Something has to happen." It hadn't yet, Denny thought to himself, but his computer science degree ought to result in something. Eventually.

"No, Denny. It's not like that. We went to coffee the other day, and we made plans to go to a movie this weekend. This all happened before the job thing came up."

"But you took advantage of your . . . 'status' to get me the job, didn't you?"

Deirdre colored again. "Maybe," she said with a sly smile. "Listen, I know you're going to get a job in tech. This is just temporary until you do."

Denny looked at the business card. "Okay, I'll call him. But just so I can check this guy out. Is he nice to you?"

"He's a good guy, Denny. I know you'll like him."

"We'll see," Denny said. "At least if I'm working with you, I can keep an eye on you."

"You sure you're doing okay?"

"Yeah. It's just . . . That was Sadie on the phone. She got a job working in Tahoe this summer. It's a great job for her. In her field. Environmental something. I'm happy for her."

Deirdre looked at him for a while but didn't say anything.

"What? Is my hair sticking straight up or something? Did I grow a horn?"

"Does she know?" Deirdre asked gently.

"Does who know? Know what?"

"Sadie. How you feel about her."

Dennis finished up his last day of work and knocked on his partner's door.

"You outta here?"

"Yep. Listen, I appreciate you giving me this time."

"No problem. Have a great vacation. I'll see ya in a couple of weeks."

Dennis walked out to his car and drove through the stop-and-go traffic to Jack London Square, where he was meeting Denny for dinner.

Denny was sitting at a table by the window. He lifted a hand when he saw Dennis.

"How's the job?"

"It's fine. I don't hate it."

"Any leads from the tech world?"

Denny shook his head.

"Listen, I've said this before, but please don't feel you have to work in a restaurant just to pay me back. Consider it retribution for making your young life miserable."

Denny laughed a short bitter laugh. "You didn't make it totally miserable. I was kind of a miserable kid."

"That's fair," Dennis said. "But really, I don't need you to pay me back."

"But I want to. So, let's leave it at that."

A server came to take their order, interrupting Dennis's further objections.

Denny looked out the window after the server walked away. It was July 3 and sunny on the Oakland side of the bay, but he could see fog starting to roll in from the west.

"You head out tomorrow?" Denny asked Dennis.

"Yup. I'm going to drive up the coast at least to Oregon, maybe even Washington. Might check out Seattle, then Portland on the way back south."

"Sounds great."

"Have you heard from Sadie?"

"Yeah. We talk on the phone. She loves her job. She gets to go out on the lake in a research boat every day."

"She told me that too. Maybe I'll stop in Tahoe on my way back south and check out the research boat myself."

CHAPTER FORTY

Meg, Brenna, and Sadie sat out on the patio watching the bedlam out on the lake. Boats of all shapes and sizes buzzed past, and kayakers hugged the shore to avoid them. Other powerboats chugged more slowly toward Tahoe City, most likely to get a good spot to view the fireworks later that evening. Sailboats glided by further out, propelled by the winds that funneled down from the mountain passes.

Jack emerged from the house with a platter of thick steaks, which he then placed on the barbecue. As the steaks began to pop and sizzle, Sadie felt that familiar anxiety in her stomach. Anytime she was presented with a meal—which was often—she flashed back to purging and starving herself. Rationally, she knew she was at a normal weight, but she felt fat and heavy and kept running her hand over the slight belly she had now.

She'd decided to leave Stanford and the Bay Area for good. Her supervisor at work had said she could finish her last year of undergraduate work at UC Davis, then apply to graduate school there but study and work in Tahoe at the research center. It was perfect. She'd move to Davis in the fall after her job ended.

Jack appeared beside her and placed a plate before her. The massive steak sat there looking completely unappetizing.

Brenna got up and went into the house; she returned with a green salad and a loaf of bread.

Jack served the rest of them, sat down, and began sawing into his steak. Sadie couldn't help but notice that her mother and grand-mother were watching her while trying to look as if they weren't. Sadie reached for the salad and a slice of bread and began to eat. She laughed as both Brenna and Meg visibly relaxed.

"What's funny?" Jack asked.

"The food police. They're now at ease."

Dennis arrived in Tahoe City just as the fireworks started. As he turned south along the West Shore, he thought, *Perfect timing.*

He'd left Oakland that afternoon, stopped in Auburn for a quick transaction with a guy he'd defended a couple of years ago, then headed up into the mountains. The drive had been stunning. The cloudless, deep blue sky, green meadows, and silvery granite peaks were out in all their glory.

It was good to be back in Tahoe, he thought, as he drove just to the head of the driveway. He cut the engine, got out, and watched the fireworks explode to the northeast for a few minutes. Then he started walking, not along the driveway, but through the property. He knew the way and didn't need a flashlight.

When he reached the garage, he stopped, still out of view of the house. He listened. He could hear conversation coming from the direction of the house. It sounded like they were outside, on the patio.

"This must be the finale!" he heard Meg say, as bursts of color and loud booms filled the night sky. Horns sounded from the boats out on the lake, and some boats motored by on their way back to wherever they were going.

"Well, I'm heading in," he heard Jack say when the commotion died down.

"Thanks for the steak, Grandpa." Sadie's voice.

"Yes, thank you, Dad," Brenna said.

"I'll come with you. Good night, my darlings," Meg said.

Dennis waited. He could hear Brenna and Sadie talking in low tones. He would continue to wait, patiently.

"I could meet you in Davis and help you find a place. I can help you move too," Brenna said, tentatively.

She thought she and Sadie were fine, but they'd never really talked about what Brenna had told her about Dennis. Brenna had been so focused on getting her out of the Bay Area, and then Sadie's eating disorder had become apparent. Maybe it was better not to talk about it. Brenna still did not want to know the results of the paternity test. It wasn't important. Peter had been Sadie's father, as far as Brenna was concerned. She felt immense relief that Sadie was not returning to Stanford. She also felt a slight twinge of guilt for having engineered it, but it had worked out so well!

"Yeah, that would be great, Mom. I'm probably going to find a roommate situation, hopefully in a place already furnished, since I'm only going to be in Davis for a year."

"Do you think you'll row for UC Davis?"

"Nah. I doubt it. I'd have to row openweight. I think I'll just focus on school."

Brenna nodded, reached over, and took Sadie's hand.

"I'm proud of you, you know."

"Back at you, Mom."

Brenna didn't feel like she had done anything anyone could be proud of—except maybe taking the stand with Dennis. Useless as her threat to turn in Denny had been, Dennis had not tried to contact her. What was annoying, though, was that Brenna still thought about Dennis. A lot. Everyday. She missed him. But she was also repelled by him. He was her drug, and she was in withdrawal.

"You okay, Mom?" Dennis heard Sadie ask.

"Just tired. I think I'll call it a night. You coming in?"

"Soon. Think I'll sit out here for a while."

"Okay, see you in the morning."

Dennis peered around the corner of the garage. He saw Sadie sitting on the patio, alone. He waited a couple of minutes until he saw the kitchen light go off. He slowly walked toward the house.

"Hello?" he said, trying to keep his voice down but not startle Sadie by sneaking up on her.

Sadie jumped up and whirled around. "Who's that?"

"It's Dennis. Sorry, I was trying not to scare you."

"Dennis? What are you doing here?"

Dennis approached Sadie and gave her a hug.

"Happy Fourth," he said. "I'm on a road trip and thought I'd stop by and say hi."

"Oh right, your trip north. I thought you were going up the coast?"

"I decided to reverse it. Head north, east of the Cascades, then south along the coast."

Dennis glanced at the house to make sure no lights had come on downstairs.

"Everyone else went to bed."

"Right, I got here a bit later than I had thought. But I'm glad you're still up."

"My mom's here, so . . ."

"Yeah, best not wake her up."

"Can I get you something? I think Grandpa's got beer. I was thinking of getting some lemonade," Sadie said.

"I'll get it. You just sit tight."

Dennis let himself into the house and headed for the kitchen. He didn't hear a sound from the bedrooms upstairs. Even if someone heard him, they'd think he was Sadie. He opened the refrigerator, took a pitcher out, found a glass, and poured lemonade for Sadie. He grabbed a beer for good measure. Setting both on the counter, he reached into the pocket of his jeans and pulled out the small vial he'd gotten from the guy in Auburn.

Sadie woke up lying on the backseat of a car. She was groggy and her head ached. She tried to sit up but soon realized her hands and feet were tied. It was dark, but she could see that Dennis was driving.

"Hey," she said weakly. "What is happening?"

"Oh, hey. You're awake," he said brightly as if everything were perfectly normal.

"Why do you have me tied up? Where are we going?"

Dennis actually chuckled. "I'll answer the second question first. I think Seattle is our destination. I've heard it's beautiful. You could finish college at the University of Washington. Row there. Once we find a place, I'll get Denny to come up. Lots of tech jobs in Seattle."

Sadie shook her head. This must be a dream. But she wasn't waking up.

"What? What are you talking about? Can't you untie me?"

Dennis chuckled his weird little chuckle again. "I think you might need a little while to get used to this idea. Before you do, though, I'm afraid you might try to run away."

"I won't run away. I promise," Sadie said, trying not to cry. *What was this? Was he kidnapping her?*

"I wouldn't advise it, anyway. We're not near anything. Just miles of empty desert all around us."

"Please, just untie me. I won't run." Sadie managed to get herself up into a sitting position. She was dizzy and her head throbbed, but she could see he was right. There was only darkness out the car window. No other cars, no building lights.

"Okay, you can sit up front with me."

Dennis pulled the car off the road and reached back. He was holding a knife, and Sadie recoiled.

"Sadie," he said, looking at her gently. "I would never hurt you. I'm just going to free your hands."

She moved toward him and held up her bound hands. He cut the rope, then he handed her the knife so she could release her feet. She thought about stabbing him but knew she couldn't do it and handed the knife back.

"Now climb over into the front seat and we can talk more about Seattle."

As he put the car in gear and pulled back onto the highway, Sadie started to climb over the seat. She felt something in the pocket of her shorts almost fall out and realized it was her cell phone. She still had her phone! They passed a sign that read SUSANVILLE 40 MILES.

Dennis yammered on about how they would finally be a family: he, Sadie, and Denny. How he'd call his partner and tell him their practice needed a Seattle office, and they'd get a house overlooking the water.

"Seattle's surrounded by water—and mountains," he said.

Sadie was barely listening. Her mind raced. Maybe she could ask to go to the restroom in Susanville and call for help. Cars occasionally passed going the other way. Maybe when they slowed down or stopped at a light she could jump out and flag one down or run for help.

Finally, she saw the lights of a town up ahead.

"We'll stop here real quick for gas," Dennis said. "That oughta get us as far as Bend."

"What's Bend?"

"It's a town in central Oregon."

~

Dennis made her wait to go to the restroom while he filled the gas tank, then he followed her to the Porta-Potty at the side of the building and stood outside the door. There was no indoor restroom with a window she could jump out of as she had hoped.

Sadie knew she didn't have much time and was afraid he'd hear her if she tried making a call. So, she texted Denny with shaking fingers: *Help! Dennis taking me to Bend Oregon. Think he drugged me. Please help!*

Dennis knocked on the door. "You okay, Sadie?"

"Yeah! Almost done."

She typed: *Don't text or call please!! He doesn't know I have my phone.*

She made sure her phone was silenced, put it back in her pocket, and opened the door, where Dennis waited, smiling.

She hoped to God Denny would know what to do.

Sadie had tried to stay awake, but she was still groggy and couldn't keep her eyes open. When she woke up, the sun was streaming in through her window, and they were driving along a highway surrounded by evergreen trees with snow-capped mountain peaks off in the distance. She felt a little better, except for a stiff neck from sleeping slumped against the car door.

"Where are we?"

"About an hour out of Bend," Dennis said. "There's coffee in the thermos on the floor behind you if you want some. I'll bet you're hungry. I know I am. We'll stop in Bend for some food."

Sadie reached behind the seat for the thermos.

"Want some music?"

"Sure," Sadie said, smiling at Dennis. "Really excited about Seattle."

"I knew you'd get with the program," Dennis said, reaching over and squeezing her knee. "We'll finally be a real family. Just the three of us. A fresh start."

"Great!" Sadie chirped, the coffee not helping the knot in her stomach. But she kept drinking it. She needed to stay alert from here on out. She'd have to try to break away and find help in Bend.

They passed a highway patrol car sitting by the side of the road, and Sadie fought the urge to open the window and yell for help.

⌒

Dennis fiddled with the radio and found a country-western station. He turned up the music and started singing along.

"I walk the line. I walk the line," he sang. Sadie thought she heard another sound above the music. *Was that . . . a siren?* Sadie glanced in her side mirror, and, sure enough, a patrol car was bearing down behind them.

Dennis noticed it just then and turned down the radio.

"What the hell? I'm not speeding. Must be after someone else," he muttered, his ice-blue eyes hardening.

Suddenly, up ahead of them, three other cars came over a rise in the road right toward them, sirens on, lights flashing. They drove three across the empty highway, forcing Dennis to slow, then stop. The four cars surrounded them, and seven officers emerged with guns drawn.

CHAPTER FORTY-ONE

The day before the wedding, Sadie and Brenna took a walk along the Truckee River path. The early September day was warm and clear, and the forecast called for a similar day tomorrow. The small ceremony would be held at Meg and Jack's, outside, with the mountains and lake as the backdrop. Jack would give Sadie away, and Brenna would be her matron of honor.

The guests would include Deirdre, Denny's aunts and uncles, a few of Sadie's coworkers and school friends, and Denny's childhood friend Eddie, who would be the best man. Dennis would not be there, even if he weren't in prison.

After a week on Hawaii's big island—Jack and Meg's wedding gift—Denny and Sadie would return to their rental cabin in Tahoe, and Sadie would begin her graduate work at the Tahoe Environmental Research Center. Denny would continue working at the Tahoe House restaurant as a line cook until he could find an IT job.

Brenna and Sadie walked in silence, neither of them sure how to start the conversation. Finally, Brenna said, "So, you're really doing this. Marrying the guy who killed your father, while trying to kill his stepfather, who basically acted like a mean big brother for most of your childhood, but then rescued you from his stepfather who kidnapped you and tried to take you to Seattle."

"Yeah."

"Okay, then."

Brenna was struggling to accept Denny, and it hadn't been easy. She kept telling herself that he'd been only a child when he'd decided to go and ram who he thought was Dennis with a stolen powerboat, but what kind of child behaved that way? She was slowly understanding that the answer was: a child who was scared and angry and trying to protect his mother.

As for Denny and Sadie, she hadn't seen this coming but probably should have. She knew they'd grown closer. Denny had always shown up for Sadie, in hospital waiting rooms and, ultimately, by contacting the police in Bend, Oregon, and giving them a description of Dennis's car.

Brenna sighed and said, "So, we know that you and Denny are not blood relatives, but I guess I'm ready for you to tell me if you and Dennis are."

"Really? I've been wanting to tell you for so long. Are you sure?"

"Yes."

"No, Dennis is not my biological father."

Brenna stopped walking and reached for Sadie's arm to steady herself. She realized she hadn't expected that to be Sadie's answer.

"You're sure?"

"Yes, Mom. One hundred percent. I wanted to tell you, but you were so adamant about not knowing."

"I just . . . I was so afraid it was Dennis."

"Well, it's not. Peter was—is—my dad."

They resumed walking again, and Brenna felt some of the stress and worry that she'd carried all those years melt away. Eventually, Dennis would get out of prison and probably try again to get back into their lives, but they had a few years of reprieve. She also knew that Jack would kill him if he ever came near any of them again, even if it meant going to prison himself.

"Denny really has cut his ties with Dennis?"

"Yes, Mom. He said he never wants to see or hear from him again."

"I have to tell you something, Sadie."

"Oh, no. Not another amends."

"I'm afraid so."

"What is it?"

"I asked your grandfather to talk to his friends here about getting you a summer job. He arranged for you to get hired at the environmental research center last year. I wanted to get you out of the Bay Area, away from rowing, and, most of all, away from Dennis."

Sadie smiled. "I know."

"Did your grandfather tell you?"

"No. He didn't have to." Sadie stopped walking and turned toward Brenna. "Thank you, Mom. For trying to protect me. You were the only one who saw Dennis for what he was."

"You know, for a while, I thought he might have changed. Or maybe I just hoped he had. But he hadn't." Brenna paused. "But Denny . . . I'll be keeping my eye on him."

Sadie stepped forward and embraced Brenna.

"I know you will," Sadie said.

When they arrived back at the house, Jack and Denny were sitting on the patio, deep in conversation. When they saw Sadie and Brenna, they waved them over.

"Oh boy," Brenna said. "This can't be good."

Denny looked a little nervous as Brenna and Sadie sat down.

"Of course, it's good!" Jack said. "We're talking about resuming the plans Peter and I had."

"Which plans were those?" Brenna said, narrowing her eyes.

"Opening a restaurant here in Tahoe. Ptarmigan II! Denny can run the kitchen, and we can hire Deirdre to manage the front-of-the-house staff."

"In honor of Peter . . . ," Denny said, eyeing Brenna with trepidation.

"You know, like an amends to him . . ." Denny trailed off under the pressure of Brenna's stare.

"Wow, that's a cool idea," Sadie said with great enthusiasm. "What do you think, Mom?"

Brenna thought for a bit, then said, "A final amends for Peter. Yes, it's a cool idea."

EPILOGUE
2020

Dennis squinted in the hot desert sun as he exited the prison and began walking down the road. He heard the gate slam shut behind him, but he didn't look back. Slung over his shoulder was the bag he'd packed for his road trip up to Washington State thirteen years before. Other than that, he figured he had nothing and was starting from scratch.

His arms were covered in tattoos and his hair was nearly shaved off. He had spent his time in Club Fed behaving as a model inmate: fixing engines in the motor pool, working out in the gym, dispensing legal advice to his fellow prisoners, and doing research in the library. Oh yes, lots of research.

He searched the San Francisco and Tahoe news websites obsessively and found out many interesting things: Denny and Sadie had gotten married (which Dennis considered an abomination since they had practically been brother and sister); Jack had financed a new "family-operated restaurant" in Tahoe City (which even Deirdre and her new husband had gotten in on as "dining room and kitchen managers") the décor of which included "artist Meghann Riley's watercolors,"; and Denny and Sadie had produced two children, a boy named Peter and a girl named Kelsey.

He also found out his father had died. Dennis's mother had started writing to him. She had moved into an assisted-living facility, made friends, and was enjoying life. He was glad for her, and he planned to visit her soon. But first, he had business to attend to up north. He'd built some useful connections in prison, formulated his plan, and it was finally time for action.

After about an hour of walking, he reached Highway 395 and stuck out his thumb. Cars blew by him, and a hot wind began to blow, kicking up sandy dust and tumbleweeds. Thirty or so minutes later, a motorhome rolled to a stop.

"Where ya headed?" said the driver, a very large, middle-aged man with a shiny, bald head.

"Lake Tahoe."

"I can get you as far as Reno if that works."

"That works just fine," Dennis said and climbed in.

"What's in Tahoe?"

Dennis's ice-blue eyes flashed. "Family reunion."

ACKNOWLEDGMENTS

finished the first draft of *The Handyman* in 1994. With the help of many, it has evolved into its present form.

I owe much gratitude to David Shields, my creative writing professor at University of Washington, who was always brutally honest about my work. I also thank writer friends, Kate Trueblood, Rick Clarke, Fran Mason, and Diane Shope, who served as role models and shared their experiences with me on all things writing and publishing.

My beta readers were invaluable resources and sounding boards, and they include Karen Boudreau, Nancy Lockett, Sarah Lyngra, Shaun Jahshan, Caleb Powell, and Matt Johnson. Thank you all for reading and offering your insights. Sharol Hofstedt functioned as both beta reader and proofreader with her usual keen eye and impeccable attention to detail.

I'm grateful to Alma Garcia De Lilla, at Hugo House in Seattle, who delivered exactly what I asked: a no-holds-barred critique that took the novel to the next level. I'm also deeply indebted to the Honorable Mary Alice Theiler for her expert and thorough legal review.

A big thank you to my Tahoe friends, Sha and Tim Schroeder, who spent a day driving me around to see the marina, the courthouse, and the estates along the west shore of Lake Tahoe. Thanks go out to the rowing community, who inspired many of the characters and plotlines.

And finally, many thanks to Brooke Warner and Lauren Wise at She Writes Press for shepherding this book to publication, along with Mikayla Butchart for her stellar editing and Cait Levin for marketing guidance.

ABOUT THE AUTHOR

photo credit: Nancy Lockett

M aura K. Deering studied creative writing at the University of Washington. She worked as a writer and communications director at the University of California, Davis, and practiced law for fifteen years. Deering retired from her practice in 2019 and returned to writing. She has published essays in the *Seattle Weekly* and *Bird Watcher's Digest*, along with articles in *ParentMap, UC Davis Magazine,* and the *King County Bar Bulletin*. She lives in Seattle.

SELECTED TITLES FROM SHE WRITES PRESS

She Writes Press is an independent publishing company founded to serve women writers everywhere. Visit us at www.shewritespress.com.

I Like You Like This by Heather Cumiskey. $16.95, 978-1-63152-292-5
In 1984 Connecticut, sixteen-year-old Hannah Zandana—cursed with wild hair, a bad complexion, and emotionally unavailable parents—is miserable at home and at school. But when she gets the attention of Deacon, her high school's handsome resident drug dealer, her life takes an unexpected detour into a dangerous and seductive world.

I Love You Like That by Heather Cumiskey. 16.95, 978-1-63152-616-9
In this sequel to *I Like You Like This*, Hannah—reeling from the loss of Deacon, her dark and mysterious former boyfriend and first love—lets herself fall into the arms of the wrong boys, even as her mother's growing addiction continues to pull her family apart.

Copy Boy by Shelley Blanton-Stroud. $16.95, 978-1-63152-697-8
It's 1937. Jane has left her pregnant mother with a man she hates, left her father for dead in an irrigation ditch, remade herself as a man, and gotten a job as a copy boy. And everything's getting better—until her father turns up on her newspaper's front page in a picture that threatens to destroy the life she's making.

How to Grow an Addict by J.A. Wright. $16.95, 978-1-63152-991-7
Raised by an abusive father, a detached mother, and a loving aunt and uncle, Randall Grange is built for addiction. By twenty-three, she knows that together, pills and booze have the power to cure just about any problem she could possibly have . . . right?

Salvation Station by Kathryn Schleich. $16.95, 978-1-63152-892-7
When committed female police captain Linda Turner, haunted by the murders of two small children and their pastor father, becomes obsessed with solving the harrowing case, she finds herself wrapped up in a mission to expose a fraudulent religious organization and an unrepentant killer.

Shrug by Lisa Braver Moss. $16.95, 978-1-63152-638-1
In 1960s Berkeley, teenager Martha Goldenthal just wants to do well in school and have a normal life. But her home life is a cauldron of kooky ideas, impossible demands, and explosive physical violence—and there's chaos on the streets. When family circumstances change and Martha winds up in her father's care, she must stand up to him, or forgo college.